MW01278202

KAI LUNG
RAISES HIS VOICE

.

By the Same Author
THE WALLET OF KAI LUNG
KAI LUNG'S GOLDEN HOURS
KAI LUNG BENEATH THE MULBERRY TREE
KAI LUNG UNROLLS HIS MAT
THE MOON OF MUCH GLADNESS
KAI LUNG: SIX
THE MIRROR OF KONG HO

Kai Lung Raises His Voice

by

Ernest Bramah

Durrant Publishing
Norwich, Norfolk, England

First published by Durrant Publishing, 2010
Paperback ISBN 978-1-905946-10-5
Hardback ISBN 978-1-905946-11-2

Durrant Publishing is a trading name of
Durrant Software Limited,
82 Earlham Road, Norwich, NR2 3HA

Contents

Preface. vii

The Subtlety of Kang Chieng 1

Ming Tseuen and the Emergency. 20

Lam-hoo and the Reward of Merit 39

Chung Pun and the Miraculous Peacocks. 47

Yuen Yang and the Empty Lo-Chee Crate 54

Sing Tsung and the Exponent of Dark Magic 65

Kwey Chao and the Grateful Song Bird. 74

Li Pao, Lucky Star and the Intruding Stranger. 86

The Cupidity of Ah Pak 101

The Romance of Kwang the Fruit Gatherer 140

The Destiny of Cheng, the Son of Sha-kien. 182

Colophon 224

Preface

HARDLY REMEMBER when I was not an admirer of Ernest Bramah. A master at my preparatory school introduced me to Kai Lung, and my mother, who liked detective stories, put Max Carrados into my hands. When I was doing my National Service I obtained from Betram Rota the four Richards collections of Kai Lung stories in beautiful uniform bindings by Riviere; and they, along with eight volumes of *The Decline and Fall of the Roman Empire*, helped me through two years of extremely inactive service. In 1994 I retired from teaching philosophy in Scotland – I liked the teaching but was homesick for England – and thought I might occupy my empty time with work on Bramah. He was reported to have had an eccentric, almost paranoid, aversion to publicity, and those who wrote about his books said that hardly anything was known about him personally. To a fan of Max Carrados the challenge was irresistible. I thought I would dig up the facts of his life and put together a biography, a collection of literary 'remains', or both.

My researches into his life were a failure. I looked up his will and that of his widow, in which there was mention of houses, nephews and nieces; I hunted after those houses and relations through London, Manchester and outlying Pennine villages; I wrote letters to addresses in Somerset and Devon; and I drew blank after blank. Bramah seemed to have vanished without trace. I could not find a single person who had set eyes on him and only one octogenarian farmer who had any personal recollection of his family.

I gave up too soon. A lecturer and later consultant on management named Aubrey Wilson, like me retired and fond of

Bramah, was persuaded by his wife to engage in similar research, and management prevailed where philosophy had been found wanting. Through Aubrey I eventually met a surviving nephew and niece, and in 2007 he published a biography, *The Search for Ernest Bramah*, which gives far more information about Bramah's life than I thought would ever emerge.

In finding unpublished or uncollected work by Bramah I did rather better. Bramah left his papers to his widow, and after her death the bulk of them was acquired by the Harry Ransom Center at Austin, Texas. I spent a week there in 2000 and discovered treasures beyond my dreams: occasional pieces published in magazines between 1900 and 1941, two complete unpublished novels, and best of all, four long unpublished Kai Lung stories, dating back to the most creative years of Bramah's life, the early Edwardian era. I transcribed these works and made two collections, one of Kai Lung stories and the other comprising tales of shady ingenuity and tales of the preternatural, two genres in which Bramah delighted.

And now at last Paul Durrant is bringing out the Kai Lung collection. There are six stories which appeared in *Punch* in 1940–41, the last two years of Bramah's life, and which, I think, were written at about that time. There is 'Ming Tseuen and the Emergency', which appeared in *The Specimen Case* and was written in 1923. And there are the four long stories I found in Texas, to which Bramah refers in letters written to his literary agent between 1901 and 1905. 'The Subtlety of Kang Chieng' is mentioned in 1901 and Bramah expresses anxiety that it may be too long, and so it is possible that what is printed here is a shortened version. 'The Cupidity of Ah Pak' and 'The Destiny of Cheng' are mentioned in June 1903. The fourth exists in two versions, one of which is typed and entitled 'The Emperor who Meant Well', the other is written in a notebook in handwriting which is extremely hard to read. It is quite possible that I am the first person since Bramah's death to have read it. It is earlier than the typed version, and more than twice as long. In 1905, fearing that it was too long to 'place', Bramah asked his agent to substitute the shorter version for it, but that would have been a most regrettable loss, and I am glad that Mr. Durrant has chosen to publish the longer version here under Bramah's original title, 'The Romance of Kwang, the Fruit Gatherer.'

Reading these stories now, I find them as fresh as I found the four Richards collections when I was a soldier. They confirm my belief that Bramah is one of the really great humourists of our language. Of writers who overlap him, P.G. Wodehouse, Evelyn Waugh and Ivy Compton-Burnett, all have their own excellences; but none surpasses Bramah in his flair for the simply funny. To those who have come to love Kai Lung from the Richards volumes, this collection will be a huge and unexpected joy.

— William Charlton, October 29th, 2009

The Subtlety of Kang Chieng

As Kai Lung the story-teller, seated on his well-worn mat in the open space at Wu-whei, prepared to raise his voice and invite the leisurely-inclined to draw near and listen to a new and veracious story, two persons suddenly presented themselves before him and demanded his judgement on a matter lying between them.

"O amiable Kai Lung," exclaimed Hi Seng, the water carrier, "this unprepossessing person and the accomplished but obstinate-minded Wang Yu who accompanies him, hearing your engaging footsteps had already carried you into Wu-whei, agreed to submit the matter in dispute for your decisive pronouncement, rather than carry it to the court of the Mandarin Ting-pi-en at Shan Tzu. For since the salt dues have been diverted into the Imperial coffers the heavily burdened Mandarin has become unswerving in his ideas of justice, and it is now his habitual custom to fine heavily all persons who appear before him, be they accusers, defenders or witnesses to the truth."

"Your decision is a wise and enlightened one in the circumstances," said Kai Lung pleasantly. "Let your difference, as it stands between you, be stated accurately and without hesitation."

"Benevolent and sagacious Kai Lung," exclaimed Wang Yu, pressing forward eagerly; "intelligently stated, as you suggest, the entire matter may be adequately laid within the hollow space of a three-fanged dragon tooth; but the mind of the garrulous Hi Seng is as tangled as the skein of a storm-tossed cocoon and his mouth is as effective to hold back the torrents of highly unnecessary words as are the barriers of the Hoang Ho to restrain the waters at flood time. At an early gong-stroke today, then, it chanced that this well-meaning one—"

"O evilly-intentioned Wang Yu!" cried Hi Seng indignantly, "do not, under the semblance of flattering words, endeavour to represent matters as being contrary to what they really are. Indeed it was by no chance, as you state, but with deliberate intention that—"

"It is well said in Wu-whei that truth from any person is as refined gold, but from the lips of Hi Seng it is more precious than opals," replied Wang Yu. "Honourable Kai Lung, it so chanced—"

"There is a jest throughout this province," retorted Hi Seng, "that Wang Yu, in endeavouring to persuade persons of the reliableness of his statements, may be fitly likened to a domestically-inclined duck trying to produce offsprings by persistently sitting upon a nest of porcelain eggs, for although the practice has no result in affecting the credulity of others yet in time each creature comes to believe in the merit of its own efforts. It was no chance—"

"Alas!" exclaimed Kai Lung, "the manner of behaving of the illustrious Mandarin at Shan Tzu begins to assume the characteristics of a heaven-sent wisdom. Clearly, unless one is endowed with a span of life beyond that generally allotted, it is impossible to learn even the outside facts of a matter arising in Wu-whei."

"Nevertheless," reiterated the mule-like Wang Yu, "the affair was the outcome of chance and—"

"Let it then be so judged," said Kai Lung, as Hi Seng prepared to make a passionate assertion to the contrary effect; and stretching forth his hand the story-teller took up a winged insect which had at that moment alighted on a branch of the mulberry tree, saying as he did so, "Now, O Wang Yu, is it not a fact that chance may be said to have destroyed this creature by leading it, from among all its fellows, into my power so that I shall kill it?"

"Such a statement is indeed uncontroversial," replied Wang Yu confidently.

"Yet," remarked Kai Lung, opening his fingers, "has it not chanced to escape?"

"It is a view of the incident that cannot reasonably be denied," admitted Wang Yu, whose assurance began to diminish as the matter grew more involved, for his intelligence was never really acute.

"Then chance has both caused the death of the insect and caused its escape?" demanded Kai Lung. "O mendacious Wang Yu!" he exclaimed; "in order to maintain your unjust demand you speak with two tongues. Assuredly it is shown that there is no such thing as chance and in founding your contention upon it you have failed and must pay to Hi Seng the full amount of his claim."

"Alas!" said Wang Yu, who did not grasp intelligently how the decision had been arrived at, "the estimable philosopher Ni-Hyu was certainly right when he propounded the sage advice, 'do not dispute with a scorpion concerning the length of its tail, but rather let the argument turn upon the weight of your own heavily-shod staff,' thereby delicately suggesting that one should not be enticed into allowing disputes to be judged by omens of which one has no actual knowledge. It would have been well for this necessitous pipe-maker had he persistently refused to let the matter be settled by the manner of behaving of so unreliable a creature as a winged insect, but had, on the contrary, adhered to his original contention – that when he overturned Hi Seng's water jars it was from no malice or irresponsible impulse but entirely by accident."

"Such a course might undoubtedly have affected the issue," admitted Kai Lung. "Yet things are not to be wholly weighed by their immediate result, for in that case there would not have arisen in this person's mind the story of Kang Chieng, which it is now his presumptuous intention to relate to those persons gathered around, as proving that in the life of one of fixed purpose and unswerving aims chance has no definite existence."

Kang Chieng was the only son of a person of illustrious descent who at one time held a high position in Pekin, as a member of the Board of Censors. About that period a distinguished commander in the Imperial forces had been attacked by a tiger while passing unarmed through a dense forest, and would inevitably have been torn to pieces had he not, in despair, unfurled the silk umbrella which he carried and rushed forward uttering cries of terrifying menace. This bold stratagem was successful and the tiger betook itself to flight in the most ignominious manner; whereupon Kio-Feng, the official in question, not unnaturally concluding that a weapon which had proved so efficacious against the fiercest beast of the forest would be even more overwhelming if employed against men of merely ordinary courage, commanded that the soldiers in that part of the Empire should discard all other arms and immediately provide themselves with paper umbrellas of exceptional size and embellished with designs of an awe-inspiring nature. From this cause it came about that when the father of Kang Chieng made one of his periodical inspections he found a considerable army equipped in the manner indicated, all inflated with an ill-disguised pride in the skilful dexterity with which they manipulated their new weapons in movements of perfect and well-balanced unison. Not understanding how the circumstance had come about, the father of Kang Chieng reported upon the matter with a complete absence of enthusiasm, and in a spirit of no-sincerity he was even so unfortunate as to suggest the re-arming of the entire army with other equally formidable weapons which he enumerated at some length. This inopportune spirit of levity did not go unpunished for Kio-Feng was high in Imperial favour and had recently had the degree 'Unimpeachable' conferred upon him.

This unique honour carried with it the enviable distinction of rendering him officially perfect and incapable of committing an error of judgement. In consequence, therefore, when the report of Kang Chieng's father was communicated he was at once degraded from office as a person of unnatural incapacity, if not acting with deliberate treason towards his country, and banished from the Capital.

In the meantime the affairs of the inventive but not really discriminating Kio-Feng had undergone a complete and similar reversal. An insurrection broke out in the Province of Kwei-chau and although his soldiers opened and closed their umbrellas with unconquerable determination and a marked precision to the spoken words of command that compelled the admiration of all unprejudiced beholders, the rebels, being for the most part persons of a low standard of intelligence, were quite undisconcerted by the display, and before the circumstance of the valiant Kio-Feng and the ferocious tiger could be explained to them, so that they should regard the hostile demonstration at its proper value, the greater part of the Imperial army had been slain. In consequence of this disaster it was decided that Kio-Feng had exceeded the limits of his unimpeachableness and in order to spare his feelings as much as possible the considerate Emperor accordingly sent him a yellow silk rope of the finest quality, with the intention of affording him a means of expiating his faults at once painless, expeditious and high-minded.

Kio-Feng did not pause to consider how undignified a course he was taking. He at once fled to a remote spot, where, following the narrow-minded and somewhat intricate process of reasoning which marked his career throughout, he denounced the father of Kang-Chieng as the real cause of all his misfortunes and bound himself by the solemn oath of his ancestral Temple and Virtues to remove him from his path, fully assured that the person in question was still unfavourably controlling his destiny by means of charms and witchcraft.

While these unpropitious events were taking place, the father of Kang Chieng – in reality a person of inoffensive manner and extreme benevolence of disposition – had retired to Pel Hing in the province of Yun Nan where he passed a consistent but in no way remarkable existence as a merchant in precious herbs and healing substances. He also studied omens and the reading of the future and in this way he was enabled to decide with assurance the meaning of certain matters which had been revealed to Kang Chieng as he slept.

"Illustrious sire," exclaimed the youth, presenting himself before his father and prostrating himself respectfully, "a dream in which this person took part last night while he floated unconscious in the Middle Air has ever since been troubling him with vague misgivings. Therefore, if the thing may be honourably effected, disclose to him the meaning of the omen, so that he may prepare himself for the destiny which it portends."

"The petition so far is a discreet and fitting one," replied his father. "Do not hesitate to reveal the occurrence fully."

"In spirit I floated motionless above the outer court," continued Kang Chieng; "seeing, indeed, yet having no power to move a hand or raise a voice. The time seemed to be midnight and all things had the appearance of being wrapped in sleep, yet upon a pole of smooth bamboo a malignant eye sat, watching the house unceasingly. 'This is the revengeful eye of Kio-Feng,' said a voice from out of the vast space around, and I awoke."

"It is a matter of no importance," said the father of Kang Chieng with an expression of unconcern; "yet in what direction was the eye fixed and to what point in height did the bamboo reach?"

"The eye was unceasingly fixed upon the centre of the house, upon the very shutters of your inner chamber," replied Kang Chieng; "and the staff was as tall as the highest pinnacle within the walls of Pekin."

After an interval of seven days Kang Chieng a second time presented himself before his father, saying, "The vision of the eye again appeared last night; but the pole was no higher than an ordinary house. Is the hour not reached when the true significance of the display should no longer be withheld?"

"It is a matter which need occasion no immediate apprehension," replied his father with manifest evasion. "Yet should the vision occur a third time the interpretation will be made."

It was after a like interval of seven days that Kang Chieng for the third time approached his father ceremoniously, but so great was his inner apprehension and so firm his resolve to betray no unseemly feeling that he was unable to do more than stand with downcast eyes before him.

Then said his father in a voice as smooth as jade, after the young man had for a period stood silently before him, "There comes a time when it is fitting to procure a certain robe so that all may be ready and suitably prepared for the last eventuality. Judge, therefore, the height of this person, so that he may, without delay, procure an adequate supply of silk."

"The height, O my venerated father," replied Kang Chieng, controlling his voice as by internal cords of steel, "is as the height of the bamboo rod which again stood last night in the outer court of the house."

"The cold breath of night begins to draw near," said his father, still speaking as though the matter were one which scarcely concerned the two persons speaking together; "call, therefore, an attendant so that he may draw together the curtains of the door."

"Even as the eye, which on the two former occasions was unceasingly open and shooting forth beams of vindictive light, was last night closed," replied Kang Chieng.

When the father of Kang Chieng understood thereby that the vengeance-laden Kio-Feng had, in accordance with his oath, sought him out stealthily from afar and had at length discovered him, he took his son by the hand and led him from chamber to chamber, disclosing to him where such store of money as he possessed was concealed, and initiating him into the more important and remunerative secrets of his calling. Having spent the greater part of the day in these conscientious occupations he embraced Kang Chieng, and taking no weapon (for in the face of so explicit an omen he wisely recognised that no resistance would avail him), but concealing about his garments certain charms and sacred sentences which could be relied upon to work disastrously towards Kio-Feng in the future, he went forth cheerfully alone to meet an obviously destined end.

The actual manner of his death was open to no doubt, for when his body was discovered in a plantation of wild apricot on the following day, a double-edged knife bearing the seal of Kio-Feng indicated the guilty one as by a pointing finger; nor were signs lacking to show that Kio-Feng, to make his vindictive purpose sure, had called unlawfulness to his aid.

When Kang Chieng had deposited the body of his father in the family temple with every token of ceremonious admiration and filial regard, and had also caused to be inscribed an appropriate tablet recording the unostentatious virtues of his mother (who had consumed a jar of gold leaf in order that her lord might not be deprived of her services in the Upper Air), he called together all those persons in Pel Hing who had any claim on his consideration. Desiring their attention to the delicate nature of his words and actions, he placed upon a table before him a variety of symbols representing the earth and the heavens and the diverse spaces between, fire, all manner of created beings, the waters both sweet and bitter, and good and bad spirits of every kind. He then kindled the flame within an incense vessel charged with sweet-smelling cassia wood of the finest quality floating in an essence subtly distilled from the roots of sacred herbs, and having in this manner made it clear that the ceremony upon which he was engaged was no ordinary affair of commerce or of elaborate courtesy he maintained his face unchangingly before them.

"It may be objected," he began, speaking in such a tone as that with which one might remark on the lesser affairs of existence, "that the voice of the panther crying for the flesh of the musk deer is unheard in the forests of the Kin-ling valley though his beard is never free from the redness of their blood. Yet the unswerving determination of a son to devote his entire life to the accomplishment of a clearly-defined aim cannot be likened to any passing ambition, nor is the utterance of a divinely inspired oath to be regarded as the mere waving of a paper banner." At this point the devout and unassuming youth placed a finger of his left hand so that it should be encircled and consumed by the flames of the burning incense, and continued thus: "Kang Chieng, the person who is now speaking and offering up this sacrifice so that the vow may be ever before him, binds himself to these things by the altars of his ancestors, by the Signature of the Emperor, and by the Face of Buddha. This is my unbending word: I will seek for Kio-Feng as silently and as surely as the roots of the desert palm-tree working underground towards the distant and unseen fountain; I will fall upon him as swiftly and as unexpectedly as the yellow-billed osprey dropping suddenly upon the unsuspecting pomfret in the shallows of the Yang-tse Kiang; and taking him between my two hands I will crush him until his bones press out between my fingers. Then shall I find internal peace and leisure in which to cultivate the domestic virtues and to continue a distinguished line which may think fit to inscribe my history in letters of gold as an encouragement for posterity; but should I fail through lack of obstinacy or by ordinariness of character may my spirit hang simmering over the mouth of the tenth hell of unbelievers to the end of all time and may my body be left unburied and taken possession of by a wandering band of unclean demons!" Perceiving that by this time his finger was consumed through, Kang Chieng ceased speaking, and sinking down suffered himself to be led to an inner chamber.

When this matter reached the ear of Kio-Feng his stomach grew very small in the sight of those who watched him closely, although he endeavoured to create the impression that he regarded the entire circumstance in the light of a passing jest; and he even made continual public reference to an imagined encounter between a voracious fire-breathing dragon and an unnaturally feeble earth-worm, he himself assuming, for the purpose of the metaphor, the characteristics of the former creature. But even while he puffed out his cheeks around a trembling tongue he took a step that cried his fear aloud, for learning by his hired spies that Kang Chieng was one of the league of the Stealthy Brethren without delay he took the oath of membership himself and was admitted to their society. As by rites which imposed unutterable penalties all of the Brotherhood swore not to shed each other's blood Kio-Feng hoped that in this ingenious manner he had placed an insuperable obstacle in Kang Chieng's way, not remembering the wisdom of the proverb, "Against two things iron walls and three-times welded bolts are of no avail: the smile of a maiden and the vengeance-laden oath of a devoted son."

When Kang Chieng heard of the artifice he cheerfully set himself to accomplish Kio-Feng's destruction without breaking through the set conditions of either oath in the enviable spirit of unmoved composure which had always been his chief characteristic. Again warned by those within his pay that Kang Chieng showed no indication of deviating from his purpose Kio-Feng next urged one in authority among the officials of the Stealthy Brethren to protect him more fully, declaring that otherwise the influence of the League would be subverted and the internal sanctity of its brotherhood set at defiance; but to the well-intentioned caution which the official in question transmitted to Kang Chieng the only answer was a doubtful assurance. "This person, rest assured, will in no way depart from the words of his oath and undertaking," he replied. "He will not spill the blood of Kio-Feng; he will greet him with a hand stretched out. He will lick him as the dromedary licks her young; as the ringed snake of the marshes licks the kid which it embraces so will he cover him with affection."

But in spite of this amiable self-confidence the barrier which Kio-Feng had thus placed in the path of Kang Chieng's honourable ambition was indeed of a most insidious nature and the latter person plainly understood that he might now find it prudent to devote a greater span of time to the necessary preparations than was really agreeable to his innermost nature. Kow-towing devoutly, therefore, to the state of things as it actually existed, rather than filling the air with undignified lamentations that matters had not come about in a less complicated fashion, he spent the next years in making himself proficient in the varied accomplishments of a wise man, and one who was prepared to advise persons in all emergencies. Then selecting a day when every omen was favourable he set out and after overcoming many obstacles and wandering through the length and breadth of five provinces in pursuit of wisdom suited to his end, he returned to the neighbourhood of Kio-Feng's residence and took up his abode in a cave at the distance of some half score li from it.

The great sky lantern had not grown and faded many times before it began to be whispered among the people of Sun-wei that a sorcerer of exceptional intuition was to be found among them. Thus it became the habit of those who were involved in any kind of difficulty to present themselves before Kang Chieng and to act in what seemed to be the way his words indicated; for so proficient had he become in his manner of expressing himself that his advice either proved to be advantageous on every occasion or else it was so worded that the person who failed to profit by it could be shown that he had been guilty of a gross misunderstanding and had, in reality, acted in precisely the manner which Kang Chieng had counselled him to avoid.

At length upon a certain evening in the month when the bees bite off the restraining gum-tips of the peach buds there came to the cave of Kang Chieng a maiden whose face was concealed behind an embroidered veil; yet, by reason of his deep studies in certain subjects not usually understood, Kang Chieng had no difficulty in recognising her as the daughter of Kio-Feng. After receiving his assurance that he was a person of high-minded honourableness, and that nothing of what passed between them should be disclosed to others, the maiden, without revealing herself, continued:

"There is a certain youth, towards whom this person's father is most aggressively opposed, who, presuming upon some slight encouragement which he may have received in the past, continues to present himself in the orchards and chrysanthemum gardens every evening with the avowed purpose of conversing with this one, nor upon some occasions has he hesitated to penetrate as far as the outer court when she has withheld herself. Greatly does this one fear discovery and the unbending wrath of an enraged sire, yet by no persuasion or other means in her power can she discourage the youth in question. Advise her, therefore, how the danger may be successfully averted and no reward will be too great in return."

Then Kang Chieng, desirous of learning exactly what degree of discouragement was really desired by the daughter of Kio-Feng towards the persistent youth, replied, "There is a district, lying among the Nan-ling mountains, which is famed throughout the Empire for the speed, bloodthirstiness and unquenchable tenacity of the hounds which are there to be obtained. A single couple, sparsely fed, would—" but at this point a wail of unendurable anguish from the maiden clearly signified that the solution was one that did not meet with her regard. Then said Kang Chieng, "When a person, expecting nothing, perceives a cloud of smoke arising, he searches diligently and will not be drawn aside until he has discovered fire; yet had a trusted one reported to him before the matter took his attention, saying, 'This person has caused a fire to be constructed for such or such a purpose,' then even the pungent odour of burning pine would not have stirred his tranquillity. Should there chance to arise a substantial rumour that the orchards and gardens to which reference has been made have attracted the favourable notice of a pair of amiable and well-disposed spirits who there disport themselves in a variety of virtuous attitudes, the frequent appearance of the two figures walking together in the dusk of the evening will neither occasion disquieting suspicion nor humiliating pursuit."

Evidently turning over in her mind the reasonable simplicity of this stratagem the maiden departed, and from that time it came to be rumoured in the neighbourhood of Sun-wei that the glades around Kio-Feng's house were inhabited by a pair of affectionate but retiring demons who shed prosperity over the whole surrounding district. Kang Chieng, when the matter was referred to in his hearing, admitted that from certain signs around he was expecting such a manifestation, whereupon the reality of the vision was universally admitted.

This necessary detail in the somewhat elaborate plan of vengeance which Kang Chieng had been driven by the unexpected course of events to adopt, had scarcely been satisfactorily arranged when the person in question was approached by a young man of elegant personality who entered his presence with the rather offensive air of one who is driven by the opposing force of expedience to prostrate himself before a being for whom he has no real veneration.

"Expert and incomparable wizard," he said politely, yet not troubling to suppress an inner ring of satire in his voice, "prepare for me a secret potion that will enable me to present the silk-bound gifts of mutual agreement to a certain maiden openly, and when I have received her marriage lot I will honourably reward you."

Divining at once who the one before him was, Kang Chieng veiled the emotion of contempt with which the other's words and attitude inspired him, and after consulting a highly burnished mirror of untarnished metal he answered courteously,

"The most efficacious love-charm in your case, O benevolent young man, will be the conscientious esteem of the maiden's father. In what spirit is his face turned towards you on your approach?"

"Alas!" exclaimed the young man with an expression of the acutest mental distress, "the one you have referred to is not only inordinately deficient in refined sympathy, but is, moreover, most objectionably expert in the use of all manner of weapons. This person has never yet found it prudent to remain long enough in such a position as to enable him to speak with authority on the exact expression of his countenance. But as regards the elaborately-embroidered pattern on his unnecessarily-heavy sandals—"

"Nevertheless," said Kang Chieng, "there scarcely exists the person who is insensible to the delicate flattery of a really well-selected gift."

" 'How exquisite in flavour is said to be the flesh of the ring-dove' exclaimed the pike to the bull-frog. 'Let us climb into their nests and grow fat upon the young,'" quoted the youth in a spirit of subtle bitterness.

"Yet," remarked Kang Chieng, "the insidiously-growing sum which in the length of a year is inevitably expended in melon seeds preserved in honey, sweet-scented ointments, expensively-worked veils and gifts of a like character for the maiden would, if diverted into one channel, very soon be sufficient to procure such an offering and thereby remove the necessity of the lesser matters for the future. Therefore, as I am well disposed towards the young and guileless, take this pearl and when your object is attained at a convenient season restore it."

"Your system of philosophy is profound, esteemed," replied the young man with a marked increase of cordiality. "What variety of gift would be the one most likely to bring about an honourable reconciliation?"

"Undoubtedly the most pleasing and esteem-promoting offering which one person can lay at the feet of another is a spacious and richly-decorated coffin," replied Kang Chieng. "Let it be of a rare and fragrant wood, carved with representations of the three thousand and three score torments of the lost or some other scene of recognised appropriateness. The highly embossed plate should be already inscribed with the name and virtues of the one for whom it is destined and not even a person of the most austere unapproachableness can receive it without at once entertaining an exceptional regard for the discriminating bestower. Act in the manner which has been suggested and amid your future happiness coffins and ornamental bridal wreaths will for ever be pleasantly associated."

The last detail of Kang Chieng's well-matured scheme was now almost at hand. One day there came to solicit his inspired advice a closely-veiled woman, whom he nevertheless at once recognised as the wife of Kio-Feng.

"Distinguished personage," she said, betraying unmistakable signs of her agitation, "the fame of your diabolical accomplishments has reached me from every side, but indulge this abject-minded one by omitting to manifest any signs of an infernal nature, and, especially, by not at any time causing fire to proceed from your open mouth while conversing with her. It is a proof of the unfathomable agony which possesses her that she has at length called up the necessary courage to visit even so polite and honourably-spoken-of a supernatural Being as yourself."

"The formality of fire-breathing and the other matters in question shall be withheld on this occasion," said Kang Chieng pleasantly. "Proceed, therefore, to enlighten this incapable person as to the manner in which he can serve so select and gracefully-outlined a one."

"The exact happening and the cause of this person's continuous mental distress, stated simply and without any ornamental forms of speech, is as follows. She is the meaner part of a person of very fierce and courageous disposition, who is so far removed from her in temperament that he is little disposed to gladden her face by conforming to her wishes when, from time to time, she is assailed by fears and apprehensions occasioned by the half-seen and the dimly-understood. For example, although the plantations encircling their abode are the acknowledged resort of a band of outrageous spirits, who frequently disport themselves openly within sight of the upper windows, yet this person is not allowed to employ one skilled in the art of removing such inconveniences. On the contrary her lord will not permit them to be disturbed at all, persisting that the fact is of incalculable value in reflecting dignity and reputation on us throughout the province, and asserting that many excessively wealthy mandarins of recent creation would willingly devote half of their possessions to be similarly honoured. An even more disturbing circumstance has now arisen, for the one in question having been recently presented with a sumptuous coffin of admittedly noble proportions insists on keeping it prominently displayed in the inner chamber, where it is an unending source of agonised vibration to this one's most delicate and susceptible internal cords. So overwhelmed with admiration for the article has her lord become that he spends the greater part of his time in an ecstatic contemplation of its excellences and it is no uncommon thing for her, when recalled from the Middle Air suddenly in the dead of night, to open her eyes and behold by the pale and unnatural light of the great sky lantern the coffin door slowly opening and the person referred to stepping out in a condition of exalted mental introspection. Unless matters can be adjusted to a more ordinary state without delay it is probable that another coffin will very soon be required elsewhere."

"The complication is a delicate one," said Kang Chieng, submitting the facts as they had been stated to the judgement of a variety of sacred devices, "and the only possible manner in which relief can be permanently afforded is, of necessity, rather intricate."

"Sooner than continue in so distracting an existence, this person would submit herself to any penance not actually degrading, and would, moreover, sacrifice to a practically un-limited extent," replied the wife of Kio-Feng steadfastly.

"The matter is not one which can be adjusted in that en-gaging manner," replied Kang Chieng. "There are certain formalities which must necessarily be performed but it is neces-sary first to convince your undoubtedly self-willed lord that his behaviour is ill-advised and is, in reality, dangerous to himself and not respectful towards his house."

"Alas!" exclaimed the wife of Kio-Feng, "if such is indeed an essential part of the arrangement this person will return and study the records of her race so that she may not incur the reproach of displaying an unbecoming ignorance when she shortly meets the spirits of her illustrious ancestors."

"By no means," replied Kang Chieng firmly. "Protected by his immaculate reputation and rendered secure by the sacred nature of his profession, this person himself will cheerfully carry out the obligation for you. Conduct him unperceived to the inner chamber, therefore, and he will then conceal himself within your lord's coffin, so that that person may learn, when he throws open the swinging door as his custom is, that the unexpected sight of a living being suddenly emerging from such a place is not conducive to a settled tranquillity of mind. As a natural consequence he will then be more susceptible to the unassuming moderation of your request."

Filled with a new hope at having obtained the services and the discriminating advice of so conscientious and painstaking a person the wife of Kio-Feng readily agreed to this expedi-ent, and entirely ignorant of the fact that she had been drawn into the meshes of Kang Chieng's elaborately-planned scheme, she met him at an appointed hour beyond sunset and secretly brought him past the guards to the door of the inner chamber where she left him on the understanding that he should act in the manner already indicated.

Then Kang Chieng, knowing that the precise moment permitted him for vengeance out of his entire life was not far distant, took brush and ink and wrote a certain sentence upon a specially prepared sheet of parchment. This he burned, accompanying the act with many ceremonies with which he had become acquainted during his long course of initiation, so that the written sentence immediately sped to the Upper Air where it searched until it discovered the spirit of the father of Kang Chieng to whom it made itself known, summoning him to the earth without delay and intimating that the moment of his triumph was at hand. When, therefore, Kang Chieng observed the form of a white butterfly enter the chamber and alight on the coffin of Kio-Feng he knew that the spirit of his father was at hand to play an allotted part, and taking up his position he brought his preparations to a close and purified his mind from all materialism by deep inward contemplation.

The hanging curtains had been drawn aside and the chamber was pervaded by a most engaging splendour of the great sky lantern when Kio-Feng entered at his accustomed hour. With no disturbing emotions he approached the coffin for the purpose of gratifying his eyes by a renewed admiration of its beauties, but no sooner had he thrown open the door and prepared to step within than the air became filled with sounds and portents which even he could not fail to recognise as a definite omen that all the converging lines of destiny pointed to an immediate conclusion of his depraved and ill-spent life. This was the welcome signal assuring Kang Chieng that the matter had come about in such a way as he had planned it by elaborate calculations in the past years. He now stepped slowly forth, and at the sight Kio-Feng threw up his hands with an undignified gesture of terror and despair, for Kang Chieng had concealed all but his face in a winding garment of white cloth from which protruded the handle of Kio-Feng's own double-edged knife, while by various marks he had caused his face to assume the external likeness to that of his father. Furthermore, he had sprinkled around him the distilled essence of apricot blossom, an odour which had hung within the nostrils of Kio-Feng since the day of his crime in the orchard, and as he advanced he stretched forth his hand as he had specifically assured the agent of the Stealthy Brethren that he would do.

"It is the end predicted by the magician Lin Tzun!" cried Kio-Feng at the sight, and without expressing himself any further he sank down to the ground although no blow had been dealt him.

"Now is your hour, O my father," said Kang Chieng. "Descend, and do not spare the guilty."

Then the spirit of the father of Kang Chieng flew down from the coffin and taking another shape it entered the body of Kio-Feng and squeezed his heart between its two hands until it became as dry and devoid of life as an uprooted sponge cast upon a burning sandbank by the receding waters of the Tong Hai.

Having in this manner acted in accordance with both his oaths, Kang Chieng took an affectionate farewell of the spirit of his father. He then defaced the inscription upon the coffin and leaving in its place an inscription of appropriate contempt he passed unchallenged from the house and was soon beyond pursuit in the direction of Pel Hing.

Ming Tseuen and
the Emergency

T WAS THE CUSTOM OF MING TSEUEN to take his stand at an early hour each day in the open Market of Nang-kau, partly because he was industrious by nature and also since he had thereby occasionally found objects of inconspicuous value which others had carelessly left unprotected over-night. Enterprise such as this deserved to prosper, but so far, owing to some apathy on the part of the fostering deities, silver had only come to Ming Tseuen in dreams and gold in visions. Yet with frugality, and by acquiring the art of doing without whatever he was unable to procure, he had supported himself from the earliest time he could remember up to the age of four short of a score of years. In mind he was alert and not devoid of courage, the expression of his face mild and unconcerned, but in stature he lacked the appearance of his age, doubtless owing to the privations he had frequently endured.

Next to Ming Tseuen on the one side was the stall of Lieu, the dog-butcher, on the other that of a person who removed corroding teeth for the afflicted. This he did with his right hand while at the same time he beat upon a large iron gong with his left, so that others in a like plight who might be approaching should not be distressed by hearing anything of a not absolutely encouraging strain. About his neck he wore a lengthy string of massive teeth to indicate his vigour and tenacity, but to Ming he privately disclosed that these were the fangs of suitable domestic animals which he had obtained to enlarge himself in the eyes of the passer-by. Ming in return told him certain things about his own traffic which were not generally understood.

Across the Way a barber was accustomed to take his stand, his neighbours being a melon-seller to the east, and to the west a caster of nativities and lucky day diviner. Also near at hand a bamboo worker plied his useful trade, an incense vendor extolled his sacred wares, a money-changer besought men to enrich themselves at his expense, and a fan-maker sang a song about the approaching heat and oppression of the day. From time to time the abrupt explosion of a firework announced the completion of an important bargain, proclaimed a cer-emony, or indicated some protective rite, while the occasional passage of a high official whose rank required a chariot wider than the Way it traversed, afforded an agreeable break in the routine of those who found themselves involved. At convenient angles beggars pointed out their unsightliness to attract the benevolently inclined, story-tellers and minstrels spread their mats and raised their enticing chants, the respective merits of contending crickets engaged the interest of the speculative, and a number of ingenious contrivances offered chances that could not fail – so far as the external appearance went – to be profitable even to the inexperienced if they but persisted long enough. It will thus be seen that almost all the simpler require-ments of an ordinary person could be satisfied about the spot.

Ming Tseuen's venture differed essentially from all these occupations. In Nang-kau, as elsewhere, there might be found a variety of persons – chiefly the aged and infirm – who were suddenly inspired by a definite craving to perform a reasonable number of meritorious actions before they Passed Beyond. The mode of benevolence most esteemed consisted in preserving life or in releasing the innocent out of captivity, down even to the humblest creatures of their kind; for all the Sages and reli-gious essayists of the past have approved these deeds of virtue as assured of celestial recognition. As it would manifestly be unwise for the aged and infirm to engage upon so ambiguous a quest haphazard – even if it did not actually bring them into conflict with the established law – those who were of Ming Tseuen's way of commerce had sought to provide an easy and mutually beneficial system by which so humane an impulse should be capable of wide and innocuous expression. This took the form of snaring alive a diversity of birds and lesser beings of the wild and offering them for sale, with a persuasive placard, attractively embellished with wise and appropriate sayings from the lips of the Philosophers, inviting those who were at all doubtful of their record in the Above World to acquire merit, while there was still time, by freeing a victim from its bondage; and so convincing were the arguments employed and so moderate the outlay involved when compared with the ultimate benefits to be received, that few who were feeling in any way unwell at the time were able to resist the allurement.

Owing to the poverty of his circumstances, Ming Tseuen was only able to furnish his stall with a few small birds of the less expensive sorts, but, to balance this deficiency, he could always traffic at a certain profit, for so devoted to his cause were the little creatures he displayed, as a result of his zealous attention to their natural wants, that when released they invariably returned after a judicious interval and took up their accustomed stations within the cage again. In such a manner the mornings became evenings and the days passed into moons, but though Ming sustained existence he could add little or nothing to his store.

Among the crowd that passed along the Way there were many who stopped from time to time before Ming Tseuen's stall to admire the plumage of his company of birds or to read the notice he exposed without any real intention of benefiting by the prospect he held out, and by long practice the one concerned could immediately detect their insincerity and avoid entering into a conversation which would inevitably be wasted. Thus imperceptibly the narration leads up to the appearance of Hya, an exceptionally graceful maiden of the house of Tai, whose willowy charm is only crudely indicated by the name of Orange Blossom then already bestowed upon her. Admittedly the part she had to play in this stage of Ming Tseuen's destiny was neither intricate nor deep, but by adding to the firmness of his purpose when the emergency arose she unwittingly supplied a final wedge. No less pointed than when he first fashioned it is the retort of the shrewd Tso-yan: 'Not what he is but how he became it concerns the adjudicating gods.'

Orange Blossom had more than once passed the stall of Ming Tseuen before the day when they encountered, and she had paused to observe the engaging movements of the band of feathered prisoners there, but for the reason already indicated he had not turned aside from whatever task he was then engaged on to importune her. When she spoke it was as though Ming for the first time then beheld her, and thenceforward his eyes did not forsake her face while she remained.

"How comes it, keeper of the cage, that your stall is destitute of custom," she inquired melodiously; "seeing that it is by far the most delightful of them all, while less than an arrow's flight away so gross a commerce as the baked extremities of pigs attracts a clamorous throng?"

"The explanation is twofold, gracious being," answered Ming, resolving for the future to abstain from the food she thus disparaged, though it was, indeed, his favourite dish. "In the first place it is as the destinies ordain; in the second it is still too early after daybreak for the elderly and weak to venture forth."

"Yet why should only the venerable and decrepit seek uprightness?" demanded the maiden, with a sympathetic gesture of reproach towards so illiberal an outlook. "Cannot the immature and stalwart equally aspire?"

"Your words are ropes of truth," assented Ming admiringly, "but none the less has it appropriately been written, 'At seventeen one may defy demons; at seventy he trembles merely at the smell of burning sulphur.' Doubtless, then, it is your humane purpose—?" and partly from a wish to detain so incomparable a vision, and also because there was no reason why the encounter should not at the same time assume a remunerative bend, he directed her unfathomable eyes towards that detail of the scroll where the very moderate rates at which merit could be acquired were prominently displayed.

"Alas," exclaimed Hya no less resourcefully, "she who bears the purse is by now a distance to the west. Haply some other time—"

"Perchance your venerated father or revered grandsire might be rejoiced to grasp the opportunity—" he urged, but in the meanwhile the maiden had passed beyond his voice along the Way.

Ming would have remained in a high-minded contemplation, somewhat repaid to see, if not her distant outline, at least the direction in which she would progress, but almost at once the oleose Lieu was at his elbow.

"If," remarked that earthly-souled person with a cunning look, "you should happen to possess influence with the one who has just resumed her path, it might mean an appreciable stream of cash towards your threadbare sleeve. The amount of meat that she and her leisurely and opulent connection must require cannot be slight, and there is no reason why we should not secure the contract and divide the actual profit equally among us."

"So far from that being the case," replied Ming, in a markedly absent voice, "she to whom you quite gratuitously refer cannot even think of the obscene exhibits of your sordid industry without a refined shudder of polished loathing, and those of her house, though necessarily more robust, are doubtless similarly inclined. Reserve your carnivorous schemes for the gluttonous and trite, thou cloven-lipped, opaque-eyed puppy-snatcher."

Instead of directing a stream of like abuse in turn, as he might logically have done, the artless-minded Lieu flung his arms about the other's neck, and despite that one's unceasing protests embraced him repeatedly.

"Thus and thus was it with this person also, in the days of his own perfervid youth," declared the sympathetic dog-butcher when he ceased from the exertion. "She was the swan-like daughter of a lesser underling, and it was my custom to press into her expectant hand a skewer of meat when we encountered in the stress around the great door of the Temple. . . . But that was in the days before a mountain dragon altered the river's course: doubtless by now she is the mother of a prolific race of grandsons and my name and bounty are forgotten."

"There is no possible similitude between the two," declared Ming Tseuen indignantly. "The refinement of this one is so excessive that she shivers at the very thought of food, and the offer of a skewer of meat would certainly throw her into a protracted torpor."

"How can that be maintained unless you have first made the essay?" demanded Lieu with undiminished confidence. "In these affairs it is often the least likely that respond phenomenally. Were it not that a notorious huckster is at this moment turning over my stock with widespread disparagement, I could astonish you out of the storehouse of my adventurous past. In the meanwhile, apply this salutary plaster to your rising ardour: could I have but shown five taels of silver, she whom I coveted was mine, and yet in the event she slipped hence from me; but this one of thine is by my certain information a daughter of the affluent house of Tai, and a golden chain and shackle would not bridge the space between her father's views and your own lowly station."

"Her place is set among the more brilliant stars," agreed Ming briefly. "Nevertheless," he added with a new-born note of hope, "is it not written within the Books, 'However far the heaven, the eye can reach it'?"

"Assuredly," replied Lien, pausing in his departure to return a step, "the eye, Ming Tseuen – but not likewise the hand." And endeavouring to impart an added meaning to his words by a rapid movement of the nearer eyelid, the genial-witted dog-butcher went on his way, leaving Ming with an inward conviction that he was not a person of delicate perception or one with whom it would be well to associate too freely in the future.

It is aptly said, 'After the lightning comes the thunder,' and events of a momentous trend were by no means lagging behind Ming's steps that day. Even while he contended with the self-opinionated Lieu, in a distant quarter of the city a wealthy lacquer merchant, Kwok Shen by name, was seeking to shape afresh this obscure and unknown youth's immediate fate, urged by the pressing mould of his own insistent need. 'It is easier for a gnat to bend a marble tower than for a man to turn destiny aside,' pronounced the Venerable, the Sagacious One, in the days when knowledge was, but how many now, in the moment of their test, acquiescently kowtow? Be that as it may, having perfected and rehearsed his crafty plans, Kwok Shen set out.

It was becoming dusk, and Ming Tseuen would shortly erect a barrier, when Kwok Shen drew near. As he approached the other glanced round, and seeing close at hand an elderly and not too vigorous merchant of the richer sort, he bowed obsequiously, for it was among these that his readiest custom lay. At the same time he recognised in Kwok Shen a stranger whom he had noticed observing him from a distance more than once on recent days, and undoubtedly this incident stirred an element of caution in his mind.

"May your ever-welcome shadow come to rest upon this ill-made stall," remarked Ming Tseuen auspiciously, and looking at him keenly Kwok Shen halted there. "It only remains for my sadly concave ears to drink in the music of your excessive orders," continued Ming. "Seven times seven felicities, esteemed."

"Greeting," replied Kwok Shen more concisely, though as an afterthought he passed the formal salutation, "Do your in-and-out taels overlap sufficiently?"

"'A shop can be opened on pretension, but ability alone can keep it open,'" quoted Ming Tseuen in reply, although, not to create the impression of negligent prosperity, he added, "Yet the shrub one waters is ever more attractive than the forest cedar."

"Admittedly," agreed the merchant politely, for not having applied the leisure of his youth to an assimilation of the Classics, he felt himself becoming immersed in a stream beyond his depth and one that was carrying him away from the not too straightforward object of his quest. "Your literary versatility is worthy of all praise, but for the moment let us confine ourselves to the precise if less resonant terms of commercial usage," he suggested. "Here is a piece of silver for your immediate profit. Thus our meeting cannot involve you in loss and it may quickly tend to your incredible advancement."

"Proceed, munificence, proceed," exclaimed the delighted Ming. "You speak a tongue that both the scholar and the witless can grasp at once," and he transferred the money to his inner sleeve.

"Is there about this spot a tea-house of moderate repute, one affected neither by the keepers of the stalls nor by the most successful class of traders, where we can talk unheard and at our leisure?"

"Almost within sight the tea-house of the Transitory Virtues offers what you describe. Had the invitation come from me, a somewhat less pretentious one might have been chosen, but doubtless to a person of your transparent wealth—"

"Lead on," said Kwok Shen consequentially. "The one beside you is not accustomed to divide a mouse among four guests," and having thus plainly put beyond all question that the settlement did not affect himself, Ming was content to show the way.

The conversation that ensued was necessarily a slow and dignified proceeding. Kwok Shen had so much to conceal, and Ming Tseuen had so much to learn before he knew what it was prudent to admit, that for an appreciable period their intercourse was confined to pressing an interminable succession of cups of tea upon each other. Ming, however, had the advantage of his literary abilities, which enabled him to converse for an indefinite time upon a subject without expressing himself in any way about it, while Kwok Shen laboured under the necessity of having to achieve a specific issue.

The position, as presently outlined by the merchant, stood thus at its essential angles. He was, as he declared, a trader in gums and resins, and by a system of the judicious blending of his several wares at that stage his fortunes were assured. Being of an easy-going and abstemious nature, one wife alone had satisfied his needs, and she in turn had lavished all her care upon an only son, to whom the name of San had been applied. Stricken by an obscure malady this one had languished, and in spite of what every healing art could do had lately Passed Above.

Kwok Shen suitably indicated by means of his facecloth and a discarded plate that the effect of the blow upon himself had been calamitous, but when he spoke of the despair of the lesser one of his inner chamber his voice practically ceased to have any sound attached to it. Very soon every interest in life forsook her; she sank into an unnatural languor and not even the cry of a passing comb vendor or the sound of earthenware being shattered by the household slaves moved her to action. The investigation of skilled exorcists, those who had made the malignant humours their especial lore, all tended to one end: without delay another should be found to take the lost one's place and thereby restore the immortal principles of equilibrity whose disturbance had unbalanced the afflicted mind. To this project she who was most concerned had at last agreed, stipulating, however, that the substitute should bear an exact resemblance to the departed San.

Beyond this point there could be no feasible concealment of the part that Ming Tseuen would be called upon to play, and that person's alert mind began to prepare itself for the arrangement. He had already composed the set terms of his aged father's anguish and chosen a suitable apophthegm to describe his broken-down mother's tears when the words of Kwok Shen's persuasive voice recalled him.

"At the moment of abandoning the search as hopeless, chance led this one's dejected feet into the market here. When these misguided eyes first rested on your noble outward form, for a highly involved moment it was as though some ambiguous Force must have conveyed there the one we mourned, for his living presentment seemed to stand revealed. So complicated became the emotions that this person returned home at once, unable for the time to arrange his sequences adequately. Since then he has more than once come secretly and stood apart, observing from a distance, and each occasion has added a more imperviable lacquer to the surface of his first impression. In the meanwhile, not from any want of confidence let it be freely stated, but solely in order to enlarge our knowledge of one so precious in our sight, a series of discreet inquiries have been made. Rest assured, therefore, Ming Tseuen, that everything connected with your orphaned life and necessitous circumstances is known. Lo, I have bared the recesses of my private mind; let your answering word be likewise free from guile."

"How shall the drooping lotus bargain with the sender of the rain?" replied Ming Tseuen becomingly. "I put myself implicitly within your large and open hand . . . . Any slight details of adjustment can be more suitably proposed after hearing the exact terms of your princely liberality."

By this sudden and miraculous arisement it came to pass that Ming Tseuen was at once received into Kwok Shen's sumptuously appointed house as his adopted son. No less enchanted than bewildered by the incredible resemblance was she of the inner chamber when the moment came, and together the merchant and his wife sought to mould Ming's habits to an even closer fiction of the one whose name he now assumed.

"At such a rebuke from menial lips he whom we indicate unnamed was wont to extend a contumacious tongue," perchance it might on one occasion be, and, "His manner of pronouncing 'tsze' was *thus*," upon another. All San's toys and possessions accrued to Ming's unquestioned use and he occupied the sleeping chamber of the one whose robes he daily wore. While kindly and indulgent on every other point, Kwok Shen imposed one close restraint.

"It is not seemly that a merchant having this and that to his position should be compelled to traffic for an heir among the garbage of the market stalls, though necessity, as it is said, can make a blind beggar see," observed the one concerned. "It would be still more lamentable that this abasement should be known to those around. For that reason we shall shortly go hence into another place, where our past will be obscured; meanwhile let the four outer walls of this not incommodious hovel mark the limits of your discovering feet and within them hold no word of converse with any from outside whom you chance to meet. In this respect I speak along an iron rule that shall measure the thickness of a single hair of deviation."

"Your richly mellow voice stays with me when your truly graceful form is absent on a journey," replied Ming submissively. "As the renowned Hung Wu is stated to have said—"

"He who is wanting from our midst was not prone to express himself in terms of classical analogy," corrected Kwok Shen graciously, and Ming dutifully refrained.

It was not long before Ming Tseuen had occasion to recall this charge, but as he was then in his own chamber with none other by, its obligation was not so rigorous as it might otherwise have seemed. He had drawn aside a stool that he might open a small shutter and look out, but the Way beneath was austere and void of entertainment, so that he would have retired again, when one somewhat younger than himself went by, propelling along his path an empty can.

"Ae ya, image-face!" he exclaimed, seeing Ming there and stopping to regard him acrimoniously. "So thou art still among us despite the pursuing demon, art thou? Where is the kite in the form of a vampire with outstretched wings for which I bargained with thee?"

"There is no kite such as you describe, nor have I ever bargained with you for it," retorted Ming, who might require the kite for his own future use. "Further, it is not permitted that I should hold converse with another."

"There is the kite, for these deficient hands have held the cord that stayed it, and touching the bargain we together ate the bag of dragon's-eyes that were the price of its surrender. Haply you think, O crafty son of the ever two-faced house of Kwok, because you are fated shortly to Pass Hence, thus to avoid your just engagements?"

A breath of mistrust stirred certain doubts that lingered in Ming's mind. He looked east and west along the Way and saw that none approached; from the house behind no disturbing sound arose.

"What air have you lately breathed," he ventured amicably, "in that for some time past you have been absent from the city?"

"What pungent fish is this that you thus trail?" demanded the other scornfully. "Never was I beyond Nang-kau since the day my mother had me. Doubtless you hope to lead my mind away from the matter of the vampire kite – may the dragon's-eyes lie cankerous on thy ill-nurtured stomach!"

"Nay, but my heart is clear of any guile," protested Ming resourcefully, "in token whereof here is a cake of honey, freely to thy hand. Yet how comes it that you know of the destiny awaiting this untimely one?"

"Why, it is the great talk among the inner chambers of this quarter of the city, and there is much concern as to the means by which the supple paint-peddler within will strive to avert the doom."

"What do men say?" asked Ming, veiling his misgivings.

"They say little; but their lesser ones industriously supply that lack."

"And to what end?" demanded Ming more urgently.

"The general trend is that the Fates will in due course prevail," replied the one outside, speaking with an air of agreeable anticipation despite the honey cake he fed on, "for it is recalled that when the wily mastic-monger had you adopted to the Temple banyan tree, to secure for you a powerful advocate, the hostile Ones were strong enough by a lightning flash to cleave it to the ground and leave you shieldless. Glad am I, Kwok San, that for me the geomancers foretold the threefold happiness. . . . To whom will go your bow and golden arrows, O estimable San?"

"To thee, without doubt, out of deep mutual friendship," Ming made reply in haste. "Touching this fate – when is the day—"

"I cannot stay – one stronger than myself draws nigh and the fair remnant of this cake—"

"But the bow and golden arrows—"

"Another day perchance—" came back the lessening voice, and pursuing feet sped by.

Ming Tseuen replaced the shutter and sat down. A variety of noteworthy sayings from the lips of Sages of the past occurred to his retentive mind, but although many of these were of gem-like lustre, none seemed at the moment to offer him the exact solution that his position called for. What outline that position took he was now perfectly assured – the chance encounter with that one outside had moulded vaporous doubt into a compact certainty. Kwok Shen had played a double part throughout. His son had not Passed Hence at all, but the foretellers had divined that he lived beneath the influence of some malignant spirit and that at a predicted hour its vengeance would be wrought. Driven from one protection to another, accident, in the form of his own peculiar likeness, had given into a distracted father's hand a final and decisive means to baffle its perceptions. The device was one of high classical authority and in like case Ming Tseuen would himself have hastened to adopt it, but, as the adage rightly says, "What is defence to Ho-ping is to Ping-ho defiance."

There was still time doubtless to turn his knowledge into flight; the outer door might now be barred, but he could at a stress project his body through the shutter. Truly, but what lay beyond? Everywhere Kwok Shen's bitter vengeance would pursue him and on a thousand facile pretexts could betray him to the Torments.

Nor, apart, was the idea of flight congenial to his active resolution. After a time of penury he had at length experienced a course of ease which he would willingly prolong up to its farthest limit. Among these hopes there twined, perchance, the form of Hya, of the house of Tai. If, ran his most persuasive thought, by any means he could outwit the invading demon and preserve himself alive, might not the liberality of Kwok Shen be deeply stirred and all things wear a brighter face thenceforward? The deliberate way in which the snare had been exposed to him revealed that his own protective Forces were even now on the alert.

These varied facets had held Ming Tseuen for a flight of time involving hours when an unusual sound, slight but insistent, at the shutter overhead recalled him to the moment. Scarcely daring to hope that it was that other now returned again, he drew the footstool to the wall and cautiously looked out. The cloud of night had gathered, but the great sky lantern hung above and by its beams Ming saw another, such as he himself, standing below.

"Who art thou standing there?" he whispered down, "and wherefore are you come?"

"I would see you face to face," replied a voice no less well guarded. "Thrust forth thy arm that I may clamber up."

"Stay while I get a worthier hold," responded Ming, and having done so complied. The one outside made good his claim, and twisting through the space adroitly they fell upon the floor together. As they got up the other laughed, and standing thus apart regarded Ming.

"Canst thou not guess?" he demanded artlessly. "I am that San, heir of the one who is lord here, and this is my own chamber."

I know who you are though I must not speak the name. So that is as I am!" and he continued to regard Ming closely.

"Should he chance to come this way our skins will bear witness of the meeting to the day when that last measurement is taken," observed Ming darkly; then going to the door he pushed home the wedge above the latch so that none could enter.

"That I well know," admitted San, "but we shall have warning by his sonorous breathing from afar and you can then speed me through the shutter."

"True," agreed Ming. "Yet whence are you?"

"For seven days and nearly seven days more I have dwelt at the elder Kong's, under a very strict injunction that confines me there. But I may not tell thee why."

"Then how comes it now that you have disobeyed?"

"The way is left unguarded and I adventured down. There came an irk to see the one who was, I heard him say, the double image of my living self – and as I likewise heard it would be too late to-morrow."

Ming Tseuen did not waver in his listless poise nor did he vary the unconcerned expression of his features.

"Why should to-morrow be too late?" he asked neglectfully.

"That I could tell also, but I will not lest you should guess too much," wisely replied the other. "But give heed to this: my shutter opens on an empty space where none pass by, and beneath it stands a water-cask on poles by which I scrambled down. Couldst thou have done as much?"

"If it gives you the foothold to descend, I doubt not that I could get up again," said Ming consideringly. "What is the place called where the elder Kong abides?"

"It has the symbol of a leaping goat and stands against the water-gate, a short space to the east – but why should you seek to know?" demanded San.

"I do not seek to know save in the light of converse," answered Ming, feeling his cautious path. "There is something to talk about in this exploit of thine – few of like age could have achieved it. And to have learned so much that would only be spoken of behind barred doors reveals a special aptness."

"As to that," declared the other proudly, "there is a passage close against the inner room where he and she recline that has a moving board unknown to them. Hadst thou not found it yet?"

"What need had I, seeing that we two are alike in everything, so that the one should tell all to the other?"

"That does not rejoice my face entirely," decided San, after he had thought upon it. "For seven days now and almost seven days more you have possessed my toys, while I in turn have been bereft of yours. . . . Where is my phœnix upon wheels whose place was here? Have you incapably destroyed it?"

"Not I," declared Ming Tseuen, though mildly. "It is laid by. This person is too old for such immature devices."

"How so?" demanded San indignantly. "My years are twelve, while among the outside I freely pass for more. How many years are thine?"

"Mine are somewhat more, though I freely pass for less," admitted Ming. "Therein we meet upon a middle ground."

"Further," continued San vaingloriously, "I am affianced to a virtuous maiden of the worthy house of Tai, whom I shall in due course marry and have a hundred strong sons of my own. Are you—"

"Which one is that – this maiden?" interposed Ming Tseuen, more sharply than his wont.

"How should I say – not having ever seen her? But she has a sweet-smelling name and all the nine delights. Are you thus pledged or married?"

"Not yet," admitted Ming, "but I may some day attain it."

"I do not think so – though more I may not say lest I should tell too much. . . . Why, when I move my head or hand, do you do likewise also, and why should you change your voice to follow mine?"

"Consider the gladness of thy father's eyes when even he fails to discriminate between us," replied Ming, with an appropriate gesture such as San would use, and speaking with the counterpart of that one's voice. "Is it not – but hasten, one approaches from the inner hall. Here! Crouch quickly down behind this screen and eat your breath, or much bamboo awaits us!" Ming Tseuen only paused for a single beat of time to assure himself that San was adequately concealed before he sought to unwedge the door. Before he could reach it the latch was tried and the handle shaken.

"Why is the door barred against this person's coming, seeing that you have not yet had your nightly cup of wine?" inquired the one who stood there, a close attendant on Kwok Shen himself. "This is not apt, O San."

"I had forgot," replied Ming sleepily. "My mind is strange and dubious to-night. Regard it not, accommodating Tsoi."

"That may well be," assented Tsoi, with a hasty glance around and fingering a written charm he wore upon his wrist protectively. "For as I came I seemed to hear resentful voices in the air, and qualmous rustlings."

"Those also," agreed Ming more wakefully. "And wind-swirls overhead and beating wings, with sudden shrieks of mirth and other unclean sounds. What do these things portend, much-knowing?"

"I may not stay – he bade me hasten back," replied the weak-kneed Tsoi, taking a firm grasp upon the handle of the door. "This cup is from his own preparing hand. May you float tranquil in the Middle Air to-night!"

"May your constituents equalise harmoniously!" responded Ming, and they heard him bar the door on the outer side and marked his speedy footsteps down the passage.

"I also would withdraw," exclaimed San, coming forth and in a sudden tremor. "That matter of the creatures of the air did not appease my inner organs. I had not thought of that. Nor was the door barred thus when I slept here."

"Peace," said Ming reassuringly; "I have a new and most alluring artifice to show you yet. Where is the vampire kite that has a trusty cord attached? It turns on that."

"I do not care. I will not stay; at least, I will not stay unless you share with me the wine that Tsoi has brought. I was wont to have a cup of sweet spiced wine each night, and thou hast had it here while there I have had none."

"The wine: assuredly. That is but fair," agreed Ming Tseuen. He had already raised it to his lips to quell a sudden thirst that parched his throat, but now he turned aside to wipe his mouth and then held out the cup. "Your engaging moderation fills me with despair. Put my self-reproach at ease by drinking all."

"Yea; that is but fair," repeated San approvingly, "seeing how long you have enjoyed it. . . . It has a bitterish taste that was not wont to be."

"The rarer kinds of wine are often thus; it indicates a special sort of excellence."

"But this weighs down my eyes and sways my mind," objected San, with twitching limbs already. "It begins to burn my mouth. . . . I will not drink the rest."

"Consider well," urged Ming, "how humiliated would be the one who sent the wine if any should be left."

"I cannot—Why does the room thus spin—"

"Cannot!" protested Ming, and by a swift and sudden move he held the other's head and raised the wine until the cup was empty. "Cannot! But see, thou hast!"

"That was not well," gasped San, turning to bite the hand that held him, ere he fell senseless to the ground. "Tonight thou art outdone, misgotten dog!"

"Perchance; but the deities ordain," acquiesced Ming trustfully, "and this works to an end." He continued to regard the one stretched at his feet, and then he turned to wedge the door inside and to listen for a moment to the sounds about the house. San had not stirred nor did he move again.

"Much of this arises from an ordinary person interfering with the guiding hand of destiny," was the burden of Ming's thoughts, for in addition to his other qualities the one in question was both reverent and devout. "Even had he been content to leave matters at a middle stage there is no telling what the outer end might not have been, but by so ordering the wine that the demon should definitely understand that his vengeance was complete, the too painstaking Kwok Shen has stumbled. Yet with one so consistently inept it will be well to certify assurance."

Accordingly he took San up and raised him to a couch, and pressing a cushion down upon his face he held it firmly there. Meanwhile, as he waited for his self-imposed task to be complete, his grateful heart rejoiced:

"Plainly the spirits of my hitherto unknown but henceforth venerated ancestors have been at work and brought this thing to pass. Henceforth I will sacrifice to their very useful memories on a really worthy scale, nor will outside and comparatively second-rate deities be forgotten, so that all who have upheld my cause will receive something solid in return. Never again let it impiously be said, 'He who sets out to make his fortune should leave his gods at home.' Has not this person maintained integrity throughout and, behold, his poverty is changed to affluence, affectionate and influential parents are raised up to take the place of those whom he has never known, and the loadstar of all earthly desire is automatically reserved to minister to his future happiness? Assuredly there is more in this than formless chance."

By this time there could no longer be any reasonable doubt that Ming Tseuen's task was done. With a seemly regard in the observance he despoiled San of his robe and all he carried, wrapping the one that he had worn around him in return, and he also made certain changes in the room of a consistent nature. Then he drew himself up to the shutter and cautiously looked out. The way was clear and the great sky lantern for a moment auspiciously withheld her light; Ming Tseuen dropped noiselessly to earth, and again reverently committing himself to the protection of his necessarily anonymous ancestors, he turned his trusting footsteps towards the elder Kong's, by the water-gate, a short distance to the east.

Lam-hoo and the
Reward of Merit

N THE EARLY DAYS of the Tuang dynasty when a formless
mist covered most of the inhabitable world and Hysi Khang
(called 'The Hard-lined') ruled over our now delectable and
flower-strewn land, a poor but industrious and exceptionally
devout villager, Lam-hoo by name, lived in a small but well-
swept hut under the hand of a mercenary and despotic official.
Fang Jung, the noble thus described, had been both envious
and depraved from his milk days upwards, so that before long
the sight of Lam-hoo's untroubled face despite his penurious
lot, and the high repute his character had attained, began to
erode that corrupt functionary's sense of pleasure. He therefore sought his liegeman's disgrace, and having no default to
impugn him with he planned an unworthy pitfall.

When Lam-hoo heard that Fang Jung required his instant
presence he put aside his working garb and went without
misgiving. It is nothing to Fang Jung's credit that he was a
smooth-speaking mandarin whatever his mood, for this was
the outcome of a profligate habit that left him inert, but it was
noticed that when displeased he gnawed the ends of his long
and unbecoming moustache with an air of menace.

"It is always a privilege to reward unostentatious worth, Lam-
hoo," began the two-faced oppressor, "and the report of your
exemplary way of life is familiar to one whose ears are both
large and ever widely open. It so happens that a state appointment of unique distinction has now become vacant and nothing
could be more appropriate than that you, who have set yourself

tenaciously against wrong-doing, should fill it. The necessary insignia of office require only your discharge of the trifling court fees and the inscriber of our spoken word will draw up the needful authority at the cost of his usual exaction."

"Alas! High Excellence," replied Lam-hoo, "it is greatly to be feared that any public office will find this incompetent earth-plodder wholly lacking. What, therefore, is the precise service entailed for which he has been deemed fitting?"

"The appointment," leisurely announced Fang Jung, dropping the words with pleasurable precision, "will be that of Public Carrier-out of Magisterial Decrees and Bestower of Corporal Infliction. In the course of your enviable task it will fall to your entertaining lot to decapitate, bowstring, incinerate, throat-press, piecemeal-slice, crucify, impale, flay, rack, hang, drown or otherwise fatally dispose of hardened offenders of the recalcitrant kind; to little-slice, thumb-suspend, heavy-squeeze, pillory, shorten at one or both ends, or similarly reprove those of a less contumacious bend, and to apply rattan in merely routine cases."

"Forbear, Pre-eminence!" besought Lam-hoo, "and let the unfulfilled word be cancelled. Among your vassalry there could scarcely be found one less competent for this honour. Not only is your suppliant slave unused to deeds of force but he is an enrolled member of the 'Pacific Knife,' a community who are under a binding vow not to take life, even that of the most insignificant of created beings."

At these becoming words, although spoke in a tone of deep respect and with Lam-hoo's face still pressed to the ground, Fang Jung began to assail the ragged ends of his already unsightly moustache.

"There is an apt saying, 'Give a beggar a joint and he will throw the bone at you when the meat is eaten'," was his arrogant rejoinder. "It is one thing, however, to raise your defiant voice in the restricted confines of the Lotus Blossom tea-house and other low-caste resorts of treason: it is quite another to question the authority of the wearer of an exalted button.

Whosoever neglects or omits to constrain offence when formally called upon to do so is himself automatically guilty of the same misdemeanour, so that you stand in immediate jeopardy of having committed murder, arson, rape, evasion of ya-men dues, pig-stealing, disrespect of official news, forestalling, spitting at shooting stars, tomb-haunting, annoying silk-worms, degeneracy of character and indiscriminate thuggism. Turn how you will, Lam-hoo, it is difficult to see how you can avoid either the hempen tie or the wooden collar."

Doubtless Fang Jung would have continued further in a like strain, it being congenial to his ill-regulated mind to dwell on the unpleasant. At this point, however, he was seen to change to an inferior tint, and it required some adroitness on the part of his personal guard to recover the excess of moustache which, in order to relieve his feelings while maintaining an appearance of exterior calm, he had inadvertently swallowed.

That night Lam-hoo left his mediocre but cherished home and with Hea-an, his allegiant lesser one, who led Kwong and Tsoi by either hand, he pressed forward into an unknown existence. A wheel-barrow contained such of his meagre possessions as could be the readiest stacked, and laboriously propelling this, Lam-hoo maintained an undeviating path while confidently awaiting an omen.

When several gong-strokes had passed since they set out and the time of no-light approached, Lam-hoo bethought himself of the need for shelter throughout the night, and choosing a well-spread banyan tree he gathered there a sufficiency of fallen twigs, covering these with dry leaves and suitable litter.

"Before you make use of what you have prepared," said a voice from the shadow beyond, "consider the claims of one whose need may be even greater."

"We have come on a long and toilsome path, having abandoned our protective roof and covered many an exacting li to escape a despot's malice," replied Lam-hoo mildly, "In what way does your meritorious case transcend this hardship?"

"I who speak am the most essential thing on earth, for without my part there would be no existence," declared the voice with dispassionate assurance. "I am the Bearer, and my need is at every beat of time throughout the cycles, while my pains are eternal."

"This cannot be other than Koom Fa, the Universal Mother, who thus indicates the debt that all men owe," maintained Lam-hoo in a discreet whisper. "Take what is yours by every test, Imperishable; already we have two dutiful and well-formed saplings."

"Your unassuming merit has not passed unmarked, Lam-hoo," was the gracious reply. "I who begin all cannot see the end of any, but sooner or later —" at this point the presence faded.

Although Hea-an, whose tightly-bound feet were now incapable of further progress, went so far as to uphold that there would be no impiety in their occupying the pallet as well, since what was intangible could not be deprived of space by those who were corporeal, Lam-hoo rejected this as almost profane and led them to a respectful distance apart, where they spent the night on the bare ground and beneath a tree that admittedly afforded less protection than the banyan.

At daybreak they resumed their arduous way, refreshed (as Lam-hoo pointed out) by water from a rain-fed pool and such sparse herbs and berries as they could gather. Yet scarcely had they set out when one whose disarray betrayed an untidy mind rose from the stone where he sat and approached with a petition.

"Invoking the cause of the sublime among the arts, he who is the most impractical and careless of all mankind – an inspired poet – begs you to preserve a classic. During the quietude of the night eight hundred lines of diamond-like brilliance came to the one who speaks, but in the space of a gong-stroke or two they will have faded from his prolific but vagarious mind and be lost to a bereaved world for ever. Devote to this service the recording tablets which you no doubt have and you will have earned the gratitude of seven generations of our romance-loving race – to say nothing of a dedicatory sonnet."

"This must certainly be Tou-Fou, now called the God of Verse," confided Lam-hoo apart, "by whom we are thus greatly honoured.

"It is not to be denied," he replied aloud, "that only a single tablet is among our trivial possessions, but your claim to it must prevail since this mentally bankrupt person has never yet evolved even one line worth preserving."

"It is as the arranging powers ordain; doubtless you are supple with your hands or have other ways of giving expression," suggested the poet with easy complacence. "In any case, the All-Seeing, the All-Providing will repay you in due season."

The next to greet them with a request was a saintly recluse in a way-side cell who for the greater part of his well-spent life had endured every variety of privation.

"At the same time," he confessed, "there must inevitably be some limit even in what is certainly the most devotional form of existence, and the persistent drip of calcareous moisture through an utterly inadequate roof threatens at last to harden the surface of this anchorite's sympathetic outlook. To pose as a stylite on a column is a recognised if slightly ostentatious display of piety: it is scarcely to be imagined that he who retires to the obscurity of a subterranean cave has any ambition to become a stalagmite."

"All you say not only goes to reproach this ungrateful person with his own enviable lot," admitted Lam-hoo contritely. "Whatever you see among his threadbare store to assuage your present state – to that you are unstintingly welcome."

"Since you press munificence to such an extreme the weather-resisting fabric of your wheel-barrow cover would serve –" and he also assured Lam-hoo that the meritorious deed would not go unrequited. The latter person considered that he was thereby heavily overpaid, but Hea-an, though too dutiful to express dissent, commiserated Kwong and Tsoi openly on their unnatural plight until their sobs withheld her.

Not to impose too excessive a strain on the polite forbearance of an ever-indulgent band of listeners (apologised Kai Lung), let it be admitted that before the boundary of Fang Jung's authority had been reached not only the entire contents of the wheel-barrow but even the barrow itself had passed into the service of those whose need was demonstrably more acute or their claims more pressing. Against this, Lam-hoo could rely (as he frequently reminded Hea-an) on the assurance of a variety of obliged and undoubtedly sincere personages that the All-Seeing, the All-Providing would scrupulously reimburse him in every particular.

How near at hand that occasion was Lam-hoo had been too diffident even to surmise, until a hint was dropped by a grateful bee (the instrument of a Superior Power) in return for the cheerful bestowal (wherewith to mend her hive) of his own outworn straw sandals. At that early stage of the Empire's growth, when the Constituent Elements were not fully resolved nor the Essential Equipoise properly balanced, the lesser deities frequently came down and assumed other outward forms, so that Lam-hoo experienced no surprise at being spoken to by a loquacious ass or even to have converse with more insignificant creatures. A song-bird, claiming to be the blithest and most light-hearted thing alive, had required a skein of thread to restore a damaged nest; an aged tortoise – 'the wisest and most uncommunicative of all,' a salve for outworn joints; an ant, asserting its industry to have become a proverb, "anything wherewith to assume an air of importance." It was when nothing remained of Lam-hoo's former store that the bee – "nature's thriftiest product," she maintained, pointed to the material needful for her use and explained the brood's dependent condition.

"Take what you ask," was Lam-hoo's humane reply, "since your need is thus and thus, for in any case this one and those of his hearth have now reached the limit of their cable."

"That is as it seems to you," reproved the bee, "because, being mortal and bound to earth, you only command a foreshortened vision. Actually, you have now passed the ultimate test and have thereby attained the ninety-ninth degree of merit." Then dropping its voice significantly the bee added: "More may not be said, but the All-Seeing, the All-Providing, has both noted and taken measures."

That night Lam-hoo, naked, hungry, parched and cold, and destitute of all that he had set out with, slept on the open waste with the three around him, covered by his cloak as they slept, but otherwise in little better condition. About the middle gong-stroke of darkness he was visited by a Shape which took him by the hand and floated him upwards into the Presence.

"Lam-hoo," said the Voice of the Unseen (and the sound was as compelling as the clash of many brass cymbals), "you have completed the circle of your earthly trial and are now in the process of Passing Upwards. As you leave two dutiful he-children to extend your Line this is only a temporary inconvenience at the most, and to commemorate your unselfish life a very special reward has been instituted in your honour. From the ground receiving your outer case a tree has been commanded to spring, and this unique growth, bearing your characteristic name henceforth, will supply every want which an ordinary person need encounter. Thus a variety of palatable and sustaining foods will be yielded by its tender shoots, a grain only slightly inferior to rice comprising its seed, while its hollow stems will provide a convenient and inexpensive system of bringing water from even the most distant sources. A sugary sap may be extracted from incisions at certain points and this in time will be found to have medicinal properties. The uses to which the leaves are destined to be put – as hats, fans, umbrellas, screens, roofing material, light household ware, upper and even under-clothing – are so many and diffuse that it would tax the ingenuity of a Recording Being to tabulate them. Scarcely fewer are the services to mankind that the various grades of its fibre offer, ranging from the delicacy of a silken thread to the sturdy rigidity of a junk's cable, and combining between these extremes material for fabrics of almost every texture. As regards the wood of the trunk and its smaller parts it will ultimately become a commonplace that not only an entire residence of superior build – a 'Lam-hoo built house' in fact – but every detail of its equipment and fittings will be within the grasp of any capable handyman, wielding, moreover, tools fashioned out of the toughest lamhoo and sharpened on a lamhoo whetstone. By this comprehensive scheme every article that you have so generously bestowed will be procurable from this one source alone so that future generations will repeat your venerated name an incalculable number of times each day and unceasingly have cause to bless you." It is not to be thought that the Voice indicated even a fraction of the countless uses to which lamhoo (or bamboo as for some unexplained reason it subsequently became) could be put, but with truly celestial consideration it curtailed the list when it became apparent that the one addressed had, for all practical purposes, Gone Onwards.

Lam-hoo thus became the greatest benefactor of his race and his name attained (with the unfortunate transformation of its outline) an imperishable lustre. His two sons both rose to high official rank and were thus in a position to reverse the regrettable oversight of their former persecution. Justice requires that the detestable Fang Jung should come to an ignominious end, and this accordingly took place; for being detected in a treasonable plot he was deprived of all that he possessed and condemned to stand in a public place wearing a board recounting his many offences.

Chung Pun and the Miraculous Peacocks

"IT IS TO THE CREDIT of an authority if he administers praise and blame impartially; the fault lies at the door of the one concerned if either praise or blame is taken wrongly. This," reflected Kai Lung, "suggests the story of Chung Pun, who may be said to have justified it."

When Chung Pun returned from the provincial capital with no distinctive characters to adorn his name it did not require the aid of an enlarging-glass to disclose that his home-coming failed to create successive waves of gladness. It was in vain that he drew attention to the harmonious balance, both in design and hue, of the robes he wore, to the novel and pleasing arrangement of his gracefully-looped hair, his long and work-unsullied finger-nails, the refined and expensively-maintained associations he had formed, and his carefully-displayed air of no-interest. The elder Chung, a person of simple habits and extreme reticence towards any taste, whose one ambition had been to see Pun add a literary flavour to his own commercial strain, was not appeased by this evidence of glamour.

"Peacocks do not necessarily lay rainbow-coloured eggs," he declared, "nor has the variegation of your many robes brought the expected lustre to our Family Tablets."

"Peacocks do not lay eggs of any colour, Esteemed," was Pun's perhaps indiscreet reply, "that function being the jealous-ly-guarded prerogative of the lesser ones of the species."

"The objection is both superficial and inept," warmly contested Chung, "seeing that the apothegm was to be understood only in the general terms of analogy. However, since the extent of your acquired knowledge would seem to comprise a single agricultural fact, henceforth your destiny shall lie in that direction."

Despite Pun's well-expressed protests that to be confined to the society of goats and oafs would stifle his better instincts, the one whose word he must obey was not to be swayed in his project.

"Whether your path will thereby lead up or down remains for the Deciding Beings to say," Chung replied to all his pleading. He thereupon directed Pun regarding the journey he should make and the point of his destination, supplied him with food and wine and a few small pieces of money for the way, and, as an after-thought, added his blessing.

It did not take a moon to fade for Pun to discover that the qualities that had so deplorably failed to impress the elder Chung harvested less snow with a gross and tyrannical earth-tiller. Commanded to rise at an unseemly gong-stroke of the day, and with the aid of a perverse-willed tool to remove from the pig-yard to a distant spot a distressingly offensive load that would be more nutritious elsewhere, Pun found his carefully-preserved nails to be of no assistance in the task, while his richly-laced robe came apart several times under the excessive pressure. Those to whom he applied, seeking to know how he might acquire a more effective grasp, replied with derisive shouts, inaccurate advice that tended to involve him in undignified straits, or merely allusive gestures. Forced by the ill-conditioned attitude of those around towards a wholly introspective mood, Pun began to reconsider the past, and before long he was willing to admit that there might be something on his side that would not be entirely pleasing to the fastidious. From this point onwards he progressed so far that before the rice was sown he would frequently declare aloud that to toil for the one whom he did, and be compelled to associate with the ones who were there, was only a just and suitable return for the misspent years he had squandered.

Doubtless the time had now arrived when the Deciding Beings, upon whose shoulders the elder Chung had rather craftily thrust the responsibility of deciding his son's future, would have made up their sacred but complicated minds what course to adopt; but in order to extricate Chung Pun from the position into which he had been led, now that some expiation and an admission of his unworthy past justified his emergence, it is necessary to contrive a reasonable excuse, and towards this end Shin-tao must be pressed forward into the recital.

Shin-tao lived alone in the darker part of an impenetrable forest that stretched towards the east, and on this account he was generally reputed to be either excessively wise or else of deficient understanding. Driven by the forbidding front of those among whom he moved to seek other paths, Pun had frequently turned his footsteps towards Shin-tao's retreat, nor, when they chanced to meet, had the latter person shown any desire to avoid him.

"Yet how comes it," had been one of his earliest demands as they conversed in a free and convenient manner, "that you who are shunned and remote should have a cheerful and benign outlook, while those who hold you in undeserved contempt are both morose and domineering?"

"That is the nature of our several moods," Pun generously admitted, "they being thus and thus in temper. Formerly I would have bewailed my lost inheritance and sought to constrain their love, but while I have my own thoughts I now count myself neither poor nor friendless."

This answer so pleased Shin-tao that he burned the substance of it deeply into a block of teak, using a pointed nail, and he afterwards hung the wood above the entrance to his dwelling.

It was at a later period of their mutual regard that Shin-tao referred to an analogous theme, for by this time there was no constraint between them.

"Seeing that your qualities are thus and thus," he said, "and have doubtless brought you some reward and honour, why should you be content to labour for a meagre wage in a house destitute of pleasure?"

"As to that," replied Pun, though with less freedom in his speech, "the answer must necessarily be long and involved and our time would be much more profitably spent in discussing the obscurer Classics." Then, remembering the elder Chung's apothegm on his return, he added: "The qualities to which you so amiably refer, Shin-tao, were not always apparent. Peacocks do not necessarily lay rainbow-coloured eggs nor he who is flamboyant produce epics."

At this Shin-tao regarded Pun somewhat closely, but seeing nothing in the other's face to disturb his confidence he said, "It is in the nature of a fore-ordained sign that you should quote that paradox to me, seeing that I am the one person alone who is able to expose its falsity."

"Disclose yourself more fully," urged Pun. "Not only are the eggs in question of inconspicuous hue but the statement contains a double incongruity."

"Yet that which exists cannot be disproved," asserted Shin-tao, "for not even demons can do what is impossible. . . . In the depths of the forest here lurks a secluded glen, the spot being known to none beyond the one who is now confiding the circumstances to your ear, since this would seem to be necessary for your destined future. In the past certain deities made this hidden valley their resort and called to it all manner of delightful things to add to their entertainment. Thus it came about that T'a Kwey, the divinity tutelary to the chromatic arts, seeing a peacock for the first time here, laid an injunction on the place that the species should propagate there for ever."

"That is likely enough," assented Pun, "as regards yourself, the deities and the valley. But peafowl eggs are of an unrelieved brown, as this one can definitely say, he having frequently eaten several at a time during his vainglorious days in order to enhance the brilliance of a naturally dull complexion. Nor is there any reason to believe that they are produced other than in the normal routine of nature."

"Doubtless that would have been so here, but the deity's injunction had been precise, and it so happened that by an oversight none of the lesser ones of the race involved – destitute as they are of external charm – had been transported to the sacred valley. It thus devolved upon the peacocks themselves to, as it were, adapt their habits to a new and obviously miraculous role which has now persisted for a number of æons. It is to signalize the higher Powers' approval of this devotion to their word that the eggs found there are rainbow-hued and scintillate with an iridescent lustre."

This explanation threw Pun into a deep concern, for it did not seem feasible that so intricate a chain of events should not be connected with his own development. At length he said:

"What you disclose, Shin-tao, only goes to confirm that this one – as he has always dimly foreseen – is in some way marked out for a very distinguished career."

"That is my own opinion as well," agreed Shin-tao, "and it is for this reason that – having been advised in several dreams – everything has been laid bare without reservation."

"Since we are at one to that extent, would not your magnanimity allow you to go a step further?"

"In which direction?" inquired Shin-tao. "Do not hesitate to put your advancement before any thought of high-minded feeling."

"Bearing an offering of these sacred eggs, added to a recital of their miraculous origin, is it to be thought that any door will be closed against a reasonable petition for recognition? Thus a venerated if obtuse-witted father's no doubt excusable annoyance would be appeased, the short-sighted decision of a corrupt and intellectually knock-kneed Board of Examiners reversed, and the way open for an obliged and influential Central Authority to express tangible approbation."

"All this has been foreseen through the instrumentality of accorded visions," replied Shin-tao, "and the path is thereby paved for your speedy departure." With these encouraging words he produced a double hand-count of eggs such as he had described, as well as an adequacy of nourishing fare to sustain Pun in his mission. They then exchanged a suitable farewell verse from the Book of Odes and turned their reluctant footsteps into opposite directions.

Thereafter Pun's progress was necessarily upwards and smooth, for bearing such a gift it is not to be thought that any obstacles would presume to impede his movements. The local mandarin to whom he at first diffidently applied fell on his face and kowtowed several times when he beheld the eggs and understood the nature of their origin. Declaring himself quite unworthy to do more than beat his head on the marble floor in the presence of such a wonder, he provided Pun with a pink-upholstered chair and a bodyguard of three intrepid bowmen with an embroidered flag and directed him to the district superior. Here Pun was received with scarcely less ceremony, the functionary bowing almost as many times as the last, while adding a blue-lined chair as well as five unarmed but loud-voiced warriors and a silk-tasselled banner. Thence he was sent to the departmental overlord, who cordially shook hands with himself with effusive warmth and, contributing lavishly to the dignity of Pun's suite, passed him on to the viceroy of the province. . . .

When, finally, Pun entered the capital of the sovereign land, to be received by the Sublime himself, he led a procession of three-score variously coloured chairs, five state chariots drawn by elephants or camels, innumerable wheel-barrows laden with seasonable food, flags, banners, trophies of war on poles, wild animals in chains, many changes of raiment to denote his superior rank, and several thousand ordinary persons.

When the enraptured Monarch (who dispensed with formality to such an extent that he gratuitously permitted Pun to raise his face slightly from the ground to relieve his breath when speaking) actually received the semi-sacred eggs and beheld their prismatic splendour, he called the inscriber of his spoken word and commanded him to set down in irrevocable form whatever Pun chose to ask for the service.

"If it can be done without unduly straining the Code, Omnipotence," was Pun's modest reply, "the bestowal of a suitable literary degree would not only restore your abject suppliant's momentarily displaced face but should reinstate an ever-dutiful if occasionally outspoken-tongued son in the affection of a revered though admittedly concave-stomached parent."

"Nothing could be in better taste," heartily replied the All-Supreme, immeasurably relieved that, in accordance with his hasty pledge, Pun had not claimed something of a pecuniary or territorial nature. "As there might be some slight technical difficulty in conferring a heath or flower-plot degree, we will institute for the purpose a new distinction, to be called the Order of the Brilliant Fowl (its contracted colloquialism being styled 'B.F.'), to be conferred henceforth on similar honourable occasions."

"Your illimitable condescension fills my unworthy entrails with fervent song," was wrung from Pun's grateful throat. "Let it be said —"

"While we are about it," continued he Most-All, with a truly royal determination not to stint merit, "there is no good reason why your praiseworthy father should be left out, seeing that bereft of his timely share this memorable occasion would not have arisen. He also, therefore, together with your commendable greatfather and all your opportune male forerunners in fact, may, on similar grounds, be styled honourable B.F.s henceforward."

To this fresh evidence of the Greatest's fostering care for subjects so negligible as themselves Pun could only reply by the passionate clashing of his overflowing head on the onyx pavement of the Hall of Ten Thousand Stars in Motion. The usual loyal cry, "May you live for ever, Revered, and beget a countless tribe of lusty he-children!" would have sounded too thin and circumscribed to express an insignificant drop from the fathomless depths of his unbounded devotion.

Yuen Yang and the
Empty Lo-Chee Crate

*'Opportunity,' declares the trusty proverb, 'may be grasped
either in front or sideways but is destitute both of pig-tail
and of trailing robes.' Let him who sees a favourable chance
approach consider the implication.*

"HE WHO CAN ADAPT HIMSELF to the needs of each new arisement possesses the qualifications not of a single person
but of many," propounded Kai Lung, when, at the call
of the hollow wooden duck, he deemed that he had attracted
a sufficient circle. "This concerns the many-sided attributes of
White Jade, who pervades the story that follows."

In the reign of that enlightened monarch the Emperor
Ng Hong (distinguished from several rulers bearing the same
melodious name by the well-deserved title, "All-embracing'),
an amiable but not otherwise intellectually-endowed youth of
the upper lower middle toiling caste, Ah-Yang to his chosen
friends, his line being that of Yuen, earned a meagre sufficiency of taels by the combined exercise of strict frugality and
a close application to his calling.

At that bygone era the considerable city of Ying-chou, in
which dwelt the various personages who take part in this lam-
entably ill-told story, was enjoying an enviable spell of prosperity by reason of its unique position as an essential link in the
lo-chee industry. Situated on a sharp bend of the river Wei,
and at no great distance from the capital of the province, with

the fertile valley of the great lo-chee growing district spreading fan-like beyond the vision of the keenest-sighted on the
other side, Ying-chou had from a time immemorial been the
natural centre for repacking the fruit. To those badly informed
strangers who in a spirit of narrow-minded intolerance enquired why it should be necessary for Ying-chou to exercise
this function, any one of the three-score hundred persons
who subsisted by the traffic (the entire population of the city)
would compassionately explain that in the swamps and marshy
districts of the river grew an inexhaustible reserve of pliant
osier shoots, so benevolently adapted by the arranging deities
for weaving into the skeps and baskets that formed convenient
vehicles for an enticing display of the luscious product. If the
opaque-witted interloper still further persisted that his enquiry
was rather directed at the need of thus handling the commod-
ity in Ying-chou at all since it could be equally well transported
to the capital direct, he would be pointedly asked whether he
was a Superior Being in disguise, so to question what had been
good enough for others since the days of Yu, the original law-
giver; or should the one addressed be of a morose disposition
or not apt in the art of retorting, the officious busy-body incurred the risk of being bodily cast into the Wei and advised to
consider whether it was not a desirable spot for landing.

It was amid these placid scenes of conscientious toil and
commensurate reward that Yuen Yang had spent the years
from the braiding of his hair until he had reached early manhood nor had any yearning to advance his cause unsettled his
organs of digestion. To excel in the skilful performance of his
simple task comprised the four walls of his ambition and in
this way Yang may be said to have struck the loudest gong for
among the marts and packing-sheds of Ying-chou his superiority would be universally admitted.

It has already been disclosed that the three-score hundred dwellers in that place were one and all, from the most
menial labourer on the soil to the chief city mandarin, his

High Excellence Pu You himself, in some measure or another dependent on the entirely superfluous but zealously upheld custom of receiving the annual crop of lo-chee from one direction and despatching it in another. Not the least important detail of this process consisted in the dextrous manipulation of the prepared osier slips to form suitable receptacles in which to pack the immature fruit whereby it might ripen naturally and display its tempting perfection to advantage. It was in this art that Yang outshone all his fellows for although there were many who could fashion the containers so as to create a wholly illusory impression as to the bulk of fruit they held, he was able to interlace a single strip of wood in such a manner that while it bulged outwardly and suggested a generous capacity within, it also protruded inwardly and successfully counteracted so unprofitable a failing. Nor in the packing season was Yuen Yang less apt for by some inspired touch he could create the impression that the uppermost layer of fruit he arranged was actually representative of all that lay beneath. Yet in spite of these natural gifts Yuen Yang was profuse and straightforward in his bearing nor could an impartial looker-on have predicted any other prospect for him than an obscure middle life and an abject and penurious old age.

Had it chanced that any in authority lurked about his paths as he left the store-house one portentous day it is not distending the probabilities to hazard that Yuen Yang would not have negligently caught up and carried away one of the substantial wooden cases in which the unsorted lo-chee reached the city. No tinge of reproach can attach itself in this transaction as an unspecified number of cases were inevitably destroyed or mislaid beyond the overseers' power to trace in the course of every season.

As Yuen Yang bent his footsteps on a homeward path, cheered beneath the burden of the weight he carried by the truly filial thought of the sounds of gladness with which his aged parents would greet so welcome an addition to their sparsely-fed hearth, he presently became aware of an unusual press of onlookers who thronged the Ways. At the Open Space of Malefactors, where all the more spectacular beheadings took place, further progress was almost barred and there Yuen Yang set down the crate and sought to learn the occasion.

"It is Tso Tso, the notorious lo-chee smuggler, who is to be piecemeal-sliced here today," pleasurably reported the one whom he addressed. "May the headsman's knife be blunt and the ceremony protracted – he who would cheat our noble mother city of its ancient privileges!"

As the entertainment was one that involved no sort of outlay Yuen Yang continued to stand beyond the pressure of the crowd, assured that his commanding height would enable him to miss no detail of so adequate an act of retribution. Not all were so happily placed, however, for becoming aware of a heavily-sustained breathing at his elbow, Yuen Yang looked down and found by his side a person of deficient growth who was endeavouring by a succession of very undignified leaps into the air to learn something of the progress of the ceremony.

"O excellent and truly opportune young man," said that one when he grasped that he had engaged Yuen Yang's attention, "since you are so generously equipped by Nature, would you, for a liberal hand-count of cash, permit this distressingly-stunted individual to mount your empty crate and thereby enable him to enjoy this meritorious act of justice?"

"You are honourably welcome to the little that you ask," hospitably replied Yuen Yang, "for why should I, who have incurred no charge, seek to profit from the needs of your affliction?" With these humane words he not only thrust aside the offered price but taking the dwarf by a convenient hold set him up in the desired position.

Later, as he was preparing the leave the Open Space of Malefactors, a gracefully-restrained cough impelled him to turn. Near by, poised in a refined attitude of virtuous unconcern, one of the other sort was undoubtedly glancing in his direction.

"Since you have, by the unconcealed way in which you are regarding her presence, betrayed a not absolute state of no-concern in this quite commonplace person's trivial existence, there can be no impropriety in her admitting a passing shade of approval at the charitable action of one who is both well-moulded and alert himself, in not only placing an empty wooden case at the service of a repellent cripple but also assisting the one described to avail himself of the advantage," remarked the maiden in a voice that Yuen Yang likened to a carillon of silver bells stirred by a perfume-laden breeze in the dusk of evening. "But doubtless you are used to being greeted with frequent expressions of approval from the many grateful ones whom you have benefited?"

"As to that," replied Yuen Yang with some constraint, "there is a relevant saying, 'It is as profitable to expect compassion from a disturbed adder as gratitude from one to whom you have lent a bar of silver.' But rather than pass the scanty beats of time on so notable an occasion with such empty subjects as this negligible one's altogether pointless doings, tell him rather the distinguishing sign of your honourable father's house, your own harmonious name, and whether it is your agreeable custom to frequent these enchanted paths at about the same gong-stroke of congenial evenings."

From the general trend of circumstances already related it should occasion no surprise to the discriminating members of an ordinarily intelligent circle of hearers that thereafter Yuen Yang's manner of life underwent some variation. Without actually depriving his revered parents of anything absolutely necessary to sustain their failing powers, he frequently spoke of the need for a person to safeguard the requirements of the future, of the advantages of preserving a Line intact, and the like. At the lo-chee-packing sheds he successfully led a movement which by the mere threat of casting down their tools in unison exacted an added copper piece for the day's labour. No longer absent-mindedly, as it were, but claiming it now as an established right, he frequently picked up and carried away an empty chest, and whenever there was an event that drew together a throng in a public pace (and this was seldom lacking) the Omens were ill-arranged if Yuen Yang, loitering about the outside of the mass, could not engage one in conversation who should ultimately hire his standing. On these occasions he invariably found White Jade (as she disclosed her well-fitting name to be) not too far away to be easily discovered, and each time his protestations became more specific.

"It cannot be denied that the prospect you so poetically unfold invests the immediate future with an alluring glamour in this romantic person's imagination also," admitted White Jade in answer to Yuen Yang's fervent challenge. "There are, however, certain complications to be faced from which it is by no means easy to see a dignified outlet. Since you are practically, as the low-class expression goes, down on the solid strata, while the tastes of the one whom you offer to support are admittedly exacting, how—?"

"All that has been foreseen," replied Yang with modest pride, "and the requirement presents no difficulty. Hitherto Yuen Yang has allowed a too lethargic disposition to clog the more remunerative attributes that must surely have been, so to speak, embedded somewhere in his composition. He has now devised a scheme by which a continuous flow of silver taels will be – when once it starts – more or less unavoidable."

"O noble-stomached Yang!" exclaimed White Jade rapturously, "reveal without a single beat of time's delay this wonder-working contrivance."

"Understand then," expounded Yuen Yang, "that for a period to be counted now by moons a searching test has been devised from which it has been definitely confirmed that a persistent demand exists for empty lo-chee crates from which to obtain an uninterrupted view of public ceremonies. He who first supplies this pressing need and associates his name with the supply will establish an unshakeable hold on the public mind that his empty lo-chee crates are superior to all others. Henceforth, before every important wedding procession, official funeral, public torture, execution, or similar attraction, through whatever Way it is to pass, there will be freely displayed at prominent points the confidence-inspiring message: 'You require the best empty lo-chee crates: Yuen Yang possesses them.' The successful outcome can never be in doubt, and when the brilliant and variegated wedding procession of our illustrious law-giver and tax-gatherer, the exemplary Mandarin Pu You (who takes his eleventh wife when a lucky day has been predicted by the yamen foretellers), passes along the Ways and through the Open Spaces, trusted emissaries of the one who speaks will be found at every point with a practically inexhaustible supply of empty lo-chee boxes."

So immersed in the contemplation of his epoch-marking scheme had Yuen Yang become that he failed to notice the sudden change of poise that came into White Jade's enthralled attitude at the mention of their cherished administrator's high-born name, but when she spoke the irregularity of her usually pearl-like voice recalled him.

"It is generally agreed that if there are times for observing a maidenly restraint in speech there are occasions when it seems almost imperative to divest an unpalatable fact of any embroidered trimmings. Thus positioned, since you have unstoppered – as may be said – the subject, it becomes necessary to admit that a second complication arises now, inasmuch as she who speaks is the destined eleventh wife of that dominant official."

With these words White Jade arranged her face in an expression of resigned despair and waited for Yuen Yang to compose his reproaches.

"It is hardly to be denied that this is excessively abrupt," admitted Yuen Yang, "but none the less the sage remark of the philosopher Ho-ping in somewhat analogous circumstances holds good, that 'It is no worse to be suddenly run through the body with a sharp sword from behind than to be clubbed to death with a heavy bludgeon while fully conscious.' Matters being positioned as they are, there would seem to be no actual need to disturb any of this person's elaborately-contrived plans – indeed your gracefully-bestowed patronage extended to his lines of empty lo-chee crates could not fail to enhance their lustre."

Without seeming absolutely gratified that the involvement had been so amiably flattened out, White Jade signified an abrupt gesture of assent, but their parting on this occasion was shorter and more ceremonious than had hitherto been their usage.

Thereafter Yuen Yang applied himself assiduously to furthering his scheme, devoting all his energies and the lavish use of White Jade's decorative name to making the occasion of Pu You's wedding the threshold, as it were, to a position of becoming widely known and extremely affluent. Thus occupied, it was not entirely with a surfeit of delight that when the nuptial day was no more than a single quarter of the moon away he surprised White Jade loitering in an angle of the paths at a spot that she knew he must resort to.

"Prosperity: may your winning number always come up." was his formal greeting, and he shook hands with himself – but with no more warmth than politeness demanded.

"It is useless to place a pebble over the source of a mountain stream," was White Jade's ambiguous reply, but without waiting for Yang to match the analogy she proceeded to enlarge her meaning.

"In the time that has elapsed since she hastily announced her future state this one has continually analysed her innermost feelings. The prospect of losing Yuen Yang is more bitter than the flavour of thrice-distilled almonds, while the vista of an entire lifetime spent face to face with the obese and unutterable Pu You is worse than the imposition of a dragon-dream prolonged through interminable æons. In consequence she has now definitely expressed her real feelings, with a freedom from which there can be no retreat, to that gross and extortionate functionary. Suffer no apprehension that she will again fail you, faithful Yang; Pu You will bid strings of pearls, feather robes and performing apes in vain, and it only remains for the two who are here conversing affectionately together to consult the Omens for a propitious date and then settle down to a future state of unalloyed felicity."

On this occasion it was some beats of time before Yuen Yang could select appropriate words, although his expression underwent a variety of shades, and certain sounds betrayed the concentrated nature of his deeper feelings.

"Thus and thus!" he exclaimed, when the power of coherent speech was restored, although from time to time he tore out considerable lengths of his neatly-arranged pig-tail and ground his powerful teeth aggressively together. "How, if the ceremony is to be set aside by a lesser one's irrational whim, should there be any procession at all, and therefrom what emerges in relation to this person's elaborately-laid plans and the vast store of empty lo-chee crates already stacked at every convenient point of the traversable Ways and Spaces?"

"That certainly is a detail that had hitherto escaped this usually capable person's nimble-witted mind," confessed White Jade. "But as our leading play-writer has so aptly put it, 'Out of this thistle, annoyance, we will yet extract the assuaging down of comfort.'"

"Never was it more truly written than that if every woman were to gum her hair before she spoke and wait for it to set before she embarked on what she intended saying, there would be fewer cases of self-ending among the peace-loving inhabitants of our favoured empire," continued Yuen Yang, without according any consideration at all to White Jade's helpful suggestion. "How is one who will be henceforth bankrupt to provide for the sustenance of another who has already proclaimed her inherent disregard of thrift? Indeed, setting aside any thought of his own scanty needs or even an adequate provision for the seemly requirements of two idolised parents, it is more than likely that in the Upper Air his pale and emaciated ghost will be held in bondage by the well-fed ghosts of those to whom he has given legal undertakings of repayment here in the Beneath World."

"When we are definitely made one your merest word will be this inferior person's unwritten law, but at this beat of time it almost seems as though you are taking a trivial miscalculation too austerely," replied White Jade with a slight corrugation of her expressive eyebrows. "Lean heavily on the resource and pertinacity of her who speaks, and have no fear of the eventual happening."

"It is well said—"

"It is better left unsaid, adored, for this one must hasten back before her absence is discovered," interposed White Jade firmly. "Do not, however, think that she forgets your spoken words or will fail to profit by their instruction: 'Every important wedding procession, *official funeral*, public torture, execution or similar attraction' – all these were equally to found our virtuous happiness."

"That is as it was," grumbled Yang, "for is it to be thought that something really noteworthy is destined to emerge – with a date now irrevocably fixed, the empty cases hired, and a band of stalwart henchmen retained with earnest-money for their service?"

"Because you cannot see beyond a bend in the road it does not follow that there is no progression further. In any case, be well assured of this: 'To the affection of a thoroughly determined woman and the embrace of a hungry python there can be only one ending.'"

* * * * *

Deep was the consternation throughout Ying-chou when it was learned that during the night their venerated Chief Magistrate had suddenly Passed Upwards. Even the most experienced fortune-tellers were unable to agree upon the exact cause of his end, so that it was very reasonably officially ascribed to the malignity of a Revengeful Being. An added pang was inserted when it was learned that the day chosen for his obsequies was that which, had the Destinies been more suitably arranged, would have seen his wedding rites, but this soon gave place to a general feeling of pleasurable anticipation as the reported splendour and extent of the funeral procession spread and gained volume.

Weighing his bags of metal in the security of an inner chamber when all was over, Yuen Yang repeatedly assured himself that nothing could have been more timely.

As no detail has been preserved of the after-life of either of the two personages with whom this painfully threadbare chronicle is chiefly concerned, it may safely be assumed that they enjoyed an unalloyed period of felicity together and established a prolific Line to follow them.

Subsequently it was found that there was no absolute need to provide empty lo-chee cases on which to stand, as boxes that had held other commodities were equally suitable. The revolutionary innovation of fixing wooden planks in successive rising tiers did not occur until some dynasties later.

Sing Tsung and the
Exponent of Dark Magic

"IT HAS BEEN TRULY SAID," reflected Kai Lung, in order to lead up, as it were, to what should follow, "that the whole course of an ordinary person's life may be rearranged by so slight a matter as having his gravity displaced at the wrong pause during a speech by a high official.

"Had Sing Tsung not turned aside to explain to a passing stranger the elusive delicacy of shafts of light produced by the setting sun when seen through the transparent veil of a discarded spider's web, he might never have encountered Hia Cho, whereby much of what ensued therefrom would necessarily have ceased to possess any actual structure."

At the moment of their first meeting Hia Cho was standing before a copiously-illuminated scroll depicting an unusually commodious burial-box around which festoons of quam-chee sprays were lavishly entwined. Unaware of the proximity of a not-unattractive observer of the other sort, she was loitering in a pensive yet thoroughly graceful attitude by the wall adorned with this enticing sheet, at the same time unconsciously expressing her thoughts aloud in a voice of bird-like melody.

"Among the admitted deficiencies of our otherwise unblemished land may be accounted the system which condemns those of this person's sort to a humiliating ignorance of the import of written outlines," was the trend of her polished lament. "Otherwise it would no doubt be discoverable what natural bond exists between a richly-ornamented coffin of exceptional

65

bulk and a deservedly popular fruit of attractive flavour, or why the one should be presented in the act of clustering thickly around the other."

When Hia Cho had expressed herself in this cultivated strain for an appreciable count of time, Sing Tsung deemed it not inappropriate to reveal himself and, as one who had already failed three times at the annual competitions, diffidently offer to expound the symbols' meaning. After recovering from the prepossessing display of well-arranged alarm into which she had been thrown by Sing Tsung's unwonted boldness, Hia Cho ventured to glance in his direction through an opportune defect in the fan she carried, and having been reassured by the undoubted inoffensiveness of his outward guise, she decided to raise no dissenting barrier.

"For," she magnanimously added, "does not the same sun shine on us equally and one earth nourish us both? Indeed, had things been somewhat differently arranged by the Controlling Powers, might we two not have been inseparable brothers?"

On the strength of this encouragement Sing Tsung applied himself tenaciously to interpreting the written signs, and presently he was able to disclose a feasible explanation.

"This notification is put forth by the 'Ying-chou and Outlying Parts Vegetation Community,'" he declared, "and refers to its yearly assemblage of all varieties of natural growth, when that brought in by whomsoever deems it to excel vies strenuously with what is paraded by all his antagonists."

"The spectacle must be an exhilarating one!" exclaimed Hia Cho, with increased sparkle in her capably-directed eyes. "Do fatal results often attend the progress of these dire encounters?"

"Not at the time of the trial itself, though there are dark reports of the length to which rival cucumber growers have been known to go in order to thwart one another. But check the melodious rhythm of your distractingly alluring voice for a single span of time while this insufficiently-equipped student wrests the meaning from the lower part of the announcement."

"The rebuke is not undeserved," admitted Hia Cho penitently. "Even a nightingale may open its mouth out of season."

"On the eleventh day of the Moon of Ingathering the assembly of all varieties of growing things will accordingly take place," continued Sing Tsung, "and as a special attraction the highest award, that bestowed on the grower of the most attractive collection of quam-chee, will on this occasion consist of an exceptionally massive and richly-lacquered family coffin."

"If one so insignificant may now be permitted to express a thought, it is difficult to conjecture what earthly desire could outweigh that of carrying off so indispensable and enduring a trophy," was wrung from Hia Cho's excess of feeling. "Surely all who read the written words and closely examine the depicted prize must yearn to be acclaimed the victor."

"Would the possession be such that the owner of it might attain any particular degree of favour in your eyes?" asked Sing Tsung in an off-hand manner. And in order to maintain his attitude of no-concern he made several ineffectual grasps at passing winged insects.

"From the strictly detached angle of one who is not remotely affected by the happening, it is arduous to imagine how even the most ambitious and exacting of her own sort would not be swayed by the prospect of a joint-ownership and ultimate occupation of so gratifying an heirloom," replied Hia Cho, no less remotely. "Thus, in a manner of speaking, he who sets forth to secure the reward might be fitly likened to some intrepid paladin of old who sought to encounter dragons in honour of one to whom he would pay homage."

"The analogy may not perhaps be classically exact," conceded Sing Tsung, "but your excessively flattering way of arranging the facts imparts a romantic flavour to the venture. The eleventh of the Moon of Ingathering will either see the hitherto obscure name of Sing Tsung inscribed on the championship bowl of winning quam-chee or mark the extinction of that presumptuous upstart's aspiring hopes for ever."

With these significant words, which clearly indicated something beyond his normal usage, Sing Tsung bowed several times with respectful precision and passed on, leaving Hia Cho involved in a very complicated state of not unpleasurable emotion.

* * * * *

Those who are accustomed to listen to the narrations of really accomplished story-tellers (as distinct from this illiterate person's immature effort) will have no difficulty in piercing the strategy of dissimulation that Sing Tsung had adopted. He was not an obscure literary candidate, as his references might have led one to believe, but already enviably known as a successful quam-chee grower who had more than once 'brushed the floor' at some of the less conspicuous Blossom and Vegetation Assemblages of the province. Having by chance seen Hia Cho through an unguarded lattice, he had formed an ardent attachment towards her merits; but not deeming himself acceptable to her Line (her honourable father being a retired hereditary Legal Tax evader), he had secretly followed her movements day after day in the hope of securing a favourable occasion. Towards this the arranging deities had proved exceptionally complying.

With so momentous an issue involved, Sing Tsung now redoubled all his previous efforts to produce quam-chee of exceptional size and flavour; indeed, it is questionable if the excess of stimulation that he lavished upon the roots of his likeliest shrubs in a well-meant endeavour to stir them, so to speak, to enhanced fruitfulness may not have had a contrary effect upon their powers. Permit this how it will, with very few moons before the appointed day, Sing Tsung's orchard had never seemed less flourishing. Calling upon the equally-concerned spirits of even his remotest ancestors to exert their pressure, the one in question resolved to concentrate every influence upon a single plant, and with this end in view he relentlessly cut down and destroyed every other.

It was about this time that Tsung received a visit from an influential neighbour. Lowering his voice and speaking from behind an open hand, Chang Toon affected nothing more than a friendly interest in Tsung's fortunes, but not even a blind-worm could have misinterpreted the significance of his message.

"Encouraged by your record in the past, Sing Tsung, and relying upon a well-spread belief in your integritous behaviour, a few virtue-loving persons of Ying-chou have ventured even down to their undercloth upon the emergence of your winning number."

"Their confidence is a gratifying portent of success," replied Sing Tsung with effusion. "May their enterprising hazard be repaid more than a hundred times over."

"Such was the anticipation of their spirited bid when the unevens were stated," admitted Chang Toon, but without any noticeable response to the other's genial manner. "Since then, however, it is not to be denied that your merchantable assets have slid heavily in a downward direction. Pung-fu, a very sombre bird from the Upper Outlands, is known to be enlisting the support of every available Force, Influence, Presence, Substance, Shadow and Being by a lavish expenditure of joss-sticks and detonating fireworks; while it has not escaped the observation of interested crevice-glimpsers that you, Sing Tsung, are not only wholly neglecting these devotional offices but have been detected in the process of secretly counteracting your own existing efforts."

"As to that," replied Sing Tsung profusely, "there need be no apprehension. With his scanty means this one could not hope to outbid the wealthy Pung-fu in the matter of propitiatory noises, and to do less would be as profitable as to scatter nuts before an approaching tiger. None the less, your discriminating friends may well be assured that when the Eleventh of Ingathering fades Sing Tsung will be the fortunate recipient of a really serviceable coffin."

"That is what has been already decided," assented Chang Toon with an unpleasant intonation, "but whether the accommodation in question will consist of a richly upholstered teak-wood casket or an equally practicable but less ornamental crate of the sort used for storing onions will depend entirely on that day's emergence. Meanwhile, therefore, regard your footsteps with precision. Ten thousand blessings!"

In spite of the parting acclaim, this arisement wholly failed to have a beneficial effect on Tsung's drooping spirits, while the continual reluctance of his one quam-chee tree to justify the trust placed in it still further corroded his outlook. He was, indeed, considering the less objectionable forms of self-ending when an omen in the shape of a written message reached him. Following a discreet noise on his outer door, a shred of parchment was thrust into his open hand by one who fled, and on this he read as follows:

> Is it not written, 'If you desire to acquire merit, study The Sayings; if to succeed in business, sell your sacred books and therewith purchase and display a pretentious banner'? Since the foul and hypercritical Pung-fu has inveigled all Allowable Things to his malodorous cause it remains for the upright and sincere to have recourse to Forbidden Powers. Within the Capital, the street being known as Crooked, look for the sign of a Mammoth Gourd, and discovering by the latch an inconspicuous knob, press this silently and there declare your errand.

*　*　*　*　*

Early on the following day Sing Tsung went cautiously, as he had been told and, entering the city by an obscure gate, sought the Crooked Way and the house of questionable doings. This he had no difficulty in knowing, for displayed within its unshuttered lights were coloured representations from alien printed leaves showing blossoms and all the edible products of the earth conjured to a size, perfection and uniformity beyond human endeavour.

"This is that which was spoken of outside all reasonable doubt," was Sing Tsung's awed reflection, "for neither in the course of normal husbandry nor relying on Legitimate Arts could such results be obtained." Suspended from a pole hung a banner embellished with certain occult signs, among which Tsung recognised the Undeviating Lines and a coruscation of the planets. The name traced on an inscribed slab was that of Lee Q Yung, and he was described as trafficking in an Other-World power (or 'powder' the outline might equally be rendered) for enhancing the earth's fertility as by magic.

"Would you then," inquired Sing Tsung when he had ventured to obtain speech with the one within, "enable this person's single quam-chee tree to outrange the produce of all others?"

"Assuredly," replied the amiable necromancer, but speaking a pleasantly abbreviated tongue that betrayed an alien usage, "provided the other eccentrically-garbed ones have not been placed astute concerning the Lee-Yung products."

"You alone, then, possess this hidden power of magic growth?" asked Tsung, not indisposed to probe further, seeing that – except for a goat-like excrescence from his chin – there was nothing formidable in the wizard's appearance. "Is it in the nature of a Dark Secret – the incantation?"

"You are informing this person!" cryptically endorsed the gifted magician with convincing vigour. "Every can of the Lee-Yung 'Fertile Force' is guaranteed and the process fully protected."

"Thus and thus," agreed Sing Tsung, feeling that despite his simple need he was becoming involved in the trend of the conversation. "Inscribe the necessary sentence without delay and this person, having discharged a just account, will return to hang the charm in the required position."

For a few beats of time the versatile sorcerer continued to regard Tsung closely, but he made no immediate response to the request, as it might be that the substance of what was asked lay somewhat outside his powers. Then, with a gesture that seemed to imply a condition of remoteness, he placed a weighty package before that one and with a lowered voice explained its enchantment.

"Scatter what you will find herein evenly about the earth to the measure of a full pace around the trunk of the tree you have chosen. Do this in the period of falling dew and thereafter scar the ground well to remove all evidence of what has been effected. On the following day walk round the tree seven times in each direction with closed eyes and repeating suitable dictums from the Classics. This do as has been said, and in due course the fruit of that quam-chee tree will outvie all other."

"May your virtuous Line increase and she whom you select become the ancestress of ten thousand dutiful he-children," was Tsung's grateful response. "Also may your Tablets never fall into disuse and your ultimate out-passing be long deferred and painless."

"You have adequately discharged the full contents of a capacious mouth," admitted Lee Q Yung freely. "May you, likewise, never regret the three taels seventy-five cash that is the meagre extent of your obligation."

* * * * *

Much has been written about the foregoing events and some of the verse has even been set to music. But concerning the identity of the unknown charm-worker, the nature of his Forbidden Art, even the name of the distant Outland from which (to use his own harmonious phrase as recorded by one narrator) he 'hailed' have been lost in a mystifying avoidance. Elsewhere in the bamboo annals of Ying-chou it is to be found how in the third of the second of the then reigning dynasty of Mong, Sing Tsung was awarded a superbly-lacquered coffin, together with a silk-embroidered burial robe, the latter as an especial mark of the Vegetation Community's regard towards one who had 'tabled' a bowl of quam-chee so incredibly distended in size that they were also accorded an illuminated vellum address under the mistaken impression that they represented a new variety of melon. In receiving these unique honours at a ceremonial evening rice, Sing Tsung introduced an unprecedented feature into the occasion by generously asserting that some of his success that day was due to the devoted encouragement of his negligible lesser one, Hia Cho of the Line of Liang.

Kwey Chao and the
Grateful Song Bird

KWEY CHAO WAS THE ONLY BLOSSOM in the depleted Line of Mong Ho, a maritime person of the Lower Hiang Delta, who was sometimes described in official edicts as 'our faithful and highly-esteemed salt-tax collector and trusty upholder of water-way law and custom in the turbulent Hiang region,' and at other times as 'that earth-polluting thug and river-contaminating two-and-a-half cash pirate, Mong' – this according to whether the one concerned had transmitted to those in office a reasonable proportion of the exaction he had levied or whether he had for a period overlooked the desirability of so doing.

It had been a matter of unutterable – but nevertheless very fluently-expressed – regret to Mong Ho that Kwey Chao had proved to be of the sort she was, whereas the painstaking and frequently hard-pressed tax-gatherer had expended a considerable weight of silver taels in persuading the various Omens and responsible Forces involved to provide him with a he-child who should in due course lend a strenuous arm to the oft-time thankless task of urging the less formidable types of river craft to recognise both the disloyalty and the hopelessness of resisting taxation.

Positioned thus and thus it need occasion no surprise that Mong Ho resolutely took no interest whatever in the outcome of his parental ambition, so that Kwey Chao, bereft of the usual accomplishments of her own sort, grew up in a wholly illogical manner. In place of the carefully gummed tresses and studiously restrained gait of those who should have been her natural associates, Kwey Chao's voluminous hair streamed unconfined until it was frequently mistaken for a flock of migratory ravens as she sped with graceful unconcern among the glades of the neighbouring forest – especially by the close-sighted. Her unbound feet, though admittedly grotesque to the superficial, enabled her to maintain an attractive and defiant poise in the most hazardous situations, while her symmetrical-ly-shaped hands seemed to be naturally formed more for the purpose of grasping required things than that of spreading out in helpless and beseeching attitudes. From these circumstances it was inevitable that when a marriageable age was reached Mong Ho's she-child was – in the deplorable apothegm of the uncouth about the Hiang Delta – generally referred to as being 'not every pig-fancier's outlay.'

Driven by these converging lines of fate to seek entertain-ment wholly through her own resources, Kwey Chao had fre-quented the forest depths and the far-reaching stretches of the Delta waters from the time of her milk-days onwards, there penetrating into unknown parts and associating on terms of unusual mutual trust and confidence with many furtive and untamed creatures.

It is only necessary here to speak of the decisive influence of Yellow Crest, the unsurpassed songster of the lonely tracts, who now comes into the recital.

It was during one of her solitary progressions into the further wastes that, following the indication of a plaintive cry, Kwey Chao resolutely forced her way through the tangled prickly thorn-shrub growth to find a small bird of inconspicu-ous hue (excluding the single characteristic from which it took its name) confined to the spot by a broken wing and succumb-ing from the lack of water. To supply the latter need was Kwey Chao's first thought, and thereafter she applied herself to the task of repairing the fractured limb with unswerving patience and perseverance. No healing salve was too costly or remote

75

to be beyond her fixed resolve, nor did she omit to tread the most distant paths in order to obtain the services of devout recluses or those capable of bringing favourable influences to bear upon any existing contingency. Such devotion could not escape celestial recognition, and the day was not far distant when Yellow Crest was able to soar to the extreme point of discernible vision and from that height to express its unbounded gratitude in an – so to speak – ample outflow of spontaneous emotion.

"Could this person acquire but half the joyousness your discriminatory senses evidently experience," was wrested from Kwey Chao's admiring throat, "such melodious incoherence on her part would result that those who have hitherto regarded the one who is speaking as an entirely negligible sound would thereafter pay marked attention to her most trivial utterance."

Inspired by this desirable but excessively improbable attainment Kwey Chao, with no set purpose at the time, formed her far from unattractive lips into a responsive shape and sent upwards an answering note of gladness. To her gratified surprise she found that the range and capacity of her voice were not markedly unequal to the task; whereupon she continued in a like strain, and with an occasional lapse from strict precision succeeded in repeating the whole of the melody with a creditable display of appropriate feeling.

Under the stress of the concentrated emotion involved, Kwey Chao had resolutely closed her eyes during the latter part of the exertion; when she again looked out she discovered that Yellow Crest had taken up a convenient position on an adjacent branch, where he had been giving an attentive consideration to her efforts, for he now brought the extremities of his wings several times together with the measured approval of one who wishes to encourage a promising display even though he cannot commend the performance of every minute detail.

From that time onwards the high-principled bird devoted itself wholly to requiting the debt of gratitude which it considered was due to Kwey Chao by lifting her step by step to an equality of melody with its own supreme achievement. At the outset, under the exacting tutelage of so precise a teacher, the one most concerned was not disposed to raise paeans of gladness that Yellow Crest's sense of duty impelled him to this exalted standard, but presently she fell under the spell of the inspired songster's zeal and strove, no less than he urged, towards an ideal perfection. With the earliest gong-stroke of the day, therefore, when his first clear-cut jade-like notes announced the dawn, Kwey Chao gladly left her scanty pallet and together they sought an unfrequented glade where the gross-minded Mong Ho could not intrude and defile the innocent scene with offensive remarks, ill-bred signs and a derisive absence of gravity. At first Yellow Crest insisted, by the inoffensive persuasion of repeated example, that Kwey Chao should perfect herself in the manipulation of single notes, and not until satisfied that she had complete control of these, as one might say, throat-relaxing exercises would he countenance a more ambitious onslaught. That achieved, however, he let it be understood, by a complicated flourish of his own vocal range, that she might attempt some of the more elementary flights of song, and, placing himself opposite on an overhanging bough, he held himself firmly on one self-reliant claw and, raising the other, suitably indicated by a variety of appropriate beats the pattern that the melody should follow. . . . It was a green-leaf day for both when Yellow Crest announced, through the harmonious medium of perfect understanding that was now maintained between them, that Kwey Chao had nothing more to learn or he to teach, and indicated that she should, in unison with himself, essay a rendering of his most admired and complicated rhapsody – that now generally referred to as 'The Yellow Crest's Invocation to the as yet Unrisen Great Luminary of the Firmament.'

At about this time the Mandarin Chan Hing Pung, a functionary as far-seeing as he was just, who exercised supreme authority over the Lower Hiang Delta, realized that, immersed in the multitudinous and exacting affairs of State, he had hitherto overlooked the necessity of providing an adequate posterity who should preserve his imperishable Line intact. He therefore summoned the inscriber of his spoken word and mechanized transcriber of doubtful outlines to his side and charged him with a mission.

"You, Ti-ping," he explained, with the courteous forbearance that he rarely failed to extend even to a vassal, "have in the past carried out a diversity of commands with no more than the normal lack of intelligence observable in the average inscriber of our uttered phrases."

"The gracious magnanimity of your excessively high Eminence's undeserved regard is a never-failing source of nourishment to the tap-root of this inept one's fading self-esteem," protested the supple Ti-ping, hastening to assemble the four essentials of his calling. "Proceed to impose your ever-welcome task, Benign, and do not hesitate to lay on the obligations with a heaped-up trowel."

"This mission, however, impresses a greater strain upon a notoriously ill-nurtured brain than anything with which it has hitherto been called to grapple," continued the urbane dispenser of justice, closing his expressive eyes in order to indicate that he had heard no syllable of Ti-ping's tactless interruption. "For a lengthy period now the various printed leaves of our cultured land have been devoting their priceless space to such epoch-stirring topics as 'Is Monogamy a Fiasco', 'Do Secondary Wives make the Best Mothers?' and the like. Your concern during the next moon, therefore, Ti-ping, will be to pay a semi-official but confidential visit to the courts of so many other mandarins of the province as you can reasonably find an excuse for distressing – both those equal but above and those equal but below to our own insignia and button – and discover, by means of ingratiatory scandal, sympathetic condolences, personal disclosures, and as many other devices as your naturally prurient mind can embellish, why in each case matrimony has been synonymous with acute mental depression. On your return we shall tabulate and card-index the results, and this person, warned diagrammatically of what to avoid, can go forward with the certainty of a felicitous union."

"It is as near as achieved, Revered," was Ti-ping's boastful assurance as he set forth, "and the processional drums of your acclaimed wedding march may almost be heard approaching."

It was, however, with a less vainglorious front that the specious taker-down of spoken words accounted for what had been accomplished on his return, and when the one whose minion he was spoke of the coloured charts that were to display both cause and effect, Ti-ping replied with an effete gesture indicating complete absence of recollection.

"That is neither is nor was, however, Esteemed," ran his facile excuse, "since everything that tends to this affair can be contained within a hollow nail-sheath. . . . All your superficial-witted contemporaries have been swayed by the prepossessing exterior of those with whom they exchanged the silk-bound bond of promise, regardless of whether any possessed the more abiding qualities that could contribute to their lasting entertainment. The lamentable consequence is that the inner chambers of the yamens of this intellectually stagnant province are dominated by an assembly of mentally-deficient bygones who have found no incentive to preserve the only allurement they ever had nor possessed the ability to develop any other. The obvious expedient in your own specific case, great Excellence – if one so negligible as the mere taker-down of your melodious sentences should be permitted to form an opinion – would seem to point towards testing the nature of the contents in advance rather than accepting as an actual fact the picture of the maiden on the label."

"The richly convoluted trend of our flowery and romantic tongue is capable of such a profundity of variation, Ti-ping, that with so accomplished a master of terminological inexactitude as the one to whom this simple-witted person is now speaking it is often a matter of extreme difficulty to arrive at any rational conclusion," observed the liberal-minded administrator concisely. "What you would appear to be endeavouring to express, however, would seem to contain some definite germ of a concrete suggestion. If, therefore . . ."

"Pre-eminence," interposed Ti-ping with his usual lack of becoming deference, "this matter is as precise as the four sides of a parallelogram and its outcome no less rigid. Thus and thus let it be ordained . . ."

Unprecedented was the emotion engendered throughout the Hiang Delta when it was made known that their venerated chief magistrate was about to take a lesser one and – herein lay the zest – not gracefulness of outline or pulchritudinous charm were of any account, but only some quality that held out the promise of future and continuous entertainment. On an indicated date all of marriageable age who would were instructed to assemble for the trial and submit their powers to please, none save those sprung from the unclean castes being excluded. To a certain extent the result would be by popular acclaim, but the discriminating magistrate reserved to himself both the casting votes (whatever number the difference entailed) and the right of veto.

Had Mong Ho been cast in a less repellent mould it is not unimaginable that one of Kwey Chao's self-reliant build would have seen no inducement to compose an ode upon the opportunity provided by this occasion; but the insalubrious filibuster had of late accepted an unpleasant habit of spitting aggressively at intruding flies while he partook of wine, and this proved the last grain of rice in the measure of Kwey Chao's over-burdened tolerance.

"To whatever lapses from strict propriety the exalted mandarin may be prone, it is remote in the extreme that two personages, so diverse in every social attribute, should have this deplorable trait in common," was the conclusion of her scruples. She therefore signified her definite intention to undergo the test, "For," ran the sequence of her thoughts, "surely the ability to produce harmonious noises to an unparalleled extent, and in all probability to be able to continue the accomplishment until we are both senile, would constitute as tangible an asset as to pluck the strings of a zither without discord, depict actual or imagined scenes by the use of coloured earths, deceive the sense of vision through the instrumentality of pasteboard cards, revolve in a continuity of graceful attitudes, carve wood or stone until it assumed some remote affinity to a distorted human being, or any of the other efforts of those who up to now are spoken of as the probable emergers."

In this broad-minded vein Kwey Chao referred to the activities of the lottery-ticket vendors who had already established their stalls even in remote settlements of the Delta, for the event was to be the occasion for a general cessation of work of every kind, and the chances of those who had responded to the call were discussed far and wide by eager partisans who had, in extreme cases, pledged their Tablets in order to purchase the utmost limit of tickets. The equivalents ranged from 3 reputed taels 75 unbroken cash in the case of Liu-san, who was credibly declared to know the 'Book of Gravity-removing Instances and Waistband Disrupter's Let-me-tell-you' off by her inside, down to 25 unspecified cash for a complete ticket on the chances of the remote outsider Kwey Chao, of whose attainments the most ingratiatory possessor of a certainty had never heard a shadowy whisper; and even at that temptingly speculative price there had not emerged a single taker. Meanwhile Kwey Chao redoubled the effort to improve her highest notes, while she did not fail – by the means that their mutual attraction had evolved – to impress on Yellow Crest an understanding of the gravity of the occasion.

It might appear irrational at this point, in view of her unassuming charm and position as chief she-character of the narrative, to introduce an element of doubt, but let it be recalled

that an assembly of astute result-forecasters, on whose presci-
ence hung their source of life, had esteemed her chances of
success as approximately fifteen thousand to one against, and
at that had found none to gainsay their wisdom.

Something of this mood assailed Kwey Chao as she entered
the space of display on the day of trial and grasped the magnitude of the task before her.

Two score, three hand-counts, and four competitors, representing each branch of demonstrable art, from producing
garments by means of coloured threads controlled on skewers,
to gyrating on an extended toe while an ordinary person might
count a hundred, were assembling there. To each was allotted
a suitable tent wherein to arrange her 'turn' and a convenient
platform whereon in due course to display it.

"What can a mere voice – however refined – avail against
so much turmoil?" was wrung from her understanding. "This
calls for more forcible methods."

Up to this point it had been Kwey Chao's dignified purpose
to confine her efforts to the pure rendering of a few simple
ballads, such as firesides inspire, but she now tore down the inscribed placard announcing her aim and substituted for it one
set out in deeper and more lurid colours. On this she described
her qualifications as follows:

KWEY CHAO
(Last of the Line of She-pirates)
Animal, Fish, Bird and Insect Impersonator
In her notable and invariably
cheerfully received production
entitled
A DAY IN THE DEPTHS OF OUR DELTA
or
MAROONED IN THE
MOSQUITO MARSHES

Introducing for the first time in the Annals
of Dynastic History a faithful rendering of
the Yellow Crest's Invocation to the as yet
Unrisen Great Luminary of the Firmament
(The Thumb-mark of her Melody).

A certain amount of obloquy has been laid at Kwey Chao's
door on account of this move, some contending that it gave
her an unfair advantage. This arose from a circumstance that
could not have been foreseen and as a result of the far-reaching
popular response to the occasion. It had been Ti-ping's design
that every candidate should be seen or heard in turn, but when
the conscientious mandarin himself realized to what limits of
his after-rice repose this would extend he declared that so gross
an expenditure of public time was not to be endured; instead,
all must display their powers at once while he in person would
be carried in his state chair along the line of platforms, pausing
here and there before a likely entrant and – as he somewhat
familiarly expressed it – in the end encountering no difficulty
about putting a distinguishing mark upon the final emerger.

This undoubtedly brought a new element of skill to bear on
Kwey Chao's fortunes, for whenever a prominent rival reached
a culminating stage Kwey Chao contrived to reach that point
whereat one of the larger inhabitants of the wild uttered a loud
and capably-sustained challenge. Added to this, the diversity
of her range enabled her, without violating any of the stringent
canons of the classical stage, to speak prosaically, to sing in an
ordinary way, to make throat-noises bereft of actual words or
to propel wind through the lips and teeth to the accomplishment of every variety of bird language. By the use of one or
another of these expedients – all of which were logically necessary to her theme – it was unavoidable that Kwey Chao should
reduce to a state of incoherent despair every other competitor
in turn, with the result that her equivalent had risen to 3 taels
74 cash when the middle period gong was struck, and the press

before her stall was continually at variance with the guarders of open space and averters of disorder.

Yet it was this complexity of talent that would seem to have led to Kwey Chao's downfall, although the intricacy of the event has since been the subject of many conflicting essays. It has already been disclosed that the yellow crest's matchless 'Invocation' was to be the test and consummating point of that one's achievement, and it was this claim that drew both partisans and those unfriendly to her cause towards the sward before her dais; for never up to then had so exacting a course been set, and on her ability to survive the risks depended the outcome of her endeavour. Faithfully rendered, and an irresistible wave of public acclaim would carry her past the barrier; fail to surmount this one achievement that she had (it was felt) so presumptuously dared, and all her hitherto adequacy would be shattered.

The 'Invocation' as rendered in Kwey Chao's now familiar setting is composed of three changes of position, each of variable length: the first is a general survey of the yellow crest's life and daily habits; the second a short but duly harrowing interlude wherein one of the race is taken in a snare and, despite his plaintive song, held captive; the third and culminating strain a rise to ecstasy when he is freed by a sympathetic hand and passes out of sight, singing as he goes and still going singing. Therein lay the snare that was to enmesh the ill-timed bird-impersonator no less, for as she controlled her unprecedented vocal range to its lowest ebb in accord with the despairing prisoner's failing effort, his sublime Excellence's state chair was halted before her stand so that he might make his final choice, and in the same beat of time Kwey Chao realized that she had gone down so phenomenally low, as it were, in portrayed despair, that it was not feasible for her to get up again for the ensuing triumph. She therefore continued to stand in an appropriate poise, with suitably arranged face and lips but without any of the expected sound coming from them.

It was at this benumbing pause that Yellow Crest so capably seized the fleeting opportunity to prove his zeal and by an act of supreme resource eradicate the last vestige of his obligation. Throughout the day he had lurked in a convenient cypress tree that overhung the ground, unseen and unsuspected even by Kwey Chao herself but deeply concerned with every fluctuation of her progress. When the 'Invocation' was reached he – perhaps more than any other of the vast array that stood around – justly esteemed the risk and divined at what precise note Kwey Chao's fatal enthusiasm for lyrical exactitude would lead to her undoing. The testimony of the only onlooker who chanced to observe what took place then – that an object comparably 'like a cloud of fire' winged across the blue and disappeared into the singer's unconfined tresses – was universally accepted as unduly fanciful and attributable to the one concerned proving to be a minstrel errant.

With a well-ordained return to normal composure Kwey Chao did not cease to operate her lips and teeth to the extent that the theme required, while the scarcely interrupted melody continued to irradiate the scene more luminously – should that be credible – than before. When the final note passed hence, and Kwey Chao simultaneously ended her facial demonstration, the continuous sounds of approval were so unfeigned that the one signalled out had no excuse for not bowing with submissively clasped hands in all the eight directions, and thus affording Yellow Crest an easy path by which to effect an unobtrusive leave-taking.

When it is related that so precise a high official as the Mandarin Chan Hing Pung, tearing to shreds the hasty record of his preference up to that point, descended from his chair and indicated to Kwey Chao that she should occupy it, what further need of words? The Virtuous Cause had once more triumphed.

Li Pao, Lucky Star and the Intruding Stranger

THE STORY OF LI PAO might be regarded as the history of one whose life covered the period of the Three-fold Struggle – an almost legendary epoch when our flower-strewn but imperishable Empire was slowly awakening to the danger of crediting less scrupulous Powers with the same fidelity to spoken or thumb-signed pacts as that which marked her own punctilious rulers. The reference to an unexpected visitor, however, suggests that the narrative must be primarily connected with an incident in the middle period of Li Pao's career, during the hostilities arising from the rude and tyrannical Uans' treacherous bid to usurp world-wide power by reducing all neighbouring lands to the condition of vassal states, and those of an indulgent circle of listeners who are so excessively polite as to remain awake to the end will realize that this inference is feasible.

Immersed in his life-long preoccupation – that of expressing the most lucid apophthegms in the obscurest possible language – Li Pao had hitherto regarded with only a negligible concern the progress of military strife, and the incursion of the marauding Uans under their loose-mouthed and grotesquely outlined chieftain Ng-ho diminished if anything his ambition to acquire martial lustre. To the under-captain of an enrolling band, who sought him out to classify his powers, Li Pao replied that the formality was legally outside the official scope since he himself was one of those who maintained a conscientious antipathy to the exercise of force, whatever the provocation.

"Yet," urged the official in a persuasible tone, "consider well the outcome. You have here what this one would unhesitatingly describe as an agreeable if restricted place of abode; an attractive companion of the other sort lurks in the adjacent background, and you doubtless either have, or look forward with reasonable expectation to having, a virile Line of lusty sons to worship your unfading memory. Positioned thus, would you not cast in the weight of a strenuous arm to thwart those who seek to dispossess you?"

While considering the formulation of his reply Li Pao placed before the under-captain a generous measure of rich peach wine after receiving an assurance from the one concerned that his mind was not absolutely opposed to such a proceeding.

"The situation might be described in a variety of ways by the application of a diversity of analogies," explained Li Pao when they had sufficiently reciprocated compliments and each expressed a wish that the other might live for ever. "Perhaps the aptest would be to recall the pronouncement of the philosopher Tzu-pang when he awoke from an admonitory dream one night to find two demons, one seated on either side of his couch, contending about his future. 'If this person's ultimate destiny lies at the mercy of the argumentative qualities of a couple of secondary Beings,' he is reported to have exclaimed, 'he will henceforth direct a course of life irrespective of the Eternal Mandates.'"

To this, which in Li Pao's eyes had the appearance of being conclusive, the under-captain assented frankly that it required every description of personage to constitute a universe, and then, having had the misfortune to overturn his cup, he expressed a gratified surprise that it was at the time, as he irrefutably disclosed, empty of any liquid.

"Thus guided," continued Li Pao, after he had replenished the cup, despite the under-captain's determined efforts to prevent him, "the line of this one's conduct in the existing emergency is unflinching. Armed with any fatal implement of assault, he would cheerfully take up a position five-score or more paces from the most redoubtable among the Uanish horde – including the obscene Ng-ho himself if available – and continue to exchange lethal missiles across that space until one or the other fell mortally stricken."

"Disclose yourself more freely," was the doubtfully-voiced response. "Why should you then hesitate to take up arms and join a company of your heroic fellows?"

"By acting as he has set forth, either Li Pao or his selected opponent must Pass Hence, and thereby he fulfils the primary object of modern warfare. Thus he achieves all that is to be gained by resorting to arms and at the same time avoids the distressing contingency of possibly finding himself during the stress of battle locked in a noisome embrace – perhaps even clasped thigh to thigh – with an unsavoury and coarse-mannered rebel. To Pass Upwards is as the Predestined Word ordains, but to appear before one's decorous and high-born ancestors inextricably locked in the contaminating grasp of an Outland thug distends the normal limit."

* * * * *

It will readily be understood, even from the meagre evidence of this encounter, that Li Pao was not a person who was likely to be greeted with effusion by an assembly of those whose chief delight lay in witnessing athletic contests. He had been nourished on the literary style and adages of an earlier dynasty, and whatever the normal passer-by extolled produced in his internal organs an emotion of acute revulsion. Especially was this the case with the remarks of those who, on Li Pao's behoof, referred to the output of really successful essay writers and demanded of him whether he could not, by studying their form, in time acquire something approaching an equal proficiency and thereby ultimately receive at the rate of silver taels where he was now grudgingly accorded an insufficiency of copper pieces.

To this well intentioned advice Li Pao at first replied by a few carefully selected sentences, accompanying, however, an arrangement of his face that left it ambiguous in what exact sense his spoken words were to be regarded. Later he replied more definitely by describing that which he was bidden to emulate as nothing but the inner membrane of a defunct cow's digestive entrails, coupling this with the assertion that it would rend him internally as with barbed hooks of steel if by any chance he should be found devoid of life in proximity with such contaminating offal.

"Yet, delight of all beholders, your nobly-connected relatives and those of my own obscurely-descended clan grasp the bamboo by its inaccurate end when they charge this really complaisant person with obstinacy and inertness," maintained Li Pao when Lucky Star, his lesser part, hastened towards him with a cooling draught after one of these occasions. "So far from it being his deliberate purpose to despise riches or to repudiate fame, he is reasonably prepared to undergo both, and any one of the other burdens of exceptional popular acclaim – if it can be arranged on an honourable basis."

"What, then, is this formidable obstacle that stands in the way of our enhanced estate?" enquired Keih Sing, with an affectionate adjustment of Pao's ruffled pigtail. "Surely if it is anything where human prowess may avail, my all-conquering lord will be able to convince demons."

"Your words are gemmed with accuracy and good sense," admitted Li Pao modestly, "and did it rest with him alone a golden pagoda roofed with translucent amethyst would be your dwelling place tomorrow."

"The limit of this one's reasonable expectation tends towards a pleasantly-situated and flower-encrusted bower, where the outcome of mutual affection might find adequate room to expand and flourish," was Keih Sing's meek disclaimer. "As things are positioned, however, we are restricted to the uppermost space beneath the heat-engendering roof of a third-rate pallet-and-early-rice establishment. Surely if the impediment to which reference has been made can be thrust aside—"

"Therein you penetrate to the nucleus of the matter and strike the spigot of our difficulty upon its thicker end," exclaimed Li Pao with convincing fervour. "It is not to be expected that one who is admittedly producing masterpieces of scintillating texture should voluntarily renounce his style – a style whereby he can with ease employ three long words in circumstances where every other contemporary essayist would find it beyond his power to press in more than one of a single syllable – in order to conform to the degenerate standard of an illiterate epoch. Let those who now devour the crude and arid commonplaces of Tin-hi, Kow Hang and other so-described 'most wanteds' remove the wax of complacency from their undiscriminating ears and cultivate an uplifting taste for classical prolixity. Then this neglected and obscure arranger of appropriate words would find his, so to speak, stock in the literary mart resounding with an upward trend, whereat the producers of inscribed leaves, who now affect to be engaged with high officials when he submits his worthless name, would come forward with outstretched hands, carrying agreements in blank at the first tidings of his presence."

* * * * *

The union of Li Pao and Lucky Star has been aptly described as an instance of affection at the initial glance, for having noted her graceful but at the same time self-reliant poise when, for several gong-strokes, they stood side to side in a stress occasioned by a whispered word that at a certain stall within a limited supply of congealed fat was available, he lost no opportunity to engage her imagination. When, at a later period, he was able to claim her hand, not only did Keih Sing fulfil all Li Pao's expectations but she modestly disclosed a variety of engaging arts of which – deeply immersed in his themes – the reclusive essayist had never up to that time suspected the existence. For his part he strove to assure her of his regard by imparting an added excellence to whatever he undertook and attributing it to her presence. This chiefly concerned his apophthegms, which thereby became increasingly verbose and involved, and although the improvement diminished their scanty means, since fewer and fewer could be induced to purchase his work, Lucky Star never failed to applaud each one in turn as Li Pao explained to her its merits, while at the same time she foretold for him an imperishable future. Let no reproach for this be laid to Keih Sing's charge, for though she might – and in fact did – fail to grasp the significance of any single point in all Pao's efforts, the element of gratitude she felt that he should have chosen her from among the countless thousands of her own sort invested him with all the attributes of a Superior Being. Apart from serving Li Pao her chief delight lay in persuading any of the feathered creatures of the air to alight at her open shutter, and for this purpose she contrived a projecting ledge on which it was her charitable habit to scatter such crumbs and fragments of discarded meat as might be spared from her own inadequate platter. While regarding this as a harmless and even to a slight degree a gravity-removing fancy on her part, Li Pao felt that it would perhaps have been more in keeping with their present need if she had by the same means enticed in larger and more meaty birds which would have brought a welcome addition to their ill-spread table.

* * * * *

Meanwhile the press of battle had so far advanced that it was no unusual thing for contending bands of warriors to congest the outer ways and to disarrange the legitimate business of the countryside and city. Requiring to be fed, they soon produced a state of siege, so that presently a general shortage reared its head, while the far-seeing and astute sped from mart to mart unostentatiously amassing a stock of what they deemed would next be most in demand, and as they met and passed freely execrating so detestable a practice in all others. To maintain a seemly balance whereby the affluent should not possess all that was essential to the community at large and the more necessitous be able to procure nothing, the high officials devised a system of issuing bamboo slips on which were described the commodities most sought as well as the amount to which each person was entitled at a given date, and undoubtedly the expedient would have restored a more normal trend had not the harassed authorities overlooked the need of also providing the requisite supply of viands.

To add to the popular concern and lack of poise a variety of rumours began to spread, some attributing to the oncoming Uans a diversity of unnatural powers, others claiming for their own armed force an even greater preponderance of victory-bringing omens. Thus Chow Mang-hi, supreme War Lord of the Uans, had claimed possession of an undisclosed device that would make resistance futile, and while some asserted that this pointed to a rare and potent drug, by which men drinking it became invisible and fought unseen, others, who had it from influential friends in a position to know, disclosed that the boast referred to the magic and long lost shears of Umph which endowed with life and all its attributes figures of a never-ending warrior host cut out from sheets of paper. Moved by such tales, not a few declared it hopeless to contend and counselled an unaggressive compact whereby Mang-hi would become a fostering ally, but an overwhelming number rejected so pusillanimous a front, claiming that even then a relieving army from a distant alien State was marching to their aid, since Outland men, speaking an uncouth tongue and wearing long beards, who could, moreover, drink liquid fire, had on good authority been seen throughout the Province.

Unaffected by the general stress and sway, Li Pao continued to elaborate his style and contrived paraphrases of more and more diffuseness, while Lucky Star remained content to serve his hand and day after day to eke out their meagre store to the utmost limits of its sparse dimensions. Thus positioned, Pao was recording his lofty thoughts by the uncertain glimmer of a single waxed thread one night, with his lesser one pounding acorns in a bowl, when the sound of a heavy body striking the latter one's alighting shelf outside brought the immediate task of both to a sharp-edged finish.

"This would seem to promise a fowl of considerably larger growth than has hitherto filled our ration – possibly a Kien-fi goose exhausted on its homeward flight or even a storm-tossed peacock," exclaimed Li Pao, casting aside his tablets with a hopeful look and taking up instead a weighty cleaver. "Throw open the shutter suddenly, Adored," and he assumed a suitable attitude of defence at a convenient distance.

"Yet seeing that the protection of our roof has been sought, is it permissible, despite the stringency of our case, so to dispose of one who might claim sanctuary?" pleaded Keih Sing with gentle reluctance.

To this no doubt Li Pao would have replied by an appropriate and convincing verse had not the shutter-fastening at that moment incapably failed to retain its hold, thus permitting the entry of a large and disordered man whose unwieldy bulk and degenerate type of face proclaimed him to be an Uan of the most repellent description. What appeared to be the remains of a badly-made umbrella hung about his loins, and as he stumbled in he held both hands submissively above his head, at the same time maintaining that he was desirous of associating in friendship with any there and willingly yielded himself into their keeping. Becoming accustomed to the light, however, and discovering their strength, he at once assumed a defiant pose and drew a keen-edged sword.

"Since you are but two," he declared, "and neither of martial build, the position is reversed and he who speaks will decide the issue."

"It would be useless to deny what is so convincingly advanced," replied Li Pao, and he replaced his ineffectual cleaver on its hook, as the intruder made several near-miss thrusts with his formidable weapon. "If it is not too much to ask, as the matter stands, would you spare sufficient of your no doubt precious time to reveal what manner of man you are and why you have elected to come up to our far from attractive tenement home at all, and that by so exacting an approach when there exists a conveniently arranged inside ladder?"

"Is it possible that this outline is unknown to you, despite the continuous efforts of the gravity-remover face-depicters of every civilized nation – this loose-lipped mouth, these protuberant hard-boiled eyes, these fan-like ears, this fatuous look, unwieldy bulk, exaggerated warrior garb and, to add a conclusive wedge, this triple row of valour-proclaiming badges? Is it credible that any outpost is so remote, or two, not apparently in a certifiable state, so benighted?"

"Ng-ho!" exclaimed both in a single voice, "Chief of the Strategy of Invasion. How does it befall that one so very high up in authority should inconvenience himself to the extent of dropping in, as it were, with this flattering lack of ceremony upon two so devoid of any shred of influence?"

"Since you have removed an uneasy doubt that he might not be so notorious as he had hoped, your very natural curiosity may now, without too much indiscretion, be sated," replied Ng-ho, lowering the point of his hitherto aggressive blade and courteously indicating by means of a downward sweep that they might sit upon the floor. "At this moment, as we talk, countless intrepid warriors of the pure Uanish strain are descending in your midst to await this one's rallying call, when they will disperse upon a preconcerted plan and seize all the points of most advantage."

"This is sufficiently astonishing in any case," declared Li Pao, who, despite his apophthegms, was not really sluggish-minded and now desired to learn as much as could be gathered; "for the gates being closed and the walls well-manned, how will this infiltrating host reach our midst, or, alternatively, you, being here, be able to pass out and join them?"

"That concerns our ever-to-be-venerated Chief," (here Ng-ho paused to throw a variety of occult signs, and he also knocked his head three times against the nearest wall in token of abject submission) "and involves his hidden weapon. The position now being thus and thus, it is permissible to explain that our revered Leader's hitherto unknown contrivance involves the use of parchment sacks which, distended by a new and miraculously-endowed sort of air, assume the quality of volitation. Each clinging to one of these, and aided by a favouring wind, picked warriors of our intrepid Panther Guard can pass undetected over barriers of the most impregnable strength and then, fearlessly casting themselves free, descend in safety by merely pressing the spring of a self-opening umbrella."

"This, then is the secret of your arrival on our inaccessible window-sill," exclaimed Li Pao, rising in his well-merited sense of indignation, "not ascending as normally would an honoured guest, but descending like a stealthy vampire!"

"That is the regrettable outcome of this one's want of experience in the wind," confessed Ng-ho, "in that he cast off a few beats of time before it was intended. No doubt official regrets for the intrusion will be expressed if a definite complaint is made on a duly authorized form and submitted to the proper quarter. Although this war is being waged on an all-embracing scale that spares neither young nor old, no Uan warrior wearing the sacred emblem of our divine Commander-at-the-Head would wittingly deviate by so much as the width of a naiad's eyelash from the severest military usage."

"Hitherto this person has borne a strictly neutral part," declared Li Pao, "swaying, as befits one who balances antitheses as a juggler does brimming cups of boiling tea, neither to the one side nor to the other. But this irruption of winged men from the Upper Space transcends the normal code, inasmuch as it now assumes the elements of a struggle between Beings and ordinary beings. In such a case one of the latter has no choice but to range himself with his own kind, according to the rule of Yaou as laid down in his imperishable edict."

Speaking in this compact but temperate strain and moving in a very natural way, Li Pao crossed over to a shelf that held his few though noticeably heavy books and from among these he selected a volume of the weightiest proportions. Advancing this he approached Ng-ho, but instead of displaying the indicated page as that one somewhat obtusely took for granted, he dextrously swung the formidable mass with a quite unexpected force and struck the dull-witted Invasion Chief at the vulnerable point where his over-swollen neck joined his offensively obese body. Deprived of any latent reserve of power by years of self-indulgence, the discreditable example of unrestricted Uan rule sank incapably upon the rough-hewn floor and closed his ill-matched eyes in oblivion.

"Alas!" exclaimed Keih Sing, looking down on that which lay there with some foreboding, "how embarrassing an alternative confronts us now, for we must either keep the extremely inopportune Chieftain here until his proximity becomes oppressive or else contrive a scheme to dispose unostentatiously of his by no means inconspicuous body."

"Have no fear on that account," replied Li Pao, "but disentangle the cord from which our recently purified garments at present depend while this one stands guard upon our illustrious guest with the now effective chopper."

When Ng-ho had been inextricably bound – and in his determination to leave no contingency to chance Li Pao encased him from head to foot in a swathe of cordage, that one unbarred the door and taking up his staff and a swinging light went forth to complete his mission. To Lucky Star he left the custody of Ng-ho meanwhile, directing her to stand above him with the cleaving-knife and should he attempt to shake off his bonds to strike him until he became supine again, but as humanely as it might be done and at first with the blunt side of the weapon. This Keih Sing undertook implicitly.

As Li Pao traversed the now almost deserted Ways, composing a variety of apophthegms based on so unusual a doing, he encountered one here and there deviously clad, who asked how to reach a certain point where, each claimed, he was to meet another with whom he had urgent matters. Recognising these to be disguised Uans by their correct but laboured speech, Li Pao replied in courteous terms and sent them in wrong directions.

At the outer gate of the Office of Warlike Deeds he was met by a custodian who barred the way until, as he recalled Li Pao and the flavour of his jar of wine, the features of that one changed to an expression from which gravity was lacking.

"Lo, here is he who disdained to mingle in the press of strife but would engage to vanquish the redoubtable Ng-ho if it could be arranged on an amicable basis," exclaimed the under-captain – for so it was – to an over-captain who had drawn near to listen. "Doubtless the import of his message is that this has now been done and nothing remains but to hang out the banners."

"It is not unaptly said," replied Li Pao, "except the reference to waving flags, that being opposed to this one's literary code as germinant of self-laudation."

"Is it not as your underling described when he spoke of this one before?" was passed in a muffled voice. "It would be as profitable to catch eels on a spade as to pursue the sequence of his actual meaning."

"Be that as it might," was Li Pao's modest boast, "the encounter took place as – more or less – he who now speaks prescribed, and it only needs those in authority to come and remove the fallen."

It was some while before Li Pao could induce those who now gathered round to regard what he had to tell as anything but an austerity-dispelling narrative, while his claim to Uans descending in sacks compelled even the most sombre to relax their waistbands. But presently first one and then another spoke haltingly of seeing this or hearing that, until a doubt began to spread which soon gave place to credence. By this

time a bodyguard of fearless Ironcaps had been called out and
told to advance with caution, but when it was understood that
Lucky Star, provided with a keen-edged knife, stood over the
Uan Chief's insensate form, confidence returned and the advance became a valiant scramble.

Quick as the movement was, rumour had gone before and
at the barrier of his outer door a surging throng was pressing.
Many of these applauded Li Pao as he passed through, though
without understanding who he was or what part he had in the
entertainment for which they deemed they had gathered. As
they went up the narrow stair the melodious voice of the one
on guard could be heard chanting an appropriate ballad of
love and war, and they saw that she had laid aside the cleaving
blade and was repairing Pao's scanty footwear to pass the time
in thrift, but otherwise everything was as he had left it.

"Li Pao," declared the over-captain when he had looked into
Ng-ho's unsightly face and suitably expressed his contempt for
that one's prowess, "you have made good your claim and in due
course – provided nothing untoward steps in – you will doubtless be agreeably surprised by the bestowal of an adequate
recognition. Whether this should take the form of an official
degree, a pink-lined chair, some mark of honour appended
to your worthy if no-longer-among-us father's distinguished
name, or the graciously-conveyed permission to cover your
own hands with feather-trimmed gloves, it might be presumptuous to conjecture."

"If," said an assertive voice – for the room was now filled
with any who would, thrust upwards by the others – "if you
are that Li Pao whose unread themes are to be found in the
two-cash receptacles of all the discarded printed-leaf dealers
of the city, a more solid reward awaits you. Obscure and ill-
paid today, tomorrow you will find your commonplace name
will be in every mouth and – for no logical reason, let it be
freely said – countless thousands will hasten to buy your neglected essays. He who speaks thus definitely is 'Long Ear' of

the 'This Person Told You So' paragraphs in the Tang Whang *Daily Heaven-sent Leaf of Truth*, who will be among the first to resound your achievement. When you have become a 'most wanted' and have anything exclusive to make known, do not forget the debt of this obligation."

"Restrain your facile brush," besought Pao, "and let a moist sponge be drawn across the tablets of your veracious memory. It is far from this one's wish or thought to profit by the chance outcome of something not even remotely connected with his unique attainments."

"That, no doubt, is one facet of your present case, Li Pao," assented the recorder of passing things, "but let this one re-mind you that there is equally another. Those who scan the *Heaven-sent Truth* have a reasonable claim to be admitted into the precincts of whatever goes on, whether it involves intrusion upon the occupants of a pigsty or a palace. Added to this, he who speaks has not left a restful couch and stumbled upon a priceless 'swoop' to be set captiously aside by the passing whim of any; whereunto also his exertions tonight will assure a complete moon's rice for a deserving and ever-clamorous family of eleven."

"Behold how an ordinary person may become enmeshed in the converging lines of fate by which his present state is entirely opposed to what he had striven for throughout a well-spent life of effort," exclaimed Li Pao, imposing silence on all by the undoubted sincerity of his message. "For several decades the one who speaks has scattered gems of authentic lore with an ungrudging hand upon a wholly unresponsive public. While never intending to grasp the hem of Fortune's cloak, neither would he have turned churlishly aside from the due reward of industry had an approximate return been offered. . . . Observe his careworn look and threadbare garb, the incongruous roughness of a devoted helpmeet's hand and the stark inad-equacy of this ill-provided chamber. Yet today, by the mere mischance of an utterly negligible warrior chief – destitute of any literary quality whatever – descending on his inopportune window-sill, he is to be thrust into the forefront of the hanging lantern's glare and destined to suffer the indignity of becoming a 'most wanted'. To whatever extremity of conduct it may lead be well assured that Li Pao, secure in the pronouncement of generations hence, will devise some subterfuge by which to escape so detestable a climax."

"It only remains to add," concluded Kai Lung, "that by whatever means, the inflexible Li Pao must have succeeded in his effort. No reference to his work exists in the contemporary record of his day, while by the Satire of Destiny, in the light of what he claimed, his name has been equally unknown at any subsequent period."

The Cupidity of Ah Pak
or
Riches No Protection Against Thunder-Bolts

Related by Kai Lung at Wu-whei, in order to prove that a person of questionable filial piety might be relentlessly pursued to an old age by the avenging deities and finally destroyed, involving others in his overthrow.

"THE STORY OF AH PAK," began Kai Lung, "as recorded by the venerable historian Wei Ching, has been included in the sacred Classics as forming a specific example of the evil which may ultimately befall a person who becomes immersed in a too assiduous pursuit of wealth."

"Such a well-intentioned warning was doubtless acceptable in the affluent days of the amiable Wei Ching," interposed Ko-fung, the very indigent dog butcher of the village, "but in Wu-whei at the present time the character and manner of behaving of the Mandarin T'sang Hai remove the possibility of so pardonable a failing. Did not the enlightened philosopher in question by any chance record a story setting forth the ill consequences of an all-engrossing poverty and showing how the necessity of being involved in such a condition of affairs might be successfully evaded?"

"Assuredly the discriminating Wei Ching would have done so," replied Kai Lung pleasantly, "could he have foreseen that the very doubtful amusement of five-cash fan-t'an would come to possess an overwhelming attraction in the eyes of needy dog butchers, O Ko-fung. As it is, however, his only remark which can be considered in any way applicable consists of the inspired proverb, 'The person who caresses a tiger with one hand and holds the stakes against an inhabitant of Wu-whei with the other, should first acquire the art of consuming his rice through a reed stem.'"

At this unassuming rebuke Ko-fung modestly withdrew himself, and doubtless the story of Ah Pak would thereupon have proceeded without further interruption had it not been for the presence of Wang Yu, the indolent and disputatious pipe maker. This person, in addition to being almost as deficient in wealth as Ko-fung and even more easily drawn into the insidious delight of venturing his possessions upon the uncertain chances of fan-t'an, availed himself of every opportunity for displaying an open hostility towards Kai Lung's opinions. "Nevertheless," he now exclaimed impetuously, "it by no means follows that there are not many less profitable occupations than that of fan-t'an. What, indeed, to call up a particular instance, O Kai Lung, what remains after listening to one of your admittedly elaborate stories beyond a lightening of one's scrip and a movement among the upper leaves of the sycamores around; or by what process of reasoning can a person of strict honourableness justify himself in passing round his collecting bowl in return for that which it costs him nothing to produce? This industrious one, and the others who stand around, can only wrest an uncertain livelihood by the exercise of continuous labour, and, moreover, after no inconsiderable expenditure for the various essentials of their craft. Plainly the reference to the unprofitableness of fan-t'an was ill-considered."

With these self-confident words the very inopportune Wang Yu pressed forward with the authority of one who has deserved well of his fellows, while those around exclaimed, one to another, "Indeed, the matter is such as the astute Wang Yu's crystal-edged penetration has shown it to be. Kai Lung's stories involve him in no particular labour or outlay, nor does their recital here in any way impoverish his stock for the neighbouring villages. Undoubtedly in asking us to recompense him with pieces of copper or pieces of brass on every occasion the somewhat avaricious Kai Lung has been guilty of putting both feet forward at once. The enjoyment of an empty rice box for the night and a portion of cold mouse pie, or some similar proffer of inexpensive hospitality, should be a sufficient reward for so ordinary an entertainment." Nevertheless, being for the most part elderly persons of established dignity they waited for Kai Lung to express himself before making any definite suggestion touching the return of the contents of his collecting bowl.

Then replied Kai Lung, clearly understanding that unless the discussion were diverted into a more remunerative channel his own opinion of the estimable Wei Ching's usefulness would in no degree differ from that expressed by Ko-fung, "It is well said, 'When the treasury of Tung-hyi was threatened he prudently buried his jewels beneath the refuse heap.' Obviously the industrious Wang Yu has been searching his mind and has brought to the surface a clarified principle of diamond-like radiance."

At this unquestioning admission the gratified Wang Yu pressed unrebuked into the foremost position, where, indeed, it was fitting that the most distinguished alone should find a place, and repeatedly looked at himself approvingly at the same time calling aloud his name and coupling with it every adroit and engaging attribute. The others who stood around, also, did not hesitate to greet him as one reasonably entitled to their esteem, for it began to be somewhat hastily assumed from Kai Lung's words that he could not now be unbending towards the suggestion of a gratifying restitution; yet it was noticed (although the incident was not fully comprehended at the time) that a wise person present, with whom Kai Lung had frequently engaged in traffic, after observing closely the affable and ingenuous expression of the story teller's face and his extreme impassiveness of manner, retired a few paces from the crowd and calling aside his son, entrusted to him his scrip of money, commanding him that he should bear it away without delay and deposit it in a secret place of which he had knowledge.

"It would be the entire reversal of a prudent and consistent habit to contribute even brass or copper pieces in the circumstance to which the unobtrusive and clear-sighted Wang Yu has made reference," continued Kai Lung. "There is, however, a further detail to be considered. What shall be deemed of a possession which in addition to being of no particular value itself allures its bearer into the never-slackening embrace of a relentless poverty? This insignificant and, it must be confessed, exceedingly badly-made opium pipe, the handiwork of the disinterested and far-seeing Wang Yu himself, though highly priced at the three cash for which it was obtained, has, ever since its purchase, involved this really necessitous person in a large and continually-increasing expenditure. Without doubt, the first reasonable act after being initiated into the requirements of Wang Yu's inspired philosophy will be to destroy it utterly, so that—"

"Alas!" exclaimed Chen-cheng, the opium seller, who received from Kai Lung many taels of silver in the course of each year, starting forward suddenly and arresting the story teller's hand; "do not, O amiable Kai Lung, be misled from your usually penetrating insight by the badly-digested arguments of one who would be more fitly employed in impersonating the hind legs of a dragon at the Theatre of Concentrated Hi-Ti Emotions than in propounding a new theory of any possible excellence. If such a condition of affairs as that which he suggested were honourably received what, as an instance, would be the ultimate destiny of the unfortunate Sing You who stands by this person's side? For it is an uncontroversial fact that the fruit which he carries from house to house grows untended upon the trees and in due season falls to the ground naturally and with no particular exertion at his hands; nor, to urge the

comparison to its legitimate end, does that for which he re-
ceives a piece of silver today, tomorrow represent the value of
a mandarin's oath."

"O evil stomached Wang Yu!" cried Sing You, the fruit seller,
casting his staff to the ground in unrestrained frenzy, "how intolerable a state of existence will it become in Wu-whei if one
of your depraved habits and stunted intelligence is henceforth
to decide who shall flourish and who shall be conveyed to the
Establishment of Uniform Apparel and Limited Diet! Why, indeed, should the frugal and unassuming Hi Seng, for example,
be condemned to an irredeemable destitution and his children
to various poverty-engendered diseases from which they can
only hope to escape by means of painful and untimely deaths,
for no other reason than that the Wu Ho, from which Hi Seng
fills his water skins, flows past his very door and is in no wise
diminished in volume by the amount which the person in question daily supplies to his customers?"

"Wang Yu," passionately exclaimed Hi Seng the water carrier,
at once assuming that the extinction of his house and name to
which Sing You had made reference was a danger immediately threatening him, "it is a matter of common knowledge
throughout the Province that your ancestors were not of any
particular repute or attainment and that, in detail, your grandsire Kong obtained a degraded livelihood by publicly beating
his head with a brick in order to excite the admiration of the
charitable. Do not, therefore, turning your gaze inward and
beholding nothing but envy and contentiousness, imagine that
so intolerable a state of things as that which you have proposed
can ever be established in Wu-whei. It may be that in this matter
you are but the finger nail sheath of high ones, here or in Pekin,
who are desirous of testing to what length of tyranny they may
safely proceed. Understand, then, O traitorous and cross-eyed
person reclining opposite, that the Yellow-fringed Banner will
certainly be raised and the assistance of the Elder Brother in-
voked before such a course of injustice will be accepted."

"It is a climax which must inevitably come to pass if the point is proceeded with," agreed a performing leper who saw his occupation threatened also. "By his own words the double-witted Wang Yu is shown to be like Ting-hi's ducks – either ankle-deep in wisdom or overhead in treachery – and in causing him to betray himself prematurely Kai Lung is deserving of our consistent regard."

"Such an emotion has never been absent from our sentiments towards the versatile and accomplished story teller," observed a vendor of writing materials, who, having married the daughter of a literary candidate, was not disposed to be outdone in ceremonious politeness by a performing leper. "Now that the garrulous and prosaic Wang Yu has been fitly silenced, will you not, O estimable Kai Lung, proceed with the history of the high-souled Ah Pak, so that all these persons present may be diligently put upon their guard against becoming immersed in a too assiduous pursuit of wealth?"

"The occasion is one which seems to demand some such forcible moral," assented Kai Lung. "Yet," he continued, "it is an admitted fact that the sun has crossed three branches of the mulberry tree since this incompetent one unrolled his mat here, while at this moment an impatient circle of mandarins awaits his arrival at Shan Tzu, all complaining of the unendurable weight of the offerings which they have brought wherewith to greet him."

"The occasion may certainly be regarded as an unusual one," admitted Chen-cheng, who was feeling very placidly disposed towards himself in consequence of Kai Lung's unremunerative impulse having been successfully turned aside; "if, however, the collecting bowl were again passed from hand to hand doubtless the varying contentions would be adequately met."

"The solution is an honourable one, and this person will in no measure protest further against its adoption," replied Kai Lung, with an extreme air of no-concern. Nevertheless he himself carried the bowl to each person present and all contributed a second time with the exception of the wise man to whom an earlier reference has been made (who was obviously unable to do so, though, somewhat to the surprise of those who stood by, he and the story teller exchanged many elaborate bows and polished courtesies, expressive of mutual regard and appreciation) and the intolerable Wang Yu. It may finally be set forth that in the meantime this thoroughly contemptible person had been relentlessly thrust aside until he stood on the outside fringe of the throng, yet so incapable was he of grasping intelligently the true course of events which had arisen that he did not cease to protest to all who would listen to him that Kai Lung's argument was inept as the opium pipe of which he complained was certainly worth the three cash for which it had been purchased.

Period I
The Early Life of Ah Pak

AH PAK, it may be clearly expressed from the first, was a person in whom every instinct was subservient to an insatiable desire to amass taels by means of profitable undertakings. It was often pointed out to him by those who had authority over him during his earlier years, that by entering for the Examinations and becoming in time a public official he would have greater opportunities of enriching himself – in a more dignified and less laborious manner also – than could ever arise through the uncertain fortune of commercial ventures, but towards these well-intentioned warnings the arrogant Ah Pak turned his feet in an opposite direction, and it is even recorded that in a spirit of presumptuous self-confidence he maintained on one occasion that it would be more beneficial if henceforth the sacred Four Books and the illimitable Five Classics were designated the Nine Roads to Incompetence; adding, that the only public examinations which he had any design to pass successfully were those to which persons who were unable to meet their just obligations were always liable.

This outrageous freedom of expression could not fail to be objectionable to Ah Pak's father, for after spending thirty years in failing to pass the examination of the second degree, the person in question had been honoured, at the age of seventy five, with the complimentary degree of "The Sign of Golden Intention," as a reward for his distinguished tenacity. With so positive a proof of the excellence of the literary system before his eyes it cannot be doubted that the father of Ah Pak would have held himself more sternly towards his son's degraded tastes than he did had it not been for the pronouncement of astrologers, for when consulted at the time of Ah Pak's birth those persons had predicted that as the event took place on the first day of the Month of Great Sacrifices (called the Dawn of Much Bargaining; or, the Many-hued Paradise of the Lesser Ones), when his mother's mind would inevitably be filled with rainbow-like images of profitable transactions and ceaseless chaffering at the stalls of the vendors of raiment, an unusual spirit of enterprise might be confidently anticipated.

"There is a true saying, 'As the mould, so the brick,'" re-marked the father of Ah Pak on one occasion. "Yet it is a matter for unpalatable regret that the brick in question has received so one-sided an impression. As a result of this in no way ex-ceptional person's assiduousness his hitherto untitled ancestors now bear the creditable distinction of 'Golden Intention' for eleven generations back, but it is more than probable that Ah Pak's contribution to the tablets in the Ancestral Temple will be the inscription 'Unnamed on account of systematic and almost incredible low-mindedness. "Golden Intention" cancelled, and ancestors degraded as far back as the Tang Dynasty,' or some similar unfilial legend."

"It is not an alluring contemplation," admitted the mother of Ah Pak, "but it should be added that for the last three and twenty years the one we are referring to has supplied the en-tire resources of this otherwise ill-equipped establishment, and has, indeed, enabled your meritorious personality to carry to a successful end your unquenchable determination to extort from the examining officials a degree of some kind."

"Doubtless the all-seeing Buddha would have supplied any deficiency as the occasion arose," replied the father of Ah Pak coldly; for the reflection that his success was in any essential detail owing to his son's exertions did not gladden his internal organs.

"Such a source might certainly be relied upon," said the mother of Ah Pak, "but in that case it is more than question-able if the supplies alluded to would have included spiced sharks' fins during the Festival of Lanterns and other illustrious occasions and a profusion of rich viands and wearing apparel for all time. The sublime Buddha's munificence rarely seems to extend beyond unseasoned rice and plain cotton robes for those who look solely to him for their sustenance."

" 'The bee spins, the silkworm gathers honey; do not con-sult the stars by day,' " quoted the father of Ah Pak. Having committed to memory the three hundred and eleven chapters comprising 'The Book of Odes' he was able to produce a ready-made expression applicable to every possible contin-gency, although some of the lesser-known proverbs to which he occasionally resorted were certainly elusive and might even appear to the thoughtless or illiterate to be applied in a wrong sequence. "Learn, O woman, that there are exalted mental contemplations which cannot be approached by those whose intellectual outlook is bounded by visions of expensively-pre-served sharks' fins or other matters of mere earthly interest." With these words the liberal-minded person turned his eyes towards the official notification of his degree, which, framed in an elaborately-carved device of pure green jade, was suspended above the Domestic Altar and hung round with innumerable sets of complimentary verses in which he was likened to an elderly tiger, infirm but full of guile; a decrepit serpent creep-ing unperceived through the reeds and seizing the prey which might otherwise have escaped; a hollow tree unexpectedly falling on those who would ridicule its infirmities and a variety of other ingenious metaphors in which the undoubted qualities by which the person alluded to had eventually triumphed were delicately and inoffensively acknowledged by his friends.

Although the character of Ah Pak cannot be upheld at any period of his life it is not to be denied that he had, indeed, for the space of three and twenty years, maintained his parents in a condition of ease, but as the all-observing philosopher remarked, "It is an ill-omened bird that makes its own nest into soup," and in order to accomplish his end Ah Pak had resorted to means which if not actually discreditable were at least questionable. When the time of the triennial competitions drew near and innumerable lotteries connected with the chances of all concerned appeared at every stall it was his custom to buy up secretly all the tickets which bore his father's name, and then at a favourable moment to spread a well-maintained rumour about every quarter of the city to the effect that the person in question had been made the object of a most significant portent. This might be that he had obliged the chief mandarin of the Board of Examiners in a money transaction; that the golden figure of Justice had been observed to leave its resting place on the central pinnacle of the Great Hall of Impartiality, and circle seven times round the residence of Ah Pak's father before returning to its pedestal; or that some other omen had occurred which placed the success of the person indicated beyond reasonable doubt. By this stratagem his father became a popular favourite in the lists and Ah Pak was able to dispose of his tickets at vastly increased sums, and had he been content to let the matter thus remain, without resorting to actual duplicity, his memory might have been handed down as one certainly not pleasant but who, nevertheless, was not wholly bad. But not trusting entirely to the really very shadowy chance which his father had of passing the examination, Ah Pak – to use the deplorably inelegant phrase by which he himself alluded to his debased practice – effectively roasted his ancient progenitor's pig by feigning, on the very eve of the examination, to be suddenly afflicted with the grimacing frenzy or some other form of malignant distemper. From this cause his father habitually went into his cell with his mind practically unlatched by the contemplation of what he believed to be the inevitable degeneration of his line, and as a direct consequence his written papers not infrequently were of so gravity-removing a nature as to be passed from hand to hand among the examiners and finally printed by one who had collected many examples of a like character. So well-disposed did the examiners become towards the father of Ah Pak for affording them such unusual entertainment that it was solely through this cause that they recommended him for the distinguished embellishment of 'Golden Intention,' maintaining with one voice that he was a person who could enlighten and extract something new from the dullest and most obscure passages of history or philosophy. It might not unreasonably be claimed that Ah Pak had in this way materially assisted towards his father's ambition, but the chain of circumstances was doubtless too involved for the limited understanding of the inferior deities into whose hands the matter had been entrusted, for it is definitely stated that all his misfortunes originated from this unfilial manner of behaving.

It is well written, 'By the side of the magnanimous Emperor is seated the resolute and unapproachable Dowager Empress.' Thus, no dignity or heaven-sent distinction is found when it is reached to be exactly as it had been anticipated. At the age of seventeen the father of Ah Pak had flung himself into the competitions with the inspired certainty of success, and the hope of receiving without delay a lucrative appointment which would enable him, at a not far distant date, to make adequate proposals with regard to a certain maiden whose outline had long been permanently reflected on his mind in very graceful and ornamental curves. In spite of a most stringent economy, however, it was destined that he should never be able to afford more than a much inferior maiden, but it was chiefly with regard to the degree that the wisdom of the proverb is manifest, for no sooner had he reached this point in his intrepid ambition than he came under the influence of a planet unfriendly towards his welfare and passed with extreme dissatisfaction into the Beyond.

His disappointment was chiefly occasioned by the incomplete state in which he had to leave a dynastical history upon which he had been engaged for twenty years, for although he had by that time completed nine volumes they were entirely devoted to exposing the narrow-minded incompetence of all former writers on the subject and to holding up their opinions to well-merited ridicule, so that his own views and arguments were still unexpressed. Calling Ah Pak to his couch, therefore, he gave him specific and detailed commands, binding him by oaths and imprecations which even the unreliable person in question would respect, to transmit to him, when in the Upper Air, ink, brushes, and writing palates of every description, the nine complete volumes and parchment skins of the finest quality to a practically inexhaustible amount, so that he might continue his labours with the least possible interruption. He also charged him to prepare and burn ceremoniously in a like manner a profusion of raiment, both heat-resisting and that specially adapted for the requirements of a rigorous climate, a well-constructed residence and a sufficiency of furniture suitable for a person bearing the honorary degree of 'Golden Intention,' vast supplies of food and wine, and money to no inconsiderable extent. Having in this prudent manner safeguarded his future against every possible contingency he recommended Ah Pak to worship his memory unceasingly and with these devout words on his lips he passed at once into the Shadowy Land.

When Ah Pak thoroughly understood the nature of the obligation thus imposed upon him it appeared to his untrained imagination that the most prudent and respectful course for him to pursue would be to commit suicide and following his father into the Upper Air courteously point out to him the uninviting

magnitude of the command; for with his father Ah Pak's chief
source of income was lost, and what he earned by enticing
strangers into law cases and then receiving an agreed portion
of the inflicted fine from the examining mandarin could not be
judiciously relied upon, and would in any case be insufficient
to procure even a small part of the enumerated requirements.
It was while wrapped in this depression that an inspired idea
flashed upon Ah Pak and for a time benumbed him with the
illimitable magnitude of its possibilities. Up to that period in
order to transmit offerings of specific objects into the Upper
World for the use of those who had Passed Before, it had always
been somewhat hastily assumed that it was necessary to burn
the object itself in order to reduce it to a convenient substance
for accomplishing the journey. Yet, came the revelation to Ah
Pak, the solid body was not transmitted and reconstructed, for
the ashes remained behind and in order to establish this to his
own satisfaction he securely bound a change of raiment to an
upright post by means of heavy chains and was still able to
transmit it as successfully as before. It followed, to his logical
mind, that when once the purpose had been indicated a band
of attendant spirits provided a similar object, whatever it might
be, in the Above. Was it necessary, then, that so extravagant
a course should be pursued, for would not a cunningly prepared substitute of paper and bamboo be equally efficacious?
Nowadays it is difficult to conjecture a time when any other
practice was observed, for Ah Pak was right; provided ordinary
care is maintained and the credulity of the attending demons
is not unreasonably taxed, the paper substitutes are quite as effective as the solid objects themselves, and for eleven centuries
these offerings have now been economically used without a
single complaint reaching the Beneath World that they have
been found inept or have failed to reach their destination.

In an atmosphere of new hope Ah Pak at once set resolutely
to work and not many days had passed before he had carried
out no insignificant portion of his father's command. The nine

ornamental volumes of dynastic history, he had cheerfully and unhesitatingly burned immediately upon his father's passing beyond, as a sign and an assurance to that person of his energetic disposition in the matter. Without pausing to make any ostentatious display of his lavish and charitable purpose he now prepared and consumed by fire in a like manner an indefinite number of bales embellished with the names and descriptions of the finest and most expensive parchment; a profusion of boxes of delicate food, select fruit and rare and costly wines; as many cubes of wood – each musk-scented and adorned with respectful greetings and felicitous remarks after the semblance of the smoothest ink – as two agile and resolute-minded oxen could draw, and about five score well-filled sacks, each bearing inscriptions which the most careless and short-sighted person could not ignore, to the effect that they contained gold pieces of perfect and unalloyed purity. To this extent he experienced no discouragement in carrying his becoming liberality into effect, but when Ah Pak endeavoured to mould richly curtained seats, reclining stools, ornaments of jade and metal, lacquered tablets and other necessary articles of furniture from the limited means at his disposal it soon became open to his mind that the accomplishment was one which he had not inherited. Those before whom he placed the articles to pronounce upon in a strain of evenly-balanced impartiality, did not hesitate to assert that the most painstaking spirit would be reasonably excused if instead of one of Ah Pak's very ornate jade incense holders he placed before the person for whom it was intended an extravagantly garnished but somewhat badly cooked portion of dried goat's flesh; while the prospect of reposing on one of the couches, if only in a complimentary and rigidly self-sustained attitude for a few moments, was a suggestion which called forth a most engaging display of obsequious and retiring politeness among those assembled.

In spite of this confessedly sombre reception Ah Pak did not suffer his meritorious intentions to be vanquished. After a period spent in perfecting himself in the manipulation of his coloured paper and split bamboo he contrived a number of articles which he was able to transmit with the full internal assurance that their arrival would not involve his father in un-merited humiliation among those with whom he associated. In this he was not mistaken for in a dream, shortly afterwards, he was visited by his father's spirit and complimented upon the excellence of the parchment. In the matter of ink, continued the benevolent vision, Ah Pak had certainly been imposed upon, for in spite of inscriptions reserved to that of the highest quality it was composed chiefly of black sand and charcoal and the tenth volume was, as a consequence, progressing unevenly. Some of the wine, moreover, had been perniciously affected by inferior stoppers and a further supply would be esteemed. The gold pieces he admitted to be practically valueless there and the only useful purpose to which he had been able to put them had been paving the courtyard of his residence and arranging them in ornamental masses among the azalea beds. Of the furniture he spoke in a reserved but not entirely unhopeful vein which led Ah Pak to believe that it had not proved wholly reli-able, but that his father was indisposed to discourage one who had given undeniable proof of his conscientious endeavour.

In the meanwhile two circumstances had converged to exercise an influence on Ah Pak's destiny. The time and mate-rial expended in the manner indicated had reduced him to a state of quite actual poverty, while passers-by who stopped to observe him in the exercise of his virtuous labours had not infrequently praised the simple-fingered dexterity with which he contrived almost every variety of object, and at the same time freely lamented the fact that they were unable to pursue so economical a course of benevolence themselves. At length it occurred to Ah Pak that the deficiency was one which he might well supply, and consoled by the reflection of the supernatural, if not actually prepossessing, nature of the commerce, and convinced that such a venture could not fail to be exceedingly profitable, he declared himself willing to undertake any similar requirements. So successful was this beginning that he was emboldened to abandon all reserve and very shortly afterwards he audaciously displayed a sign and invitation inscribed with his name and virtues.

Period II
The Middle Part of Ah Pak

In an open space of the city, called the Square of the Three Pagodas, Ah Pak established himself beneath the sign of the Lofty Palm Tree, and by a lavish display of fireworks and a distribution of verses composed in his honour, invited the thrifty to show an affectionate regard for their friends and relations who had Passed Beyond in a practical though inexpensive manner. Success at once showered rice upon his efforts. He was the first and at that time the only person in the city to engage in such a commerce and when the reliable and economical nature of the offerings was thoroughly understood, the Lofty Palm Tree was never deserted; while after important assassinations or executions, fiercely contested examinations, or popular risings of more than ordinarily fatal result the not inconsiderable Square of the Three Pagodas was embarrassingly crowded with persons of both sexes. So expert had Ah Pak become in the art of fashioning likenesses – not only of objects with which he was well familiar but also of beings which rarely display themselves openly, as wind spirits, demons inhabiting empty bottles, and the like – that on no single occasion had he the humiliation of having to confess a weak-minded inability to produce whatever was demanded. More, not content with this he proceeded to anticipate what would be required and employing persons of average intelligence to carry his designs into effect he gradually gathered around him a store of paper creatures of every kind, both large and small, and so varied as to meet every imaginable emergency. Within a short space of time it became the custom for those who were showing honour to friends or relations from distant parts of the province by conducting them to such places about the city as were both remarkable and gratuitous to include Ah Pak's unique establishment among the temples, public tortures, displays of warriors in motion and other sights of an equally animated nature; while lesser merchants from time to time visited Ah Pak purchasing from him vast stores which they in turn disposed of to nations of barbarians living beyond the Bitter Waters. These savages, being both poor and obtuse-headed, could not be persuaded to exercise an intelligent perception of the requirements of those in the Upper Air and instead of transmitting to their ancestors weapons and armour, life-sized horses and chariots, and food of various descriptions, they insisted on procuring and sending to them fans, umbrellas, insects which when put into motion emitted life-like cries by means of hidden cords, and other useful but trivial offerings to an unreasonable excess. If any further proof of the widespread merit of Ah Pak's commerce were required in might be found in the innumerable proverbs associated with his name, while to this day it is customary to reduce evil-tempered and inordinately obstreperous little ones to a condition of trembling silence by the threat of one of 'Ah Pak's seven-headed ink-breathing vampires,' making its appearance in the chamber if the outcry is not at once quelled.

Yet in spite of the high and venerated profession which his symmetrical skill had called into being Ah Pak failed to make himself agreeable to those who wished him to become charitably disposed. To the well-meant suggestions that he should contribute freely of his inexhaustible store to festivals introduced on a philanthropic pretext or to the embellishment of temples or of the tombs of the deserving but indigent, he invariably replied by placing before those who supplicated a double-edged knife of formidable proportions, at the same time requesting them to use it fatally, but as painlessly as possible, on the one to whom he referred as "the claw-footed and totally inefficient Ah Pak," adding that his business had become unprofitable to such an extent and the mercenary propensities of those around him so offensive as to render this service the most disinterested that a friend could perform. In this certainly crafty but not very reputable way Ah Pak constantly gained his end, for he well knew that to oblige him in this way whilst engaged on such a service would constitute too grave an omen for even the benevolent to incur. In other and more reprehensible directions the inauspicious scales of avarice were beginning to penetrate Ah Pak's outer surface of deferential urbanity. He ceased to exercise any discretion whatever in the selection of the offerings which he made to his ancestors, apportioning for this weighty service merely such articles as were too insignificant to be displayed within his walls or those which after a lengthy period had become deficient in lustre and were deemed unsaleable. From this cause it was no uncommon thing for the spirit of Ah Pak's father to be practically inundated with delicately embroidered garments quite unsuited for his use while of those actually fitted to his requirements he was in a state of embarrassing destitution; or for him while lamenting a disrespectful scarcity of opium to receive several thousand empty wine casks all of which he was compelled to accept and thereby give to his orderly and well-maintained residence the air of belonging to a person of undoubted capacity but of very equivocal attainments. Ah Pak was at length, not to pursue his deficiencies further, behaving fully in the way predicted of him by the far-discerning astrologers, and the most complimentary opinion which could be expressed of him even by those not unfriendly to his welfare was that he was certainly a person of 'much head and little pigtail,' thereby indicating that he had voluntarily abandoned all dignified and graceful ambitions in his insatiable strife for wealth.

It was at this period that he made the acquaintance of Kin-sha Hing who appeared before him on a certain day upon a matter of business. Kin-sha Hing was a person who carried every external mark of prosperity, being richly apparelled, of well-shaven limbs, and round-bodied to an almost incredible degree; while from his continual smiles it might be seen that his thoughts were frequently of a gravity-removing nature. Nevertheless he manifested no unseemly disregard of fitting ceremonial and upon perceiving that the somewhat over-punctilious Ah Pak (upon whom the other's indications of consequence had by no means been lost) was slowly approaching him from the other end of the building upon hands and knees, Kin-sha Hing at once cast himself to the ground with well-timed precision.

"Estimable merchant," said Kin-sha Hing when they had passed a few gratifying moments in attempting to raise one another from the floor, each at the same time striving to resist this flattering distinction being conferred upon himself, "the subject of your fame is so general a topic among the great and enlightened that at length it has penetrated even the low-lying and noisome district in which this fever-stricken one so fittingly resides. Without pausing to make himself more presentable, therefore, he has approached to lay open his mind before you."

As these words seemed to indicate that Kin-sha Hing was honourably disposed towards acquiring some of the varied objects around, Ah Pak judged it expedient to stifle a delicate allusion to his preternaturally-acute ears. Nevertheless he very subtly obtained an equally flattering effect by shading his eyes with his hand as he gazed into Kin-sha Hing's rubicund face and quickly turning away with fluttering lids as though the radiance were too disconcerting for his only average faculty.

"The actual matter," continued Kin-sha Hing, "is one which touches another more closely than the person before you. Among the many high-minded ones who do their best to render the inadequate residence alluded to in any way presentable, by remaining within its overhanging walls and putting up with its obsolete hospitality, is one who is in the relationship of this person's father's daughter."

"It is a wise and exalted position and one which the refined being in question is well qualified to fill," ventured Ah Pak, as Kin-sha Hing paused, in order to consume a melon seed.

"In such a light it assuredly appears to one of those chiefly concerned," admitted Kin-sha Hing, in a tone of great no enthusiasm. "The essential facts of the circumstance are thus positioned: At no more remote period than last moon change the enchanting person in question – the phoenix-eyed but confessedly middle-aged Mu-mu – suffered the pang of seeing her lord pass unattended into the Upper Air. In a most commendable transport of becoming solicitude she announced her fixed purpose of following him without delay and to this end ordered the construction of an adequate pyre."

"It was a gracious and charitable resolution," said Ah Pak, by this time perceiving that Kin-sha Hing's rotundity was so well-developed that the obligation of expressing many sentences without a pause was offensive to him.

"The remark is an inspired one, for in that manner did the proposed sacrifice display itself to all who knew the accomplished remnant," continued Kin-sha Hing. "Nevertheless, on his death bed the one whom she was desirous of following had called this unworthy person to his side, and, anticipating his lesser one's unflinching devotion, had bound him by a variety of oaths to prevent such a course by every means in his power, urging that after enjoying the privilege of listening to what he termed the undulating but never entirely subdued word-music of the prolific Mu-mu's well-sustained voice for eight and twenty years, it would obviously go very evilly with him in the Upper Air if he enviously deprived the world of so capable an exhibition."

"The scruple was delicately-imagined and should have a very agreeable effect upon the accommodating person's comfort in the Upper Air," remarked Ah Pak.

"Doubtless it will," admitted Kin-sha Hing, "yet there are certain varieties of self-denial which cannot be regarded as other than reprehensible ostentation. As it chanced, however, there was no necessity for interference as on the following day the undoubtedly vexatious Mu-mu declared that she had never had the most willowy intention of acting in the manner indicated, and in spite of the unanimous encouragement of a large multitude that had been drawn together to witness the entertainment, she obstinately declined to relinquish the assured comforts of an ordinary existence. In spite of this, the thought of the one the Upper Air being attended by maidens of unknown ancestry – possibly of usurpatory instincts and certainly of peach-like appearance – did not gladden her imagination and when she heard of your entrancing versatility, O many-fingered Ah Pak, she at once determined to despatch an efficient counterpart to the Upper Air, who would, at least, exercise a dragon-eyed vigilance over the maidens referred to and restrain the mind of the one upon whom they attended from contemplating too feasibly the possibility of a state of existence devoid of her benignant care."

"The decision was a sagacious one," said Ah Pak approvingly; "yet its successful accomplishment may be neither easy nor inexpensive. Out of an experience covering many years and embracing animals of all kinds, boats, trees, residences, yamens, pagodas and temples in every variety, mandarins up to the second degree, and vampires, ghouls, spirits, demons, spectres and impalpable shadows, this person has no hesitation in saying that the representation most difficult to construct when it has to give satisfaction to the person herself and to her friends and relations, both well and ill-disposed, is that of a being of the inner chamber who is past that age when she may be fitly likened to the unopened chrysanthemum. Does the devoted and accomplished remnant by any chance bear a likeness to Yao Niang, the Goddess of Almond-Eyed Perfection, or to any of the other recognised models of female excellence?"

"On the contrary," replied Kin-sha Hing, "if a resemblance is to be found among deities it should be sought in the profile of Ngou-tang, the spirit which is said to take refuge in wine jars during the continuance of thunderstorms, and by its presence transform the pure and reliable contents into an unprofitable liquid, only useful as a pungent condiment. Yet observe how overbalanced has become this one's attitude in the matter! On the one side the vigorous and self-opinionated Mu-mu will certainly greet him with no tissue-paper reproaches if he fails to secure for her a life-like representation; and when it is considered it seems as though few greater misfortunes could attend a person than to be under the same roof with a being of the formidable Mu-mu's pertinacity, whose goodwill towards one is like the road to Pekin when one is journeying in the direction of The Wall – unavoidably before one's eyes but all the other way. But on the opposite side must be weighed the impressive oaths by which he is bound to the individual in the Upper Air to obstruct such a ceremony, and when *that* detail is dwelt upon it certainly does not seem desirable to put oneself in antagonism with a spirit possessing exceptional means of retaliating. Assuredly, in whatever direction he moves the point which this well-meaning person encounters is not a comfortable one – like Tcheng Lo's benevolent bee sitting on its own sting."

"Yet," suggested Ah Pak, whose chief anxiety was lest the other should decide not to purchase a figure after all, "yet if the matter could be confined within the knowledge of the four persons who are most intimately concerned it would be exceptional if a representation of the beautiful Yao Niang, clothed, however with the garments and distinguished emblems of the zealous-minded Mu-mu, were not honourably received by all. Doubtless the lily-footed remnant herself has not yet reached that age when to be credited with a jade complexion, hair blacker and more opaque than the cloud heralding a sand-storm from the west, and an outline of more varied gracefulness than that of the porcelain nine-terraced pagoda of Nankin, is a pronouncement to be regarded with exceptional repugnance. The estimable being in the Upper Air will perhaps be so amiably-disposed as to look upon the substitute in a spirit of broad-minded toleration; the sordid Ah Pak, also, will show no disinclination to accept so easy a solution, for he will receive the explicit regard of two conscientious and proverbially munificent persons and of one powerful and well-equipped spirit (in addition to disposing of one of his most expensive ready-made figures); and, finally, the hitherto over-embarrassed Kin-sha Hing will be able to make himself agreeable all round without in any way upsetting his own digestion – like the blind bear in the Pih Shen legend embracing the unprepossessing and neglected maiden."

At this cunning suggestion on the part of Ah Pak varying but ever-increasing emotions passed across Kin-sha Hing's face until it took the outward appearance of a very highly-illuminated paper lantern, agitated somewhat violently by a passing breeze and distended to an incautious degree. In this condition of utter absence of gravity he thrust his thumb against Ah Pak's body, the encounter taking place at that point where the lower garment meets the waist cloth, exclaiming in a tone of effusive admiration:

"O ingenious-minded Ah Pak, how crafty a black-lipped pup art thou! Command one of your obliging slaves to bear the fascinating Yao Hiang to The Extinguished Pipe of Domestic Harmony, standing by the Bridge known as Happiness Beneath, and this necessarily deceitful person, under the plea that he has received a vision from the one above, complaining of the intolerable anguish of separation and casually mentioning the admitted solicitude of the attending sprites, will induce the credulous-witted Mu-mu to transmit it without delay."

On the day following that of Kin-sha's visit Ah Pak was made aware that a being of the inner chamber was approaching the Lofty Palm Tree and presently an elegantly-designed and lavishly-perfumed piece of rice paper, bearing the titles and virtues of the not really attractive Mu-mu together with a poetical allusion to the one in the Upper Air was placed before him. Not doubting that the matter upon which she had come was one that could be very profitably enlarged he hastened to greet her obsequiously.

"O most expert cutter out of paper figures," she exclaimed pleasantly, "an emotion of appreciative gratitude has prompted this usually retiring one to let down the legs of her chair at the door of your enchantingly laid-out place of commerce. Never before, she may justly assert, although the most highly-esteemed stone cutters and picture makers of the Empire have repeatedly measured her features, never before has one attained to the unswerving fidelity both of colour and of expression which marks the production of the deft-handed Ah Pak."

"Your words," replied Ah Pak, stepping back somewhat as the one before him lowered the silk fan behind which she had hitherto remained prudently concealed, "may be fitly likened to a dragon-fly sipping water at a crystal spring, in that they are both delicately-poised and refreshing. Condescend to bend your imperceptible footsteps from one object to another among those disposed in the buildings around, confident that you may engage in this amusement without being urged into acquiring any."

Upon receiving this honourable assurance Mu-mu, not without some half-expressed doubts of the propriety of such a visit, permitted Ah Pak to lead her through the various divisions of his commerce, manifesting, as the occasions arose, a lavish exhibition of many-sided emotions. When a sudden turn brought them into the space reserved for dragons, sacred bulls, winged serpents and other formidable creatures she cast herself unreservedly into Ah Pak's arms, repeatedly calling him her "true-stomached and magnanimous protector" and imploring him not to hesitate to hold her in an even more inflexible grasp if the necessity arose. Reverting to an evenly-balanced state of mind, however, when Ah Pak cried aloud, beseeching attendants in distant places to hasten to his aid, she presently evaded his notice and concealing herself among the hanging drapery of a particularly awe-inspiring demon she uttered the muffled sounds of subdued menace generally attributed to beings of the Other Part at the moment when Ah Pak was passing the spot in search of her. As the person in question was never entirely free from apprehension concerning his standing among the deities this manifestation had the effect of almost felling him to the earth in the terrors of the writhing sickness, and only the timely appearance of Mu-mu in a state of the most abject contrition and intolerable self-reproach, restored him to his usual alert resourcefulness. So undeniably perturbed was the fragrant and sympathetic remnant that scarcely had they reached a point of the building where the hanging lanterns chanced to be sparsely displayed than she began to sink to the ground devoid of power and very soon she had all the appearance of floating in the Middle Distance. Ah Pak was preparing to withdraw unobtrusively in search of those more skilled in such emergencies when the versatile Mu-mu opened her eyes slowly and enquired what gong-stroke it was and for how long she had remained without sentiency. Nevertheless she reverted to her habitual composure so expeditiously that she would not permit a chair to be summoned to the spot, and when they had reached the spaces where they were surrounded by appointments and articles of furniture of the most massive kind she fled suddenly, declaring as she went that no matter how swiftly Ah Pak pursued he would never succeed in overtaking her. In this prediction she was undoubtedly inspired, for although Ah Pak caused his feet to simulate the continuous sound of a well-sustained pursuit, in the hope that the exceedingly volatile remnant might be thereby impelled into reaching the outer door without a pause, he did not think it consistent with a reputation for dignified restraint to indulge in so attenuating a competition. This hope, however, was not altogether realised, for the person in question was still engaged with his ingenious stratagem when his eyes were unexpectedly obscured from behind, while at the same time a voice, which by reason of being feigned resembled more than aught else the cry of an unfledged sea-fowl, demanded that he should indicate by name the one who was thus attacking him, as the price of his release.

Had the over-expressed gratitude and appreciation of the very far advanced remnant ended with the ceremonious phrases of mutual regard with which she and Ah Pak parted on this occasion the matter might in time have faded into the semblance of a particularly outrageous dragon-dream in the mind of the latter person. Unhappily, on the following day she again appeared within the Lofty Palm Tree, protesting that as she passed the fragrance of Ah Pak's unapproachable apricot tea drew her on in spite of every modest and receding impulse, and it soon became her daily custom to present herself openly, either on the plea that her bearers had misunderstood the direction they were to take and had brought her there against her will, or to acquaint Ah Pak with some omen affecting his future or to advise him on some detail of his commerce. Before the great sky-lantern had again grown small she did not hesitate to address him as 'Ah', and it was even asserted by those familiar with her inside manner of behaving that among the few of her own chamber she freely referred to him as 'Pak'.

Without submitting the matter to elaborate consideration it had long been plain to Ah Pak that he could at any time overlap the footsteps of the one in the Upper Air if he were so disposed, but in addition to regarding Mu-mu with an unquenchable dislike – to an extent which made him abandon the most lucrative trafficking upon which he might be embarked and display himself in flight at her approach – must be placed the fact that he had already honourably bargained for the possession of a certain maiden of his own district, for whom he entertained an affectionate regard. A third and still more insuperable barrier remained, for it may now be fully declared that when Ah Pak had become sufficiently intimate with Kin-sha Hing to ask him definitely, and apart from the elaborate ambiguity of true politeness, the exact value of his possessions, and had learned its formidable proportion, he became mentally over-weighted with an ambition to be proclaimed as that person's adopted son and heir. With this end clearly before his eyes Ah Pak assiduously devoted himself to the object of growing large in Kin-sha Hing's esteem. As Ah Pak himself was by many years the more venerable of the two, and was, moreover, declared by those skilled in the various arts of witchcraft to be suffering from an incurable malady, while Kin-sha Hing moved in an unvarying atmosphere of continual robustness, the very speculative nature of Ah Pak's infatuation will at once appear; but when it is admitted that Kin-sha Hing already pos-sessed a vigorous line of sons, and even descendants to the next generation, it can no longer be reasonably doubted that the avenging deities had at length decided upon their course of action and were luring Ah Pak on to a fate that would be both decisive and contemptible. Kin-sha Hing, although he could not fail to be gratified by the far-reaching details of the liberal-ity and obsequiousness with which Ah Pak hoped to entrap his imagination, occasionally suffered annoyance thereby, as in public places from the gravity-removing jests and unbecoming observations of those who stood around when Ah Pak, follow-ing his consistent habit, prostrated himself and requested the honour of being trodden upon, at the same time calling the attention of all to his own palpable inferiority but adding, with classically allusive subtlety, that in his opinion it was a greater distinction for him to be inferior to Kin-sha Hing than it was for Kin-sha Hing to be superior to Ah Pak. Weakly assuming that the only way to render his passage through the streets in any way tolerable lay in propitiating Ah Pak, Kin-sha Hing finally agreed to allot him a portion of the gains of his com-merce (which Ah Pak understood to be that of obtaining sums of money from persons of all classes on the sealed assurance of granting to them certain amounts at stated intervals until they passed beyond,) he, in return, receiving a similar benefit from the result of Ah Pak's enterprise.

It was at this period – before Ah Pak had prudently seized an opportunity of making himself fully acquainted with the precise manner in which Kin-sha Hing conducted his unusually complicated ventures – that the various angles which Ah Pak and Mu-mu had adopted in regarding the same circumstances came together with a most brilliant and irresistible velocity.

"O double-headed and very thin-bodied Ah Pak!" exclaimed Mu-mu, standing before him unexpectedly at an early hour one morning and displaying no amiable pretence of speech or manner, "what, indeed, is the truth of the whisper which has come to this person's ears concerning your excessively misleading behaviour and scheming duplicity?"

"To no degree misleading," replied Ah Pak, his only desire being towards a conciliatory evasion and for this reason feigning, doubtless undiscriminatingly, to misread Mu-mu's plainly edged words. "Henceforth within the Lofty Palm Tree it will be a gratifying feature that all purchasers to the extent of upwards of a tael will freely receive one of this person's celebrated silver-papered bricks, which alone will represent in the Upper Air many score times the full amount of their outlay." Smiling reassuringly Ah Pak placed before her one of the objects to which he had alluded and a copy of the printed words – entitled 'Ah Pak's Very Good Scheme: An Agreeable Thunderbolt from the Lofty Palm Tree' – setting forth the definite proffer, at the same time lowering himself in an obsequious attitude as though to receive her esteemed orders.

"Alas!" exclaimed Mu-mu, casting the brick from her with so diversely graceful a movement that although her eyes were fixed upon the upper portion of Ah Pak's body the one on whom the blow actually impressed itself chanced to be an expensively-moulded figure of Impassiveness which stood some paces behind her, "how is it possible to express a matter in terms comprehensible to one of so greed-dimmed an understanding without having resort to the concise and melody-devoid phrases of mounted warriors and wholesale vendors of fish! Behold how unendurable becomes this one's condition, for after being greeted on all sides with formally-expressed saluta- tions in which her own name and that of the perfidious Ah Pak have been freely entwined as by garlands of honeysuckle and orange tendrils she will now be spoken of behind open hands as only comparable with a fan in autumn. Who is Hia Fa, of the Upper Oil Market, sometimes called Harmonious Jade Perfection by the easily pleased, and by what right do they of her household boastfully display your pledging gifts?"

"Ah!" cried the one before her, easily perceiving that his well- intentioned desire to lead the discussion round to a subject less controversial had been received in a spirit of no acquiescence. "Well is the Being to whom you have referred also called the Little Black-crested Bird upon Chop Sticks! Her feet are more immaculately proportioned than the lily-curves of the new moon; her hair – which, you may have observed, after a certain period begins to assume in many cases the hue and lustre of a neglected iron cleaver – is darker and more resplendent than polished marble from the Imperial quarries of Che-kio, while her eyes are so entrancingly narrow and delicately-fringed that on several occasions persons of no intentional flattery have paid her the compliment of assuming that she was entirely devoid of these features. Her expertness in striking instruments of stringed woods is so highly developed that it is no uncom- mon thing for her to portray absolutely conflicting sentiments upon the same instrument without varying her position or even changing her expression, while her fingers, when thus employed—"

At this point the distracted Mu-mu, upon whose mind the recital of the engaging Hia Fa's charms had produced a fu- nereal effect, fell to the ground in a most proficient exhibition of the opposing emotions of the convulsive frenzy, alternately weeping and becoming inordinately amused, at the same time expressing conflicting statements about Ah Pak and his atti- tude towards the Great Principles, and finally calling by name upon the one in the Upper Air, adjuring him not to remain an unmoved spectator of her deliberately-contrived humiliation but to appear in some diabolical form and avenge the one who henceforth, she declared, would enshrine his memory by remaining a solitary remnant. Those around, who had been drawn to the spot by the outcry, did not hesitate to add their voices to the turmoil, the greater part ranging themselves on the side of the atrocious Mu-mu and representing to her that as the one in the Upper Air showed no disposition to appear as the awe-inspiring creation which she had requested, it was probably because he was confident that she herself was a thoroughly efficient substitute. In this not entirely genuine strain of encouragement they urged her to take Ah Pak up by the middle and bearing him to the Upper Oil Market there cast him into an adjacent vat before the eyes of the maiden for whom she had been abandoned. At that moment, however, Ah Pak, acting in the manner counselled by the few who were better disposed towards him, flung himself through their midst uttering cries of desperate menace, and reaching the outer square in one inspired bound sought refuge in the open country.

Period III
The End of Ah Pak

THE ELDERLY PHILOSOPHER SEN-YUEN was once asked by a favourite pupil to demonstrate out of the vast reservoirs of his experience what principle regulated the action of a maiden towards one of the opposite sex upon whom her eyes had turned not unfavourably; how she would conduct herself in various emergencies, and what deductions might be reasonably extracted from her behaviour. After remaining silent for so long that many judged the venerable Sen-yuen to have fallen into one of his introspective visions, he suddenly called the favourite pupil to his side and was in the act of embracing him affectionately when without warning he dealt him a heavily-propelled blow in the face. Expressing an overwhelming regret for the impulse Sen-yuen led the youth towards a deep well of translucent water and without regarding the fact that his own costly robes were spoiled in the process he tenderly removed every trace of the ill-judged outburst; yet no sooner had this been accomplished and the two were preparing to leave the spot together than the treacherous philosopher unexpectedly thrust the enquiring youth backwards into the depths of the fountain, where he would inevitably have been drowned had not his companions succeeded in drawing him forth. From these symptoms it became plain that Sen-Yuen's faculties had become unbalanced and he was led away in chains, and shortly afterwards passed beyond as the result of a disorder brought on by his immersion. When his body was being conveyed to the temple it occurred to his followers that he had left the question submitted to him unanswered, and as no thinker since the time of Sen-yuen has been deemed competent to deal with it, it necessarily remains very much as it was before.

Recalling this incident to his mind, and deeply regretting that the erudite philosopher had not been permitted to dispose of this last enquiry so that he himself might have some indication of the probable nature of the many-hued Mu-mu's next position, Ah Pak was returning to the city in the evening, after spending the greater part of the day among rocks and desolate places, when he became aware that events of an unusual – and probably supernatural – course were taking place. On all sides people of every class of life were fleeing as though pursued. From the still distant city the increasing tempest brought the sounds of many powerful gongs and brass instruments clashed with a ceaseless vigour and determination, while at every moment coloured lights and fireworks were discharged lavishly, the effect, as Ah Pak easily read, not being one of wide-spread rejoicing but a well-designed movement to avert evil omens and, if possible, to throw any advancing demons into a panic and to divert their flight into another path. Even as he stood motionless, a deep shadow enveloped him. At this manifestation a passing official, of high mandarin rank, prostrated himself without pausing in his flight, crying aloud that his past life certainly did not wear a very highly-burnished face now that he came to observe it closely, but that while intentionally benevolent himself he had been led aside by those whom he at length perceived to be unworthy of his confidence. Furthermore, he added, he undertook to sacrifice to a large and specified amount if the vision would charitably pass on to extortioners more worthy of its sublime omnipotence. By this time the shadow had melted away, whereupon the mandarin rose to his feet, and perceiving Ah Pak as he looked around to ascertain whether anyone had witnessed his spoken vow, he affected to be engaged in conversation with himself regarding someone else.

Ah Pak's mind, however, was immersed in contemplations more nearly affecting his own prosperity. When the apparition had withdrawn its direct influence he ventured to cast an upward glance, when some details in the form and colouring of the object held his attention. It had the appearance of being an unusually large monster, wingless though many-horned, and was doubtless urging its flight towards the I-chang Valley where the unfathomable caves offer a very attractive resort to beings of this class who avoid observation to so marked a degree that although they may be heard moving above on any very stormy night they are rarely actually seen. But before Ah Pak could satisfy himself on any definite point it had passed into the outer distance, under the influence of the ever-increasing gale.

The nature of Ah Pak's faintly outlined presentiment will at once reveal itself to all. So far it had taken no more definite shape than to diminish the sustaining power of his knees somewhat, but when he again turned his footsteps in the direction of the city he beheld a sight which felled him to the ground most effectively; for the whole intervening space was filled with companies of creatures of the most varied kind and in them the helpless Ah Pak at once recognised his handiwork and understood the nature of the implacable Mu-mu's vengeance. As he lay a band of female attendants, all very richly apparelled, passed at a considerable distance overhead, a warrior mounted upon a sumptuously-caparisoned charger, flying incautiously, became entangled in the branches of a prickly poplar near at hand, and a quantity of sea fish of the most delicate flavour, being drawn into the middle air on account of their instability, collapsed discreditably with loud explosions. To the east and west similar processions were taking place unceasingly and at the full understanding Ah Pak built a fire, collected together a variety of sharp-edged flints and prepared to inflict upon himself the most painful tortures that the rather primitive means at his disposal admitted. Yet the proverb "Wine does not intoxicate men: they intoxicate themselves," is full of significant application; for if Ah Pak had not voluntarily degraded his commerce it is more than doubtful whether the revengeful Mu-mu would have found it possible to impose a like indignity upon him. It need be no longer withheld that for many years Ah Pak had been in the habit of systematically lowering the standard of excellence with which his name and occupation had at first been identified; so that, for the sake of enriching himself to a still higher degree, the sacrifices which had originally been contrived of excellent parchment supported by frameworks of polished bamboo, had passed through varying degrees of ignominy until they consisted of nothing more than inflated creatures composed wholly of the thinnest and least expensive rice paper. To this day it is not unusual to hear a deeply-read scholar compare an arrogant and self-confident person to one of Ah Pak's tigers, adding, "Nevertheless, there will presently arise an intrepid Mu-mu," by which it is inferred that the one in question is all outside, in spite of a very fierce expression and demeanour, and will disappear entirely at the first blow or before a breath of determined opposition. Even among the low-class and ignorant it is the matter of a jest to compare the

Ever-Victorious Imperial Army to Ah Pak's legions without fully grasping the meaning of the saying beyond a clear understanding that neither has more than a paper existence and that when the presence of an enemy has become known it is no uncommon thing to find both men and horses taking refuge among the branches of the trees around.

The gongs in the watch-towers had announced the middle portion of the night before Ah Pak reached the city. The gates were barred and zealously defended, but upon receiving sufficient cash pieces to procure a jar of hemp spirit the one on guard to whom Ah Pak addressed himself readily pointed out a well-worn path through the wall by which he might enter without discomfort. Not turning aside to pass the Open Space of the Three Pagodas, Ah Pak proceeded in the direction of the lower part of the city, for it appeared to his benumbed faculties that in one way, and in that alone, could he relieve his position. In his journey back to the city further possibilities of ruin had occurred to him, for it seemed by no means improbable that those who had suffered would employ persons skilled in the recognised practice of legal pillage to extort from him not only material damages to compensate for coloured lights and other explosives, but also other and heavier sums as recompense for the disarrangement into which their digestive and intellectual organs had been thrown. For this reason it seemed to become necessary that he should procure a sum of money without delay: not necessarily to meet the unjust demands of those who would assail him, but to convince the examining mandarin of the uprightness of his cause, to gather together a company of credible witnesses who would be prepared to testify his innocence in all emergencies, and to enable him to protect himself by the exercise of similar prudent safeguards. In this difficulty his thoughts turned towards Kin-sha Hing and to the share which he himself possessed in that one's commerce. How Kin-sha Hing would regard the obligation when the tidings of Ah Pak's condition reached him was a

detail which the contemplation of the latter person refused
to dwell upon pleasurably, yet it seemed to him that if only
he could render Kin-sha Hing some marked and profitable
service beforehand the feeling of esteem which must be fresh
in his mind would lead him to regard the full circumstance in
a tolerantly-disposed light.

It had already occurred to him that Kin-sha Hing was
somewhat obsolete in his commercial methods, for it would
be immeasurably more profitable to hire assassins to remove
to the Upper Air all those persons to whom Kin-sha Hing
paid an annual sum of money than it would be to continue
so wasteful a practice indefinitely, even though the outlay to
procure their extinction might be initially large. It seemed a
strange oversight on Kin-sha Hing's part to have neglected so
simple and remunerative a branch of his business, but Ah Pak
had on several occasions suspected that although he was well-
intentioned and painstaking, the one alluded to was not really
brilliant or quick-witted. Feeling that the time had now come
Ah Pak sought out certain reputable assassins whom he had
formerly had occasion to employ as models. An agreement was
soon reached between them and having in this way arranged
everything and safeguard his future condition to the best of
his ability Ah Pak retired to his couch with worn-out feet but
feeling very well satisfied.

After a day spent in emotions so various and so widely-
contrasted Ah Pak floated serenely into the Middle Air for an
exceptional length of time. As he passed through the streets on
his way to the residence of Kin-sha Hing the sun was already
high and the unusual number of persons whom he encountered clad in sackcloth, together with the profusion of white
lanterns and other signs of mourning, clearly testified that
those with whom he had trafficked had faithfully carried out
their undertaking with expeditious celerity. It was with a very
distended feeling of self-approbation that Ah Pak reached The
Extinguished Pipe of Domestic Harmony and entered.

Kin-sha Hing was not in his receiving room nor in any of the more important chambers of the house and it was not until Ah Pak had descended into the underneath parts that a sound, hardly distinguishable from that produced by striking a stone wall repeatedly with a wooden mallet or some other object of similar density, drew him to a mean cavern. There, surrounded by stores of fuel and other obscure merchandise, he discovered a person who bore some of the external marks of the one he sought, although he was clad in rags, distressingly shrunken in outline, and wearing the general appearance of having recently come in contact with an explosion of gunpowder.

"O opulent Kin-sha Hing," exclaimed Ah Pak, confident that he would be able to remove the deeply-ingrained signs of affliction with his first breath of tidings, no matter from what cause they arose, "restrain yourself for a moment from your charitable course of flagellation. During the night an evil influence passed over the city and at daybreak it was found that the spirit of the unassuming Sung-kin Yen had been translated into the presence of his ancestors."

"The fact has already been blown in at the door by the many-tongued heralds of misfortune," replied Kin-sha Hing, not looking up from his search for a heavier and more destructively-pointed fragment of material.

"Also that of the mild Li-You," added Ah Pak: "those of T'ing-chen, the millet seed merchant, Wang-king, who conducts a lottery, and several others."

"Alas!" exclaimed Kin-sha Hing, abandoning his search as inadequate and casting himself bodily among the fragments of metal and broken jars, "alas! May disintegration attend the most remote ancestors among those who preceded this persecuted one; let woe and tabefaction be the lot to the fifteenth generation of those related to him by marriage! Is the list of calamity not yet ended?"

"To no extent," replied Ah Pak, now assured that Kin-sha Hing was merely submitting himself to bodily pain in his private capacity as a personal friend of those who had passed beyond, and apart from business forms, "but continue in your disinterested self-afflictions. Much to his own regret this one cannot join you as he was not on terms of social intercourse with the estimable persons in question, but he will finish the list referred to and make you acquainted with an important detail of the incident." With these words Ah Pak drew from his inner robe an account of the names of all Kin-Sha's clients – the counterpart of one which he had composed for the assassins' guidance – and then proceeded to explain what part he himself had taken in the transaction, not without some delicately-shafted jests at the other's expense for his obtuseness in not grasping the economy of the device before.

While Ah Pak was thus occupied the mutilated and dust-smeared surface of Kin-sha Hing's face completely veiled the succeeding emotions which may have been called up within his mind, but when the full extent of Ah Pak's crafty ingenuity was set forth and he had made an end of speaking in order to permit Kin-sha Hing to embrace him and load him with ceremonious titles, the person in question, instead of acting in this commendable way, suddenly abandoned himself to an internal disorder which swayed him from side to side and strove convulsively within him until it finally cast him to the ground in a most excessive form of removed gravity.

"O intricately-witted Ah Pak," he exclaimed at length, "how irresistibly diverting a form of enriching oneself is this which you have contrived, when expounded with your own inimitable self-satisfaction! Reveal to this unenterprising person by what voluntary acts of penance you marked your intense vexation with yourself when you encountered disaster spreading from the city to meet you upon a recent occasion!"

"The spot was a desolate and remote one, entirely cut off from the resources of civilisation," replied Ah Pak. "Nevertheless, this person procured fire and cutting stones and accomplished what he could."

"Yet," said Kin-sha Hing impartially, "*that* loss was not brought about by outrageous incapacity or one to be lightly evaded by taking ordinary precautions, nor was it utterly overwhelming or irreparably final. A state of things now exists which is without reservation wholly the other way, and the limited resources of this ill-equipped cave appear to be quite unequal to the emergency. In the circumstances permit this commonplace person to put at your disposal his well-stocked private torture chamber. 'When heaven sends calamities it is just possible to escape them, but when one invites them himself it is no longer possible to live.'"

At this point it is necessary to introduce a matter which would have been more reasonably expressed at an earlier period if a fitting opportunity had presented itself. The commerce of Kin-sha Hing did not strictly consist – as Ah Pak had hastily assumed that it did – of obtaining large sums of money from persons of all classes and then making them yearly allowances until they passed beyond, but of the converse system of receiving comparatively small annual sums of money on the understanding that a much larger sum should be allotted to their immediate descendants as soon as they themselves passed into the Upper Air. The former manner of conducting the enterprise had been in existence for many dynasties and was widely known and understood, but the other was the result of Kin-sha's untiring industry, and was regarded, even by those who fully grasped it, as necessarily intricate. For this reason Kin-sha Hing had not at first thought it desirable to explain to Ah Pak the true details of the operation; for, in his opinion, although the person alluded to was deferential in the extreme and an efficient contriver of sacrificial figures, he was not really brilliant or acute-witted and an attempt to explain to him the scheme as it actually existed would only result in confusing his perceptions and inevitably lead him to regard it with an unconquerable suspicion. It may be frankly admitted that this estimate of Kin-sha Hing was well-founded, for although Ah

Pak lived to a venerable age, and even revived sufficiently to take an intelligent concern in matters of public interest, he could never be made to understand how the gigantic loss had been brought about, nor did he cease to protest against the impunity with which the heirs of those who had passed beyond continued to press their unjust demands.

For many years after the taking place of these events two heavily-scarred individuals, one excessively round-bodied and the other very ordinary, made it a custom to expose themselves daily by the Gate of the Nine Benevolent Omens, leading to the Temple of Truth and Opulence, each bearing about his neck an inscribed board testifying that he had been blind from the time of his birth upwards, while that upon the leaner of the two contained an added claim to be regarded as one whom demonical malice had marked out from the first beyond power of resistance.

At certain hours of the day a being of the inner room, not actually deformed but in no way ornamental, and wearing the characteristic signs of remnanthood, approached them with fragments of cast-aside viands which she had received from the residences of the wealthy. Neither greeted her with any elaborate tokens of esteem, but the less of the two openly reviled her on every occasion, execrating her as the cause and beginning of all his misfortune, and entwining her name in imprecation with that of the well-meaning philosopher Sen-yuen, who, he contended, ought at any cost to have left some indication warning mankind of what might be reasonably expected from such a person. Yet it was observed by those who had occasion to pass the spot at these times that the choicest portion of grilled lizard or stewed paw was invariably allotted by her to Ah Pak, and that the very complicated Mu-mu showed every appearance of taking more pleasure in listening to his immoderate reproaches than in receiving the occasional expressions of regard thrown out towards her by the more courteous-minded Kin-sha Hing.

The Romance of Kwang the Fruit Gatherer and the Princess Suin-yu

"There are persons of so depraved a nature that they believe neither in evil spirits nor in the protecting shadows of our ancestors; how, then, do these self-opinionated ones account for thunderbolts?"

Part I

The Circumstances Inducing the Narrative.

"ALAS," EXCLAIMED KAI LUNG, the story-teller, when requested by those who most frequently contributed to his collecting-bowl in Shan Tzu that he would dignify the occasion by a story which might enlighten them as to the general manner of behaving of an Emperor or some other person of undoubted distinction, "has the insidiously-growing seed of unrest penetrated even as far as Shan Tzu, that its people begin to affect an interest in the doings of upper ones with whom they can have no possible honourable concern? Learn from this person's consistent habit of relating stories which introduce those slightly higher placed than the ones forming his audience how an intelligent ambition may be fitly encouraged without unduly exciting the imagination by a recitation of the deeds of those with whom they can never by any chance hope to compete. In the presence of the sublime Emperor, to give a specific example, he narrates histories of the inferior deities, benevolent spirits, those who have been specially singled out for worship after their death and so forth; before Mandarins he speaks of Emperors, those who have proved exceptionally fortunate in the public examinations, and illustrious historians and story-tellers both living and passed beyond; at Wu-whei he inspires them with tales of mandarins of the eighth and ninth degrees, round-bodied merchants who have escaped being de-graded for extortion and those of no particular rank who have contrived to pass a conscientious and remunerative existence, while at Shan Tzu he is compelled to search his memory for the obscure records of criminals who have evaded detection, lepers who have been markedly successful in their mendicancy, and street performers of the lower castes. Indeed, it would be as unseemly to relate episodes referring to Emperors in Shan Tzu, as it would be presumptuous to try to engage the attention of a high official with the history of a tea house attendant, and such a manner of acting could only arise from an ill-balanced mind desirous of overturning and confusing the fixed order of things."

"Nevertheless," urged Yang, the needy herb-gatherer, mod-estly, "is it not written 'The humblest winged creature may set-tle upon the mandarin's house top without fear of stumbling?' How then should a brief contemplation of the virtues of high ones affect one in an objectionable manner?"

"Such a contemplation may try your estimable eyesight somewhat, O amiable Yang," replied Kai Lung affably, "but, more than that, it must be carried in mind that winged crea-tures are not so presumptuous as indigent herb-gatherers and do not settle upon the house top for the purpose of offering the delicate incense of well-considered flattery to the manda-rin's daughter;" whereupon there was a lightening of coun-tenances of all those assembled, and many gravity-removing jests as Yang's expense; for the fruitless passion of the person in question towards the only daughter of a wealthy vendor of jade images was concealed from none and his untiring efforts and stratagems to gain the maiden's ear were the subject of widespread conversation. "Yet," continued Kai Lung, in whom the sombre emotions which had arisen at the sight of the admittedly inadequate contents of his collecting bowl when it was returned to him (which, indeed, was the true cause of the really inelegant way in which he referred to those of Shan Tzu) had passed away before the gratifying reception of his opportune reference to the affairs of Yang's private life, "yet, it must be confessed that apart from classics of the most refined excellence – those consisting entirely of the names, titles and virtues of sovereigns of the various dynasties from the very earliest times – there are few stories into which persons of all conditions of life cannot be discreetly introduced; especially as the essential characters in the history of a nation are the Emperors, obstinate-minded outcasts who assassinate them, and all the intervening ranks of princes, mandarins, students, earth-tillers, merchants, warriors, slave maidens and attendants whose destinies it is to be drawn into the various plots of the contending parties. The story of the Princess Suin-yu alone would be sufficient to prove clearly how inevitably such a condition of affairs comes to pass."

The Pronouncement of the Omen Readers

SUIN-YU WAS THE DAUGHTER of a brother of one of the Emperors of the accomplished Thang dynasty. So widespread was the report of her beauty and accomplishments and the just renown of her illustrious house that for many months and even years before she reached the age when her hand might be fittingly bestowed in marriage, the streets of Nankin were inconveniently thronged and the legitimate commerce of the city thereby thrown into a state of inextricable confusion by the immense crowds of princes and high nobles who had resorted to the capital not only from all parts of the Empire but also from lands beyond The Wall and the Bitter Waters. Some, indeed, came from countries so remote and inaccessible that until the arrival of the rulers in question, even the wisest and most venerable persons in China had been unacquainted with the very existence of their kingdoms. From this cause the intolerable state of affairs in Nankin arose; for, on account of the vast distances to be traversed, many were unable to compute the period required for the journey to the narrow compass of a few years, and therefore prudently started without delay when the first tidings of the peerless Suin-yu reached them. Others, it must be admitted, were inspired by less honourable motives, chief among these being a desire to ingratiate themselves by means of bribes and ingeniously worded suggestions in the esteem of those who had any influence in the matter.

Among the first persons to arrive at Nankin for the purpose indicated was one named Kim ô Seng, a prince of an obscure province of Yen-ah, the country lying beyond the Yun-Nan mountains. Such, at least, had been the reasonable conjectures of the most profound-witted persons in the capital, for Kim ô Seng himself was unfortunately entirely ignorant not only of the Chinese language, either spoken or written, but also of any of the civilised tongues by which persons of widely varying races are enabled to carry on an amiable and unrestrained intercourse. Having of necessity to traverse many thousand li of unknown country, peopled for the most part by wild and bloodthirsty tribes either owing allegiance to no settled authority or else ruled over by extortionate and superstitious chiefs – to penetrate, moreover, through forests and wildernesses entirely given up to the malicious influence of rapacious demons and evilly disposed dragons – it cannot be concealed that Kim ô Seng set forth in a very ill equipped manner. Instead of providing himself with charms and sacred written sentences to turn aside unfavourable influences, and with articles of an apparently elaborate but not really expensive nature with which to propitiate the undiscriminating outlaws by the way, he freely displayed banners setting out his imposing name and titles, wore a profusion of finely wrought ornaments of jade and precious stones and was openly accompanied by a retinue of umbrella-bearers, fan-wavers, gong-beaters, secretaries and interpreters and attendants of every description. By this reprehensible ostentation the cupidity of the savage tribes and the innate greed of the demons were enhanced to such a degree that by the time Kim ô Seng came within sight of the outer walls of Nankin he was in a condition of most objectionable poverty, possessing nothing beyond a few insignificant pieces of brass money and being destitute of even a single attendant. In this extremity he was compelled by the pangs of hunger to engage in the menial occupation of chair carrying, for although he endeavoured with an unquenchable and highly praiseworthy determination to become instructed in the less intricate details of the Chinese language, yet he never attained sufficient proficiency to make himself understood on any point whatever, partly because he was, through his poverty, unable to gain the assistance of one of the persons who make a profession of such instruction, partly because he was deliberately misled by those passers-by to whom he applied for assistance, either because they had been bribed to throw obstacles in the way of competitors for the hand of the princess Suin-yu, or – in the case of persons of immature age or of unformed ideas of dignity – for the sake of witnessing the degrading but nevertheless gravity-removing spectacle of Kim ô Seng courteously addressing the offensive and sometimes really unseemly remarks which they had taught him to austere and excessively self-opinionated mandarins whom it fell to his lot to convey from place to place in his chair.

It has already been expressed that the name and titles of Kim ô Seng, the details of his journey and the object of his visit to Nankin were entirely a matter of reasonable conjecture on the part of the officials connected with the College of Ceremony and the Board of Public Manners of Behaving.

So engrossing had become the interest in the nuptials of the adorable Suin-yu that it did not occur to those in authority that a stranger could arrive in Nankin from a distant land for any other purpose than that of entering his claim to compete for her incomparable hand, and accordingly as the person in question was quite unable to give them any assistance, it devolved upon them to assign to him the most probable name and rank so that he might be greeted with becoming tokens of esteem and recognition when the occasion arose. On this conclusion – which was by no means hastily arrived at – they were strengthened by the manifestation of an almost celestial occurrence, the incident arising in the following manner. It chanced that the sublime and magnanimous Emperor of that period, being desirous of knowing who was destined to win his fascinating and symmetrical niece, in order that he might privately bargain with him in a remunerative manner beforehand, called together the most successful readers of the future in the city and commanded them to ascertain the course of events. After a suitable period spent in observing the course of the stars and in consulting omens and written parchments of an obscure nature, these persons again approached the Emperor and veiling their meaning under the cloak of delicately chosen hyperbole – after the manner of speaking affected by all the most experienced readers of the future – they laid before him an unhewn stone from the wayside, a weapon of the finest steel, one edge being sharp and polished to a most unusual brilliance, the other rough and irregular to the touch, and a broken twig of the kwing-shu tree whose roots grow upwards in the marshes, which in this manner signifies a 'reversal'.

"Alas!" exclaimed the sagacious Emperor, as he looked coldly in turn at each of the ingenious symbols, "let the imperial dust remover be summoned without delay." This august monarch, though invincible in combat and expert in many other very useful accomplishments, had, indeed, the very doubtful reputation of possessing an almost undignified directness of speech, which led him to regard the more subtle and elusive pronouncements of omen-readers in a spirit of non-satisfaction.

"Are the soothsayers of this ill-regulated capital all engaged in the commerce of money-lending, using these as profitable occasions for the disposal of their unsaleable stock?" he enquired in a voice so sympathetically modulated that at its insidious smoothness the by no means imposed-on augurs beat the floor with their faces in an ecstasy of undignified apprehension and incapable foreboding. "It is undoubtedly a fact that the only reply which this prosaic-minded person can ever obtain to a simple and uninvolved enquiry is to have his usually orderly and well arranged Court of Reception degraded into the semblance of the stall of a vendor of partially worn out garments."

"Illustrious sire," exclaimed the readers of the future in accents of unfeigned mental distress, "we become exceedingly small and unsettled in the stomach before the words of your royal displeasure. Nevertheless it has ever been the custom to make known the will of the omnipotent Buddha by means of similar divine emblems—"

"Your words have every resemblance to matters as they exist," interrupted the Emperor, "for this commonplace-souled one recalls that on the last occasion when he was desirous of ascertaining merely the amount of genuine affection entertained towards him by the elegant and refined chrysanthemum-seller Nyi-lu, the omens consisted of an empty rice bowl, two entire changes of female raiment, neither of any real pecuniary value, a somewhat badly damaged sedan chair of the imperial yellow and three score and a half dried fruit of various kinds."

"Distinguished being," replied the wise men tremblingly, "it is beyond controversy that we are but as the Eye seeing the things which are revealed to us and not, on all occasions, also the mind working out the omens to their obvious conclusions. Let, however, proficient interpreters of signs be summoned, and to them these emblems will be as outstretched fingers pointing in one inspired direction."

"Perchance," said the Emperor agreeably, "the direction alluded to may lead all the persons concerned to a spot not far distant from the Open Space of Public Torture. Nevertheless, let the interpreters pronounce upon the matter without delay, and in a spirit of unbiased impartiality."

At this command the expression of appreciative amusement which had brightened the countenances of the interpreters of signs when the Emperor first began to reproach their hereditary rivals, the readers of the future, faded from their faces and reappeared on those of their heirs and of such persons as were not well disposed towards their enjoying a prolonged existence, this effect being not greatly dissimilar from that seen when the sun's radiance passes from one hill to another, leaving the first involved in an even deeper gloom than that which first possessed it. The intolerable and funereal images which arose before the manifestly distressed interpreters at the Emperor's words were engendered by a twofold cause; for while it would be an offence against the Tcheon dynasty Edict of Ceremonial Conduct (punishable by slicing to death) to be guilty of any inaccuracy in so critical an announcement, it would be an act of deliberate treason against the sublime Emperor (punishable by compressing to death) to profess themselves unable to make a specific declaration. In this dilemma they prostrated themselves with an apparently somewhat unnecessary obsequiousness – in reality that they might while in that position have an opportunity of conferring together as to their course of behaviour and manner of acting – and then rising, at once affixed to each of the symbols an inscribed parchment bearing a sentence from that portion of the Book of Verses entitled *The Crystalised Chapter of Best Digested Wisdom*: to the first, 'Distrust an outward appearance of poverty in the person with whom you may be called upon to exchange gifts. As its exterior to the unpolished gem, so is an ill made cotton robe to the discreet one watching unobserved;' to the second 'In battle the skilful triumph by valour and the keenness of their weapons, but

in negotiations by the patient and insidious wearing away of
opposition;' to the third, 'The eyes that have not seen shall
see, and to those that have seen daily shall be absence.' By
this ingenious subterfuge they undoubtedly contrived to avoid
the two very humiliating alternatives, for it appeared to the
Emperor that if he openly professed an ignorance of the exact
meaning of quotations from so exact and significant a classic
as the one in question he would be held in scarcely disguised
contempt by the more discriminating of his subjects; therefore,
affecting a look in which veiled satisfaction and well concealed
surprise were craftily blended, so that in no case should he be
betrayed by his expression, he dismissed both the readers of
the future and the interpreters of signs, and secretly consulting
a written parchment containing the names and qualifications
of all those affected he at once decided that the various signs
and portents unevadably singled out the prince Kim ô Seng as
the one destined to possess the beauteous and heaven-adorned
Suin-yu.

The Real Nature of the Supposed Prince of Yen-ah

AT THIS POINT in the histories of the various persons concerned
in the story it is necessary to explain that an important misunderstanding had arisen in consequence of the universal preoccupation in Nankin at the time of Kim ô Seng's arrival. Kim
ô Seng, indeed, was not a prince from an obscure province of
Yen-ah, nor was he, as had been somewhat hastily assumed, a
competitor for the pledging gifts of the incomparable Suin-yu.
On the contrary he had been a merchant of spices and cassia
wood in a country distant from The Wall many thousand li,
and in this honourable occupation he was amassing a satisfactory competency when the very unprepossessing manner
of behaving towards him affected by a certain maiden of his
town caused him to regard all mankind, and especially such as
were of the age, sex and peach-like appearance of the maiden

in question, in a spirit of unconciliatory malignity. Hastily abandoning his really lucrative business, and exhibiting other signs of acute mental disorder, Chen Fung – to conceal his exact name no longer – retired to a distant and almost unin-habited region where he endeavoured to efface the bitterness of his condition by immersing himself in studying the arts of witchcraft.

In this he was successful only to a limited extent, for al-though he gained the reputation of being a powerful magician he was conscious himself that he had no claim to the wide-spread veneration which the title gained for him. He could, it is true, cause various things to disappear in a most unaccount-able manner and he overcame corporeal space to the extent of being able to project his body rapidly through the air in a forward direction to a practically unlimited extent; yet in spite of the most assiduous research and inward contempla-tion he found himself totally unable to create articles of the most insignificant value or to call back into the state of an ordinary existence those which he had caused to vanish; nor could he travel through the air backwards or in a sideway or circular direction. Becoming attached to his new manner of life, these deficiencies weighed heavily upon his mind, to the inward contempt which he felt for powers of so limited an extent being added the open reproach which he frequently ex-perienced at the hands of wayfaring pilgrims to whom he had obligingly manifested his powers; which, however, they had not sufficiently considered until too late. So undignified was the resentment of those who had entrusted to Chen Fung sums of money or articles of a costly nature for him to display his engaging magic upon, that it was no uncommon thing for him to be driven to his second accomplishment in order to escape their unappeasable anger, and even though endowed with this serviceable faculty, the abraded and deeply scarred condition of his face and body plainly testified to the painful nature of his emotions when compelled to maintain a fixed and unswerving flight through the thickly wooded forests by which his retreat was surrounded. It was at this period that he chanced to hear of the world renowned treatise by the celebrated philosopher Hyui Ty, entitled *The Explanation of Most Things Not Generally Fully Arrived at Intellectually* which occupies seventy nine volumes in the Illimitable Pagoda of Reference at Nankin. Entertaining no sort of doubt that this all-embracing classic would acquaint him with those details of his art which were so greatly lacking to complete his satisfaction, Chen Fung set out for Nankin without fully considering the involved nature of the enterprise, for the rough and mountainous character of the line of his route and the presence of countless spirits unfriendly to such a design made it impossible for him to travel in the most expeditious manner. From this cause the manner of his arrival in Nankin was such as has already been set forth, while the discovery that the inimitable work which he had come so far to consult was inscribed from beginning to end in a language which made it as inaccessible to him as the central court of the Temple of Clarified and Three-Times-Pure Justice is to a person who can only reward the doorkeepers with complimentary words, added still more to the sombre channels into which his thoughts were every day diverted.

The Offensive Behaviour of the Magician Chen Fung

"A PERSON MAY STAND behind a multitude expounding heaven-sent truths, to the effect that a devout and honourable manner of living is more to be esteemed than a find of jewels and so forth, without inconveniencing a single one to the extent of turning his head," remarked the venerable Tai Loo considerably more than four dynasties ago; "yet let a solitary wayfarer crossing a desert strike his brow bitterly remarking that he has dropped a tael on the spot, and the plain will immediately become covered with eager searchers hurrying in that direction." The public manner of behaving towards Chen Fung as soon as the Emperor's ingenious conjecture came to be whispered about – for information capable of such lucrative development could not long be concealed – clearly proved that the discriminating Tai Loo was by no means one who wrote for his own age only. In spite of Chen Fung's inability to understand the meaning of any remark addressed to him it was impossible for him to be long in ignorance of the fact that he was the object of remarked and, on the whole, amicably intentioned though somewhat inconvenient attentions on the part of passers-by. Ordinary persons whom he deferentially approached for the purpose of enticing them into his chair overwhelmed him with elaborate ceremony, protesting, as they retired backwards, bowing with graceful obsequiousness, that the honour of so great and ill-merited an attention was more than the inferior deities would suffer them to accept without striking them dead in envy. High officials daily presented themselves at his confessedly inadequate place of abode, each spending many hours in the pleasurable intercourse of polished bows and other complimentary actions, plainly indicating their conviction of Chen Fung's unapproachable superiority, and by comparison, their own boundless low-mindedness; and from time to time discreetly introducing the name of Suin-yu among signs and gestures which indicated that the suit of the one whom they were addressing would inevitably be brought to a prosperous conclusion if entrusted to their care. In this way the name of Suin-yu, – which was the only word actually expressed in spoken words by those who fully understood the disability under which Chen Fung existed – came to be regarded in that person's mind as a synonym of all that was objectionable and unremunerative; for although the innate courtesy of his disposition inspired him to entertain those who presented themselves as expensively as his degraded circumstances permitted, yet the obligation of diverting hours and sometimes entire days away from the exercise of his never very highly paid occupation sat funereally upon his imagination, as a full understanding of

the inspired yet undoubtedly abstruse works of the sublime
Hyui Ty faded with each moon-change into a more untangible
nothingness. In addition to the officials and secretaries, whose
attendants and waiting chairs undoubtedly conferred a not
undesirable distinction upon Chen Fung's house in the usually
inelegant and deserted Street of Those Who Vend Rat Feet,
there soon began to arrive jewel merchants who displayed their
profusions alluringly, workers in gold and silver with specimens
of their handicraft, makers of garments who submitted Chen
Fung's body to intricate measurements in spite of his dignified resistance, protesting that the imperial ceremonial would
shortly require him to appear in certain robes which they alone
had the privilege of making. Designers of palaces, introducers
of ventures of an infallible and extremely profitable nature,
distillers of lotions, subtle drinks and charm waters, serpent-
tamers and those who made a practice of subduing the natural
instincts of wild beasts; omen readers, casters out of malignant
dragons and evil spirits, together with singers and dancers of
both sexes and innumerable aged women who, with every appearance of having arrived at a complete understanding with
him, professed themselves to be indispensable for the future,
all approached Chen Fung both by day and by night, freely
making use of the name of Suin-yu in their conversation, and,
notwithstanding the entire lack of acquiescence which it was
in the power of the one to whom they spoke to grant them,
invariably departing with assurances that the matter would
be arranged and fully carried out according to his esteemed
and beneficent orders. Most intolerably of all there came vast
hordes of picture-makers bearing in their outstretched arms
representations of the really inimitable Suin-yu, each freely
confessing – so great was the admitted beauty and adorable
elegance of the princess in question – that the picture bore no
greater resemblance to her than an expiring straw-light did
to the brilliance of the great sky lantern, yet at the same time
unswervingly asserting that no more successful likeness could

be obtained by merely human agency. These persons were accompanied by practisers of the other refined arts: sculptors and
workers in clay, who brought with them images moulded in a
resemblance of the princess, some of colossal proportions and
animated by a variety of concealed devices which endowed
them with attractive and most life-like movements; musicians
and verse-makers, both the well-esteemed and the lesser, who
would not be prevailed upon to depart until they had recited
the composed pieces in which they set forth the descent, virtues
and charitable benevolence of both persons; writers of imagined tales and historical occurrences into which the names and
descriptions of Suin-yu and the magician had been flatteringly
introduced without impairing the interest or truthfulness of the
narrative, after the semblance of serpent-corn entwining itself
among the branches of the date-palm and thereby conferring
an added grace upon both objects. All these persons, in spite
of the honourable professions which they followed, came in an
almost deficient state of poverty, and entirely drove away the
reputation of high-bred exclusiveness which the visits of the
mandarins had conferred upon the Street of Those Who Vend
Rat Feet. Failing to persuade Chen Fung into the purchase
of any of the objects which they placed before him (for these
persons being seldom received into the society of upper ones
were ignorant of Chen Fung's inability to converse in their
tongue and accepted his unbroken silence as the usual manner
of behaving affected by princes in the presence of persons of
no particular rank), each explained with very circumstantial
detail and every appearance of sincerity that a most unexpected chain of circumstances had resulted in his being at that
moment entirely deficient in the means whereby to journey to
his own quarter of the city, and praying Chen Fung to entrust
him with the necessary amount until the morrow when a large
sum was confidently anticipated; or if the request should seem
too presumptuous, at least with a few brass pieces with which
he might purchase a potion of rice spirit to inspire him to so

fatiguing a journey. Accepting the smiling bows and amicable hand-wavings under which Chen Fung concealed his real emotions of almost bloodthirsty resentment in an altogether wrong spirit, these persons departed filling the air with lamentations and impolite references, at the same time declaring that if ever the person whose presence they were leaving came into a position of supreme authority the arts would become neglected and disencouraged and China thereupon sink into a degraded condition of unrelieved barbarism.

There is a somewhat obscure saying to the effect that a person of deformed intellect is spared the expense of witnessing the masterpiece among gravity-removing plays entitled "The Winged Mule of the Ni-hysi Plains" the real significance of the remark being the undoubted fact that the practical jests carried out by the more jocular deities upon the minds and destinies of human beings are infinitely more mirth-provoking than any which have been imagined by ordinary persons. Had it been the deliberate intention of the greater part of the city of Nankin to expose Chen Fung to undeserved ridicule and to engender in his mind an undying antipathy to the people and the place in question, and, above all, a vindictive and utterly ineradicable hatred of the name of Suin-yu – which he somewhat hastily conceived to be the key-word, as it may be expressed, of the elaborate and really contemptible plot of which he assumed himself to be the victim – it could not have been carried out with a greater precision than that which naturally and undesignedly resulted from the misconception of the high ones on his first arrival. The discriminating will at once see that the entire course of events was the outcome of the malicious jealousy of certain spirits who were not disposed to allow Chen Fung even the few magic accomplishments which he possessed, so that by the stratagem of putting it apparently within his power to increase his knowledge they lured him into an unknown country where they could safely and uninterruptedly bring about his entire destruction. To this end, having prepared the conditions of Chen Fung's mind by the devices indicated, they suggested to the Emperor, through the medium of a dream, that the time had arrived when Chen Fung's interest might be fittingly aroused and his munificence doubtless increased by the sight of the incomparable princess. For this purpose trusted messengers were despatched from the Palace and reaching Chen Fung at a time when the various circumstances had reduced him to the condition of mind in which a person is not greatly concerned whether he is alive or dead, they brought him into the presence of the Emperor.

"Illustrious and anonymous chieftain," exclaimed the benevolent Emperor, striking himself twice in the face to indicate beyond all manner of doubting his polished regret that he had so inferior and commonplace a countenance with which to greet one of such delicate refinement, "it has been clearly reported to us that you affect, for reasons which display an inordinate amount of sagacity, an ignorance of our involved and offensively long-winded language. It has even been suggested that the matter is exactly as you would have it appear, but concerning this we have an evenly balanced internal vision; for it does not seem reasonable that a being endowed with an exterior so god-like should be unprovided with any detail of knowledge, however trivial. Nevertheless in either circumstance our persistent amiable glances in your direction and the unconcealed looks and gestures of disgust with which from time to time we regard our own person and apparel after rewarding our eyes lingeringly on yours cannot but reveal to you the exact nature of our friendly and disinterested sentiments. Remember well our words, even if you cannot understand them, so that at a later period you may be able to recall the incident in its true light to your immaculate and overwhelming generosity. We would now inveigle you into partaking of some atrociously made almond tea, but before doing so we have a design to confer upon you the most unmistakable evidence of our personal approbation – a distinction, indeed, which will be bestowed upon no other suitor." Speaking thus in loud and commanding tones, the better to impress the meaning upon Chen Fung's deficient perception, the Emperor led him forward by the hand and drawing aside a hanging curtain of gold-embroidered silk, exclaimed in a restrained and warning voice, "Behold, the select and altogether desirable Suin-yu!"

There is a proverb well understood among those skilled in extorting money or confessions by means of torture: "the hundredth blow need be of no greater proficiency than the ninety and nine," thereby indicating that no endurance or supernatural politeness can withstand to an indefinite extent. Chen Fung had already undergone many privations and had often been reduced to the expedient of satisfying his hunger by recollecting the ill effects from which he had frequently suffered after attending elaborate feasts in former times, encountering these and other vicissitudes to the accompaniment of Suin-yu's name as it were. When, therefore, he unexpectedly found himself standing face to face with the one whom he consistently and not unnaturally believed to be the instigator of his unending cycle of evils, all thoughts of prudent restraint were submerged in a tiger-like and utterly inelegant ambition for revenge, and summoning up the power of his most effective magic he would certainly have reduced the princess to a condition of having no actual existence had not his determination been suddenly and somewhat inconsistently weakened by perceiving the undoubted likeness which she bore to the maiden who had influenced his life to so great an extent in his own country. For a momentary space of time there passed through Chen Fung's mind a variety of thoughts and impressions concerning past events and matters which had not been realised; speculating as to how certain hopes would have been fulfilled had they not been destined to be only half filled, and conjectures of a like nature, all aroused by the resemblance to which reference has been made; then finding that his resolution had become unequal to the crime of utterly destroying so ornamental and perfect a being, he breathed heavily into her face, and thereby threw her into a condition of deep and rigid sleep. Having submitted the sublime Emperor to a like indignity, despite his violent and unceasing protestations, Chen Fung was on the point of effecting a judicious absence when the palace guards, summoned by the Emperor's really formidable outcry, appeared from all sides. Plainly recognising that no advantage could be gained by remaining, and either judging obliteration to be preferable to submitting his cause to the decision of the high officials of law, or else forgetting for the moment the irrevocable nature of his act, the magician concentrated his entire power internally and without any hesitation vanished completely from the surface of the earth.

With commendable energy and resource, precious herbs and restoring substances of every variety were applied both to the Emperor and to the Princess Suin-yu. In the meantime the whole city was given up to panic and to rumours of the wildest and most conflicting nature, some not hesitating to assert that the existing dynasty had been overthrown and the Emperor's body transferred to a place of safety by the protecting spirits of his scandalised ancestors; others steadfastly declaring that the sun had been inadvertently struck and destroyed by the badly controlled tail of a passing winged dragon, with the consequence that henceforth business of every kind would have to be transacted by the uncertain light of hanging lanterns. Doubtless the rebellious banners of insurrection would have been raised had not the Emperor's faculties been quickly restored (for on him the magician's breath had less power than it had on the princess, partly owing to the sacred nature of his office and person, partly also on account of his entire body's being permeated with the essences of opium smoke which he unceasingly consumed), enabling him by prompt and efficacious measures to prevent a similar outrage in the future and at the same time convincing the people that a fixed government and unchanging form of justice were in existence and that matters were going on precisely as before; for without any delay both the interpreters of signs and the readers of the future were publicly executed together with all their relations both by blood and by marriage, and the entire street of Those Who Vend Rat Feet was purified by an all-consuming fire in which undoubtedly perished many persons who might otherwise have spread the false teaching and barbaric enchantments of the treacherous Chen Fung. By these wise precautions all danger for the future was removed, but an irreparable blow had been dealt both at the monarchy and at the nation, for in spite of sacrifices and of every other device that could be thought of, the beautiful Suin-yu remained in a condition of fixed and profound slumber.

Part II
The Proclamation of the Charitable Emperor

ABOUT THE DISTANCE of a day's journey from the city dwelt a widow together with her only son, a youth of high-minded but unassuming honourableness. So poverty-controlled had been their lives in the past that in spite of the woman's persistent carefulness and of Kwang's untiring labour as a wild-fruit gatherer, their hut in the forest contained nothing beyond the essential constituents for the barest existence. Kwang, indeed, had never possessed, or even beheld, a piece of money of the meanest value, all his recompenses consisting at the most of a small piece of rough cloth or an insignificant measure of rice, but this circumstance affected him beneficently rather than the reverse, for being thus far removed from the possibility of greed and avarice he passed an ingenuous youth in which thoughts of profligacy and of riches gained by extortion had no part. In spite of his poverty he sacrificed freely, carving in wood and bone, for this humane purpose, lifelike representations of various animals both wild and those subservient to the will of man, and offering them by fire upon an altar which he built in the depths of the forest. This selection was inspired rather by choice than by necessity, for of so gentle and considerate a disposition was Kwang that the fiercest and most rapacious beasts as well as those by nature inordinately timorous did not hesitate to walk by his side and to receive caresses at his hands, but it seemed only reasonable to his exalted imagination that the protecting deities would more highly esteem the ceremonious destruction of objects which had required skill and patience at his hands than of creatures which could be taken without exertion at every step.

At this time, when Kwang had reached the age of manhood, there suddenly appeared throughout the two provinces of Kian Su and Ngan-whu an imperial proclamation relating in some measure to a matter which has already been adequately set forth in detail. It so chanced that one of the persons deputed by the Emperor to affix a copy of the paper containing the edict to every prominent object which he encountered, lost his way in the inextricable tangle of the forest and ultimately perished miserably through most incapably maintaining an aggressive and threatening attitude towards the otherwise peaceably disposed wood creatures of the neighbourhood, but not until he had discovered in his wanderings the spacious and well constructed altar which Kwang had erected and had embellished it with one of the decrees as he had been commanded. From these various causes it came about that on a certain day when Kwang withdrew to perform his usual prostrations he was astonished to find before his eyes the following expressive and skilfully set forth notice:

To Persons:

[An official paper concerning the upholding to the highest degree of the dignity of the Supreme Emperor, Brother of the Sun, Possessor of the Crystal Fang of the sacred Buddha, Wearer of the Imperial Yellow. Also of a lesser matter.]

It is, alas, a matter beyond reasonable questioning that even in the sublimest and most tolerantly governed country events of a rebellious and distressing nature occasionally arise.

As a specific example it may be explained that as the devout and custom-respecting Emperor was making a public procession through the streets of Nankin recently seated upon a chariot of seven heights symbolically constructed to represent the Pagoda of Heaven, graciously inclining his head from side to side in order to afford his subjects the inexpressible delight of gazing upon his sagacious and intellectual countenance, a low-class outcast named Wong (said to be of the house of Chang from the town of Ping-hi) openly and most offensively spread out his feet towards him at the same time propounding a meaningless enquiry. This utterly contemptible person would undoubtedly have been torn to pieces by those standing around had they not become so excessively amused at the thought of the mirth-compelling position which Wong's body would shortly assume when seared at every point by red hot pincers that they were placed at a disadvantage, and through this cause the depraved person effected a temporary escape. As the entire city is now engaged in searching for Wong's hiding place with the untiring assiduousness of one endeavouring to trace a certain ticket for the State Lottery after he has been warned of its success in a dream, the ultimate and not long deferred fate of the person in question may be regarded as definitely settled. It is also a detail to be remembered that a reward of fifteen taels will be pressed upon anyone who delivers up Wong to the Imperial Guard, while should there exist a person misguidedly attached to

the intolerable Wong to the extent of affording him
shelter, the magnanimous Emperor would feel utterly unequal to such outrageous cruelty as parting
two beings so cherished by one another, and they
will, in consequence, be boiled together.

*[Words concerning the prolonged trance affecting
the condition of the Princess Suin-yu.]*

It is set forth that on the eleventh day of the month
of Earth Tremblings an ill disposed magician,
skilled in certain arts not usually resorted to by persons of self-reliant capableness, gained admittance
to the Imperial Palace of Three Times Crystallised
Sacredness, partly by his power of becoming invisible whenever he pressed a certain spot on his
body which had been previously anointed with a
preparation of unknown spices, partly owing to the
treachery of an inefficient band of augurs. Passing
through the innumerable rooms and courts of the
Palace, and concealing about his person such articles as excited his cupidity, this clay-souled leper
reached at length an apartment where the accomplished Princess Suin-yu reclined elegantly upon an
inlaid sandalwood couch engaged in the amiable
occupation of embroidering a most delicately imagined coffin-cloth for her aged father. At the sight
of a being so exquisitely formed and at the same
time so charitably inspired, the evil thoughts and
debased emotions by which the magician's character was almost entirely built up confessed themselves vanquished, and endeavouring to escape
in a volume to a more congenial neighbourhood,
rushed out of their creator's mouth in the form of
a thick white vapour which completely filled the
room and by the violent antagonism to her own

161

virtuous and refined nature, threw the princess into a rigid sickness from which she has not yet recovered. By a most beneficent chance the all-observing Emperor entered the chamber at that moment and becoming possessed by an overwhelming sense of indignation at so presumptuous an intrusion he first struck the too self-confident magician to the ground by a pitiless glance from his usually mild and conciliatory eyes, and then proceeded to trample upon his objectionable body so ferociously that when the intrepid Tiger Guard rushed to the spot nothing remained but a few garments of scarcely any real remarketable interest.

This is to summon to the Palace any person who has become expert in the art of reviving princesses who have been thrown into a like condition owing to a similar chain of circumstances; or those who have by honourable, or at least not distinctly unlawful, means, become possessed of knowledge which might be prudently and efficaciously made use of. As the divine Suin-yu is admittedly of no particular value to anyone as she now is, she will, according to the law and edict of the Thang Imperial House, become the property of the person who restores her to the condition of her ordinary existence. It is, moreover, a detail to be carried in mind that, in order to discourage persons of an idle, vicious or merely curious nature, those who make the attempt unsuccessfully will be ceremoniously escorted to a seat on the sacred jade stone known as the Threshold of Ancestral Reunion.

These are set forth over the Imperial Vermilion and cannot be rubbed out, nor, assuredly, will the illimitable and well-digesting Emperor eat his word, or lose his benevolent face by these.

When Kwang had finished the reading of this gracious and encouraging announcement – which was inscribed in the most elementary of the six recognised styles of printed characters with the especial design that it should be intelligible to persons of even the most deficient literary education – his face grew red like the evening sun viewed through the mist preceding a sand storm in the deserts of the west, while his limbs trembled beneath him in a most incapable fashion; for added to the proclamation was a printed illustration of the Princess Suin-yu (given in the hope that it might by chance afford some clue to such as thought they could remove her malady) and at the sight of it Kwang's internal organs alternately grew small and large entirely beyond his control. Yet the fact need not be concealed, proving as it does the extreme simplicity and ingenuousness of Kwang's nature, that the picture in question by no means resembled the unapproachable Suin-yu either in colour or in delicacy of outline; nor was it, indeed, in any way exceptional, for when the sagacious Emperor impetuously decided at the last moment that this facility should be afforded, it became necessary that a number of picture-makers who could be the readiest seized should be urged to an almost incredible expedition and without any particular regard whether or not they had ever actually beheld the object of their really unflattering dexterity. Nevertheless to Kwang who had seen no other illustration on any subject whatever in the whole course of his life, it appeared as select as a many-hued illumination from the most sumptuously embellished classic, and hastily concealing it among the folds of his garments he at once turned his footsteps in the direction of his home.

"Venerable and well-informed mother," he exclaimed, touching the ground reverentially before her, "instruct this illiterate person without delay in the art of restoring to an ordinary condition princesses who have been thrown into a trance by the poison-laden breath of evilly disposed magicians," and he proceeded to put before her the full facts as they have been related.

"Alas," cried the widow apprehensively, "before embarking upon so doubtful an enterprise consider the proverb which says 'The longer the stem of the opium pipe the further one's lips from the flame, yet the sweeter and more pain-assuaging is the nature of the smoke.' Fire, wild beasts and persons of high rank are excellent and necessary institutions when regarded from a safe and practicable distance, but the red hot hearthstone is a seat which cannot be cordially recommended, nor is it prudent to lead an unmuzzled tiger by a hempen cord when a five pace staff of exceptional rigidity is available. Emperors and princesses are arranged centres of a beneficent system of government and are therefore to be honourably regarded but in no emergency to be approached; and in any case the unreproved contemplation of a refined and highly attractive maiden – even though a princess – is more dangerous and soul-benumbing to an unsophisticated young man of inferior circumstances than would be the poisonous breath of any magician; while the prosecution of such an attempt would be inexpressibly more likely to throw yourself into a permanent rigid condition than to relieve any other person from a similar temporary infliction. Banish to an entirely unfrequented chamber of your memory all thoughts of so distinguished and expensively ornamented a being as the Princess Suin-yu, and henceforth devote yourself even more considerately than before to the task of collecting wild fruits, so that shortly it will be within your power to bargain irreproachably with the parents of some maiden in your own low-conditioned station of life and to raise up a prolific generation who will worship the memory of the one who now gives you this conscientious and impartial advice."

"Reverend ancestor to the first degree," replied Kwang deliberately but with no appearance of ill-considered haste, "your words are discriminating and in an ordinary case, or when referring to one of the lesser events of one's existence, they would carry immediate conviction. But to a person of unswerving determination and inextinguishable ambition there is no such thing as his own station in life. The thought of the divine Suin-yu is as inseparable from this one's existence as the unperceived roots of the spreading banyan are to the tree above it, while her radiant image is ever before his eyes in colours more bright than those attained by a firework display of even unreasonable profusion. Were matters otherwise than what they are he could, indeed, persevere to an old age, upheld by the entrancing thought that some of the fruit which he gathered might, without unnatural improbability, finally reach her exquisitely-gilded lips, but the knowledge of the intolerable affliction by which she is now bound down makes so passive and disinterested a course of action impossible. Furthermore so unassumingly devoted is he to the welfare of the heaven-sent maiden in question that he would unhesitatingly give his body to be used as a stepping stone to her recovery even by another who should possess her, or would offer his internal organs to be treated experimentally as a guide of the most potent and audacious substances which may be safely employed. Failing these things, however, he will feel bound to journey to the Imperial Palace and willingly compressing his entire lifetime into the one inexpressible moment when he is permitted to gaze upon her adorable face, he will cheerfully submit himself to be disposed of according to the specific terms of the proclamation."

Then replied the widow more cheerfully "'Ki-feng once swore to starve himself to death on account of the disdain of a certain maiden: lo, the heir of Ki-feng is at the door begging for a hat with which to protect his grey hairs against the rigours of the cold.' There are many turnings both to the right and to the left in the road from here to Nankin, nor is a wallet stocked with dry wild fruit the most expeditious passport to the innermost chamber of the Palace. Nevertheless, if you are resolved to make the attempt it is undesirable that you should go to the funereal extent of adding your name to the Ancestral Roll even before you start; so that, in order to make this contingency as remote as possible, attend carefully to my words. Set out at once and by travelling with all speed to a northerly direction you will reach the mountain Hoang-Tsao at sunset on the third day. This you will recognise by the yellow barrenness of its almost perpendicular sides, for nothing but a meagre vegetation, totally unacceptable to cattle even of the most thrifty habits, can flourish in so desolate a region. When the moon rises over the highest point of the Hoang-Tsao mark well where it first touches the rocks of the valley in which you stand, and proceeding without delay to the spot you will there discover a ruined tomb. Enter this without fear and cry three times loudly, adjuring its dweller to step forth, saying 'The one who calls, O wise and inspired Fuh-Tung, is Kwang, a son of the house of Kin. By our single temple on the banks of the Ho-Chuan far beyond The Wall; by the ancient agreement between our two families, and by the obligation under which you exist since the betrayal of Chun-ah Kin and the dew of the scented myrtle grove, this person demands your specific assistance. Should it be withheld, may the dying curse of Chun-ah no longer be restrained by a million sacrifices, but, directing an unswerving course from the Upper Air, strike your unresisting body at the most vulnerable angle and fasten upon your vitals with the tenacious grasp of a hungry scorpion.'"

"Beloved mother," replied Kwang prudently, "unless the latter part of the invocation is an integral and material portion of the whole, it seems to this conciliatory one that it would be discreet to omit it, if, indeed, the solitary ruggedness of the plain and the unscaleable precipitousness of the mountains by which the formidable hermit is surrounded have not been somewhat exaggerated. With this possible exception, however, the person before you will act in precisely the manner you suggest, confident that the various forces around him are tending to bring about a flattering, or at the worst a not absolutely degraded, reward for his unswerving devotion."

Thereupon Kwang set forth on his journey, relying upon his intimate knowledge of the habits of wild fruit to provide him with the necessary sustenance on the way, and not even tarrying to sacrifice, for the entire adventure upon which he was engaged was of the most charitable benevolence and in the second classic of the Four Books – known as "The Conditions of Equilibrium" it is distinctly said: "The person who escapes hastily from his burning house and at once publicly consumes his only garment in an offering to the deity of Fire may be suspected of ostentation – if indeed of nothing more reprehensible – rather than of true self-abasement, and should be avoided by the honourable of both sexes."

The Deep-Rooted Wisdom of the Philosopher Fuh-Tung

ON THE EVENING of the third day Kwang came to the foot of the mountain of Yellow Growth, called Hoang-Tsao, and discovering himself to the venerable hermit Fuh-Tung as he had been instructed by his mother, he was courteously received.

"The hospitality of a deserted and worn-out tomb is deplorably inadequate for you, O Kwang-*ti*, who, since the passing beyond of your father's brother, are undoubtedly hereditary ruler of the Northern Sand Plains, although it must be admitted that eleven dynasties have intervened since your illustrious ancestors occupied the throne," said Fuh-Tung deferentially. "Enter, nevertheless, and partake unstintingly of the rainwater and badly cooked cold lizard which is the only repast in this deficient person's power to set before you."

"Virtuous and amiable philosopher," replied Kwang, "do not tempt this earthen-minded one with magnanimous suggestions of richly-spiced viands and luxurious ease; instruct him, rather, out of the unfathomable wisdom which deep contemplation and an unchanging habit of life had engendered in your mind, upon a matter which closely affects his future tranquillity and, indeed, his existence." With these words Kwang unrolled the entire succession of events affecting the Princess Suin-yu and himself before Fuh-Tung's understanding and then prostrating himself, as he might becomingly do before so aged and dispassionate a being, he besought his explicit advice.

In spite of Kwang's impetuous words and desire for an immediate return Fuh-Tung would by no means consent to the matter being conducted with unceremonious haste. "Nothing but confusion could arise from action of such ill-considered precipitancy," he exclaimed when the youth entreated that he might be allowed to retrace his footsteps before the great sky lantern had completed his nightly course. "Even the unlettered camel does not attempt to cross the mountain by leaping over the highest point; how much less, then, should a human being of royal descent and of more than average profundity avoid giving the impression of being swayed by menial impulse or necessity – a state of things which assuredly would only result in alienating the protection of all the more leisurely and important spirits and thereby defeating its own aim? Remain in this insufferable place until sunrise, for it cannot reasonably be expected that your exalted personality should be able to put up with its atrocious shortcomings for a longer period, and in the meantime this indifferent person will endeavour by means of his discredited and obsolete philosophy to discover what the controlling deities actually intend."

On the following morning Kwang left his couch at the earliest gong stroke, and having performed his obeisances he approached Fuh-Tung who throughout the night had unwinkingly observed the course of the star called the Third Eye of Laotsu as its image passed across a reflecting disc of polished silver upon which were inscribed many sacred characters and some details of Kwang's past life and history.

"The interpretation," said the painstaking hermit agreeably, "depends, as far as it may be fittingly revealed to creatures of the lower part, upon a proverb contained in the Book of Verses and an intelligent understanding of the behaviour of Kin Yeng."

"What is the nature of the proverb?" enquired Kwang, as Fuh-Tung paused in a delicate contemplation of the inward satisfaction he experienced at having been able to serve the young man's interests so capably.

" 'More insidious and poison-laden than the tongue of the deadly fan-tailed snake of the desert is the ingratiating breath of an evilly-disposed magician' ", replied the hermit.

"And in what manner did the estimable Kin Yeng conduct himself?"

"Upon a certain occasion the enlightened Emperor of the period was engaged in his favourite occupation of ensnaring locusts when he was bitten by one of the offensive reptiles alluded to. The faithful and devoted Kin Yeng without any hesitation whatever applied his inspired lips to the wound and drew out the poison so efficiently that his imperial master was at once restored to a condition of ordinary existence."

"And the faithful and devoted Kin Yeng?" enquired Kwang, to whom this detail of the circumstance did not appear to be devoid of interest.

"His ancestors were ennobled as far back as the eighth generation," replied Fuh-Tung in an unmoved voice, but at the same time regarding the extreme ridge of the mountain Hoang Tsao with unnecessary interest; "and a tablet of the finest marble was affixed to the Gate of Imperishable Remembrance, recording the extremity of his virtue and the loyal unostentation of his death."

Then exclaimed Kwang, unable to restrain his acute bitterness, "O venerable and deeply learned Fuh-Tung, does the reading indeed admit of only this one interpretation? Do not, this person makes a direct request of you, misunderstand the willingness of his emotions or the unquenchable nature of the obligation which he places upon himself by reason of your ingenious discovery of even this expedient; but the unfettered desires of a person may be fitly compared to the blossom of the sun-peony and instinctively turn towards the light and avoid that which is dark and oppressive. Nevertheless so enchanting is the prospect of alleviating the distress of the adorable princess and then unassumingly passing beyond at her incomparable feet – perhaps even being permitted to receive a divine glance expressive of her approbation before becoming entirely devoid of life – that those whom this person outstrips on the way to Nankin will assuredly judge by his speed and by the expression of his countenance that he has been appointed to a high mandarinship and flies to the capital to receive the outward insignia of his office. Through every detail of his quest, the fixed and unchanging intent of his purpose has never for an instant deviated from its appointed end; yet (to mention a matter which, however, has no material bearing on his determination, even with the full assurance of an immediate death) from signs and indications of a slight but encouraging nature it had appeared to this presumptuous one that out of the unbounded omniscience of the protecting deities some irreproachable way might be found by which the destinies of himself and of the heaven-sent princess should be entwined together for a not inconsiderable period. Make a last and definite assurance, O trustworthy philosopher, whether no such amiable solution exists, for it seems incredible that so versatile a being should be unprepared for any emergency, and then this really very highly-favoured one will turn his eager steps towards the radiating centre of all his desires, which lies beneath the highest cupolas of Nankin."

Without expressing himself in spoken words Fuh-Tung took Kwang by the hand and leading him through secret underground paths he brought him presently into the depths of the great mountain Hoang Tsao where it was hollowed out in the form of a cave and gracefully illuminated by a profusion of hanging lanterns. Here, before a many-armed figure which Kwang recognised as the founder of his race, stood the lost jewel of Tsin, – the cause of innumerable outrages and vicissitudes and the real object of seven invasions – an emerald two

paces in length, two paces in width and about the height of an
ordinary person; while from the unusual sparkling brilliance of
the walls around, it at once became apparent that the entire
mountain was composed of the finest gold. Prostrating himself
before the figure and explaining the nature of the act and its
lawfulness under such circumstances, the pious hermit struck
the upper surface of the rock and broke from it a fragment of
about the size of a closed hand. Instructing Kwang by a sign
that he should place this in sack which he carried, Fuh-Tung
repeated his action, continuing until Kwang cried out that the
weight of the burden of the load was greater than he could
reasonably bear.

"Yet behold," exclaimed the venerable philosopher, "priceless emeralds have been aptly compared to well-digested
wisdom, and of both the munificent deities have provided a
practically inexhaustible supply for the use of the discriminating, but it is within the power of none to take away sufficient
to meet every reverse or contingency which may perchance
be experienced." In this delicate and inoffensive manner he
conveyed the undoubted fact that the limitation of a person's
knowledge lies in his own inability to carry and retain it, rather
than in any want of forethought on the part of the deities to
provide a fitting solution for every possible occasion in life;
and at the same time he furnished Kwang with the means of
appearing in Nankin with a retinue and a supply of wearing
apparel in keeping with his ambitious object and his illustrious
descent. "Nevertheless," he continued genially, as the varied
shadows of mingling emotions crossed Kwang's expressive face,
"this detail – conveying as it does a perceptible suggestion of
divine encouragement – may be honourably revealed: towards
the last hour of the transit there came a vaporous mist over the
polished surface of the disc, as though some benevolent spirit
in his flight had passed before it, and when this cleared away
it at once appeared that the malignant influence of the chief
star of the Constellation of the Bent Bow, which throughout

the night had striven to cross the passage of the Third Eye of Laotsu, had been completely baffled and diverted to another and a harmless course. By what means this was actually accomplished the mist was unquestionably designed to conceal, and to what end it presages, the research of the one before you has been unable to discover, but the incident may well be held in mind and the assistance of the responsible spirit confidently claimed should an opportunity arise."

When they were again come to the outer air Fuh-Tung embraced Kwang with many ceremonious details of intimate regard and then permitted him to retrace his footsteps, to the last warning him against certain unpropitious influences which he might encounter on his journey, and providing him with a mystic word and imprecation by which he might test and ascertain the true nature of any unusual occurrence.

The Aged Woman in the Cedar Forest

IN SPITE OF THE UNDENIABLE WEIGHT of the burden of emeralds which he carried, Kwang scarcely left any impression upon the earth he trod, so rapid and unfaltering was his course through the woods and over every manner of obstacle. Whenever his limbs began to experience a feeling as of bodily fatigue he cried aloud in tones of unfaltering resolution "O evilly persecuted Suin-yu, to whom this person's most aspiring thoughts ever turn as to a celestial and far-removed being, do not sink beyond recovery under the overwhelming load of your affliction; for one whose heaven will be to restore you to an ordinary existence and then to sink expiring to the ground is even now wearing out the soles of his feet in his intolerable haste." In this invigorating way he continually urged both his body and his mind to more successful efforts, and at the same time – however improbable such a thing may appear – the repeated utterance of the princess's engaging name had a direct influence on the outcome of the affair; for towards evening of the

seventh day of his journey, while actually within sight of the
towers and walls of Nankin, he had no sooner made use of
this inspiring cry than there fell upon his cheek a faint touch,
as it might be the shadow of a passing spirit, reminding him
of the mist Fuh-Tung spoke of after his unceasing scrutiny of
the reflecting disc, but accompanied in this case by a faint and
most entrancing perfume of trebly refined chrysanthemum.
Turning quickly, Kwang beheld less than a score of paces away
an aged woman struggling and already overcome in the embrace of a voracious serpent. Provoked at so unequal a conflict
the youth rushed forward with menacing cries and feigning
that his real intention was rather to seize the reptile by the tail
he unexpectedly struck it so proficiently on the head with the
sack of emeralds he still bore that it at once sank to the ground
and offered no further resistance.

"Illustrious youth," exclaimed the aged woman when she
was somewhat recovered, "the service which you have rendered
this person is indeed one of no ordinary or superficial courtesy. Proceed therefore to her obscure abode which is situated
at no great distance away, and there refresh your exceptional
faculties with such inadequate fare as so menial a place can
afford."

"The proposal is delicately intended," replied Kwang, "and
if the time and the circumstances were other than what they
are it would afford this person unfeigned gratification to partake of many cups of even the coldest apricot-beer and an unlimited number of dishes of the most commonplace unspiced
rice in the company of so entertaining a hostess."

"Alas," cried the woman with every external appearance of
disappointment, "the sincerity of those who protest that the
honour of walking side by side with street beggars whom they
have known is too great, while they do not hesitate publicly to
caress the outlines of high officials of their acquaintance, may
well be suspected. Doubtless you are hastening to partake of
some many-coursed feast, where, amid the continual imbibing

of rich wines and opium smoke your gravity-removing jests will be received with flattering exclamation."

"Your words are badly digested and of a contradictory nature, O aged woman," exclaimed Kwang, whose only desire was to resume his journey without any delay. "You have plainly shown that they who provide luxurious repasts do not mix on terms of equality with mendicants and road-sweepers; yet the unprepossessing one before you is assuredly Kwang, practically an outcast, of the inconsiderable though royal house of Kin. The only feast of which he is likely to partake is a fleeting sight of the lovely and enchanting Princess Suin-yu, the only wine a brief but admittedly intoxicating touch of her returning breath, and the only gravity-removing jest which he is destined to perpetrate will be the practical illustration of how the most highly favoured person in the Empire will at the same time be the one totally unable to enjoy the full measure of his happiness."

At this unhesitating avowal there came into the face of the woman a trembling light which might be compared to the uncertain glow of the rising sun, and her voice faltered somewhat as she exclaimed in tones of vehement emotion, "O conscientious young man, do not permit yourself to be tempted by ambition or by the imagining of a pecuniary award no matter how excessive to engage in an enterprise which can only result in your not unshapely person being submitted to torture or at the best to an immediate death. In spite of her somewhat poverty-stricken appearance the one with whom you are conversing has in reality vast riches, one half of which she will give you as a reward for your intrepid services if you will abandon all hope of possessing this really greatly over-rated princess."

"It is an admitted contention among those skilled in forms of law that a person cannot dispose of that which he does not possess," replied Kwang, "yet the less presumptuous hope of restoring her to her habitual robustness and then expiring not ungracefully at her feet is one which this sordid-minded person would not relinquish for the inlaid throne of the sacred

Emperor and the unlimited riches of Feu-li who possessed the Great Secret. Permit him, therefore, to resume his journeying without discourtesy for each moment which divides him from so highly-favoured an end hangs more leaden-footed than a full moon of merely ordinary existence."

Then exclaimed the aged woman, "Behold, O Kwang of the House of Kin, it is within this one's power, by the aid of honourably acquired magic, to transform herself to the form and appearance which she formerly possessed – a condition in no way inferior to that of the Princess Suin-yu – while whatever she possesses of riches will be yours if you will put this rash and ill considered project entirely from your mind." With these words she rubbed the juice of a certain fruit upon her eyes, which from being dim and almost sightless at once assumed the most perfect colour and symmetricalness, while continual beams of incomparable violet light shot from them. "More," she continued, regarding Kwang with every appearance of affectionate concern, "it is not seemly to reveal until the matter has been definitely settled, but consider well that on the one side there awaits you a certain though confessedly not ignoble death, and on the other boundless riches and the undisguised esteem of one who in her youth was frequently complimented on her appearance by the discriminating Emperor of the period."

As the radiant eyes of the aged woman rested upon Kwang there came over his spirit a trembling similar to that which had afflicted him when he first beheld the features of Suin-yu on the proclamation in the forest. Nevertheless fixing his mind upon the spectacle of the Princess's distress he answered resolutely, "The beauty of a maiden may be fitly compared to the flavour of the different varieties of fruit, for whereas one person will extoll the colour and delicacy of a peach, another, equally competent to maintain a definite opinion, will declare that nothing can approach the sharp and invigorating taste of a lemon. Let it therefore not be regarded in the light of a hastily-formed resolution or as an impolite and disdainful preference that this person's entire being is so filled with images of the amiable and persecuted Suin-yu that his mind is incapable of change or forgetfulness."

At this final denial of her enchantments the aged woman turned away as though she would conceal the deeply-set emotions to which Kwang's refusal gave rise within her mind. Nevertheless, as he made a movement as to resume his way she sped again to his side and displaying her right arm cried aloud, "O valiant and chivalrous Kwang, remain at least until you have completed the service which you so dextrously began. Behold the wounds inflicted by the evilly-disposed reptile which lies dead before us and apply such restoring substances as will efficiently combat the insidious malignity of its poison."

"Alas," cried Kwang, perceiving that the woman's arm was already possessed of the corrupting influence of the serpent's nature, "when once so formidable a blow has been dealt nothing but the direct intervention of the all-powerful Buddha can avail. Consider, rather, what proportion of the riches to which you have made frequent reference you will devote to sacrifices and prayer money, and then compose yourself in a respectful and dignified attitude for passing into the Upper Air."

"Yet it has been said that a powerful antidote, applied but a few moments before one passes Beyond, is more satisfactory than a thousand and one pieces of the finest prayer paper burned after the Event," replied the woman, and cutting off the head of the serpent she revealed a substance of about the size and appearance of a date lying concealed behind the fangs. "Understand now, O true and constant Kwang," she continued "that there are matters beyond the wisdom of an elderly philosopher and even outside the knowledge of the faithful and devoted Kin Yeng."

With these words she swallowed a portion of the counteracting substance, whereat her arm was at once restored to its former condition, but before Kwang could recover from his astonishment she had again faded from his sight, leaving upon his cheek a warm and reassuring touch as of a passing spirit, and in his mind the lingering perfume of chrysanthemum which had first announced her presence.

The Very Opportune Arrival of Kwang

"IT IS INDEED a most intolerable deficiency that no reliable soothsayers exist," remarked the benevolent Emperor, causing his face to assume an expression of ill-destined severity. "Already the virtuous and enlightened Suin-yu has remained in a condition of unyielding rigidness for the space of more than three moons and in spite of failure being punished with a continually increasing severity until it involves tortures of really almost unfeeling barbarity, no person has been able to achieve the most insignificant degree of success. Let the twelve mandarins of the fifth degree who were yesterday appointed as temporary omen diviners to the Imperial Court now come forward and express themselves without reserve as to the most profitable and suitable course to pursue."

In response to this plainly-intended command the twelve newly created augurs advanced respectfully and kowtowing repeatedly placed before the magnanimous Emperor a variety of articles among which could be easily discerned the feathers of a newly slain peacock, a number of elaborately carved jade ornaments for the hair, some pomegranates of a kind rarely seen in Nankin and a stone obtained from The Wall by means of a band of swift and untiring runners. Having laid these impressive emblems at the foot of the richly ornamented throne they retired backwards with frequent ceremonial bows until they reached the opposite wall of the Great Hall of Audience, where in some doubt as to the real nature of their reception and not being disposed to let any material object interfere with the unfeigned depth of their self-abasement they still continued to raise their feet deferentially in an almost unparalleled display of complimentary obsequiousness.

"Alas!" exclaimed the pure-minded sovereign dispersing these inspired symbols by a well-directed movement of his expert and richly sandalled foot, "it is expressly stated that a person who has been bitten by a serpent may feel no dishonour in leaping back suddenly from the shadow of his own pigtail. With the memory of the atrocious person Kim ô Seng still fresh in his nostrils this not usually violent monarch has no hesitation in commanding the Palace Executioner to make an exhibition of his proficient dexterity. In the meantime let the Imperial Temple be unsealed in the hope that the insufferable frequency of these misunderstandings will be brought to an end by depositing the actual origin of them in the best secured and innermost vault."

"Sublime and very much magnified being," interposed a favourite slave approaching the Emperor submissively, "a person of no particular appearance or dimensions is even now craving admittance at the outer gate, protesting that it lies within his power to restore the Princess to an ordinary condition."

"Has the one in question made an inspection of the remains of those who have already failed in the attempt, and tested the various appliances used – in particular that for spasmodically working the jaws to and fro while a spiked instrument is held in the mouth?" enquired the humane-tempered ruler affably.

"It is credibly asserted that he has made the usual survey and that he was undeniably fascinated by the ingenious mechanism of the instrument alluded to, even while he was ignorant of the fact that it owed its perfection to your all-knowing versatility," replied the favourite slave. "He desires, moreover, your tolerant acceptance of this thoroughly inadequate emerald which he gracefully suggests might, in the absence of a more suitable and deserving object, be found useful for casting at offensively persistent suppliants or for some other trivial purpose."

"So agreeable and discriminating a person must not be neglected for a moment; let him be put in such a position that he may practise his irreproachable arts upon the Princess without delay," exclaimed the self-satisfied Emperor, and somewhat imprudently permitting all thoughts of the necessity of his presence to pass from his mind, he engaged in an uninterrupted contemplation of the many-hued excellences of the jewel he held; for indeed, though one of the most insignificant stones that Kwang had received, it was, nevertheless, incomparably the largest and most symmetrical emerald ever seen within the Empire.

"The Bolts of Sacred Random Light"

When Kwang was ceremoniously, and with every external mark of an assumed deference, conducted to the chamber where the beautiful Princess Suin-yu lay unconscious upon a jade and ivory divan, almost concealed by a richly-worked cloth which announced by words and by devices her titles and virtues, some incidents connected with her past life, and the malevolent event which had reduced her to such a condition, his emotions were so opposed and dignity-removing that for many moments he was unable to proceed in any direction whatever, or even to see the sublime object of his wanderings and excessive perseverance. At length somewhat refreshed by the subtle odour of thickly distributed chrysanthemum flowers, he went forward, guided by the faint but inimitable violet light which proceeded from the Princess's almost closed eyelids, and falling to the ground passionately but at the same time respectfully before the divan he exclaimed aloud "O exquisite and seven times worshipful Suin-yu, at length this distressingly unworthy person reaches the cloud-piercing summit of his secret and most internal ambition and gazes unreproved upon a countenance a hundredfold more almond-eyed and delicately outlined than the one which drew out his soul when he first beheld it. Assuredly the deities will not allow an ordinary person to penetrate any further into the Upper Air; so that, although inflated from time to time by visions and utterly presumptuous

179

hopes, this already too highly rewarded one now makes the attempt with the full conviction that some essential detail has been overlooked and that his contemptible body will either fall incapably to the ground devoid of life, or only exist to be reserved for the gravity-removing contrivance devised by the noble-minded Emperor." Thus expressing himself Kwang consumed the substance which had been taken from the serpent's fangs and then, raising Suin-yu's ornamental form within his arms, he put his lips to hers and drew from her body, and into his own, the contaminating poison of the outrageous magician's offensive breath.

For a period of which neither person had any actual re-membrance the various influences at work contended stub-bornly within the bodies of Kwang and Suin-yu, and it is even asserted by those skilled in witchcraft that for a brief space of time the former one visited the Upper Air and mingled famil-iarly in conversation with the inferior deities. In his own im-agination, however, it appeared to Kwang's benumbed senses that after being lifted up suddenly to a great height and then dashed down unexpectedly he was bound for several thousand years at the bottom of the Bitter Waters and there periodi-cally dragged violently backwards and forwards over pointed rocks by means of unnecessarily massive chains. As the fetters dropped from him and the waters parted above his head he was astonished beyond measure to hear a voice of melodious and unmistakable reality whisper in his ear "O Kwang, of the house of Kin, constant and true one, nothing did you suspect as we conversed together in the cedar forest! But my spirit, groping blindly in the Middle Distance, was caught into the bosom of Kum-Fa, who was little disposed that two such royal lines should end, and there it was instructed of many things. Assure your menial one, the preparer of your rice henceforth and the lesser being of the inner chamber, that the deception which was imposed upon her is forgiven, and the entire cir-cumstance honourably regarded."

"O sweet and adorable Suin-yu," cried Kwang, recovering his unimpaired faculties at length and perceiving that his head still rested upon the maiden's while her arms now in turn supported him; "this person has been through a variety of adventures and has experienced many visions and celestial manifestations. Has this thing come about after its destined earthly fashion or is he now in paradise?"

"That," replied the gracious Suin-yu while her incomparable eyes lit up the entire spacious chamber with a most unapproachable violet radiance, "is as my lord, the ruler of my destiny and the keeper of my most internal emotions, shall decide."

"Alas," exclaimed the considerate Emperor, entering the chamber a brief space of time later, and discreetly affecting to stumble somewhat on the threshold and then feigning to search for the obstacle; "from every outward indication it would appear that a not inconsiderable source of revenue for providing the imperial necessities has come to an abrupt conclusion. Nevertheless the occasion is one usually of especial record: let twenty-one guns go off and convey our magnanimous and humane pardon to such of the temporary soothsayers as are still undisposed of."

The Destiny of Cheng, the Son of Sha-kien of the Waste Expanses

'To the Outstretched Finger of Destiny the Earth has no Corners'
Related by Kai Lung at Iong-ho,
at the modest request of the silkworm-keeper

K AI LUNG HAD ALREADY SEATED HIMSELF upon his mat in the most conspicuous spot of the meeting of the three ways within Iong-ho, had passed round his collecting bowl and reflectively contemplated its meagre lining for a period, and was on the point of announcing the title of the story which had been selected for the occasion when the unusual sound of processional music broke the tranquillity of the midday hour. Rightly conjecturing that so important a procession would trample upon their bodies rather than turn aside from the line of its march, Kai Lung and those about him dispersed hurriedly, yet scarcely escaping the blows of the most advanced who with whips hung about with knots and spikes of metal relentlessly cleared the road of all who would have loitered. Following these came a band of attendants armed with weapons of all kinds, slaves displaying scrolls and banners inscribed with their master's names and titles, a silk umbrella of three tiers and worked in many colours, a servant bearing a paper vessel embellished with sails and flags, players upon drums, bells, wooden ducks and sounding stones, seven youths with trays of flowers, a number of persons of no particular use or description and lastly the one in authority, concealed inside a richly ornamented chair and surrounded by personal attendants each displaying a spiked iron rod of an arm's length or more and about the thickness of an ordinary person's tooth.

When this imposing company had passed beyond their sight (although the point of its destination was revealed by the still discernible strains of music to be the yamen of the Mandarin Lo Hok), Kai Lung and those who remained behind again drew together and disposed themselves in their former attitudes.

"It is the great and successful Hong Ngou, the justly famed healer of pain and averter of sickness – he who was concealed from our eyes," remarked Tang-hi in response to the many enquiring glances cast in his direction; for the one who spoke possessed a stall where pig-tails were adorned and the surfaces of the face and limbs made smooth, so that those who occupied his stool conversed freely of all they knew relating to others and there was little taking place in Iong-ho that did not reach Tang-hi's ears or pass his lips again. "Behold, he has travelled many hundred li to exercise his unfailing resources upon the Mandarin Lo Hok who can do nothing but turn in agony from one side to the other and in either position speak evil towards those around him."

"Is then the obliging Hong Ngou more expert than our own Wei Ta?" enquired a simple-minded cobbler. "Lo, when this person was afflicted with a misplaced ankle-bone the accommodating Wei Ta breathed upon it several times and having written certain mystical characters upon a shred of bark he instructed me to consume it on the ninth day of the ninth moon, secretly at the middle hour of the night, with feet pointing towards the Sacred Tortoise and my face well anointed with palm-nut oil. For this he demanded the mending of his sandals and the forepart of a dressed kid, yet it is undeniable that shortly after the observance the bone returned to its appointed place and has remained so ever since."

"Wei Ta!" exclaimed Tang-hi, who had listened to these words with ill-concealed impatience. "None but a squat-legged cobbler who has no regular opportunity of conversing with persons of elegance and refinement could display an empty mind so openly as to refer to Wei Ta and Hong Ngou, representing as they do the immature leafless shrub and the waving cypress tree, with the same expression. So dextrous is the latter person that, aided by his unfailing knowledge of one's internal arrangement, he can safely and without the slightest pain drive a spiked instrument completely through the body so that the ends protrude for all to witness. His ordinary recompense is one and twenty taels of silver, to which is frequently added a change of raiment or a richly carved tablet, and it is asserted that upon a recent occasion when he attended a very rich merchant and successfully transposed the eye from the right to a place on the left and so in a converse manner, so that he should be no longer compelled to turn his head away from an object in order to see it, he received five score taels, a state chair, eleven slaves and a contrivance which by sorcery produces harmonious sounds upon pressing a handle."

"Peace!" interposed Kai Lung. "Not unobservantly was it written, 'A rock falling in the village creates more noise than a landslip across the valley.' Hong Ngou is well enough for Iong-ho, but there are many greater even outside the walls of Pekin. Doubtless he transposed the wealthy merchant's eyes in the fashion indicated for there is no great matter in that; but it is a boastful word concerning the piercing of the body from side to side. Wan-taing was the most intrepid and accomplished user of spiked instruments who has ever lived and there exists no record of *his* ever performing such a feat – probably because he found it just as effective and much more prudent to use two needles and inserting them from different sides of the body to bring them together at whatever point he desired."

"Doubtless that was the practice in the days of the high-born Wan-taing," replied Tang-hi deferentially; "but, O widely-read

Kai Lung, if the detail is not as this person conscientiously stated it, to what end were the long and formidable spikes which
all persons here assembled must have seen borne in readiness
by the side of Hong Ngou's chair?"

"It is true," remarked many as Tang-hi looked triumphantly
around. "We ourselves beheld the instruments in question and
undoubtedly they were long enough to pierce the body from
back to front without stint."

"Alas!" exclaimed Kai Lung, "truth may be more enduring than marble but error has the disseminating properties of
thistle-down. Who has not observed that while the chariots of
mandarins of the lower degrees are in no wise remarkable, as
the rank becomes higher the wheels are placed wider apart
to mark their owners' distinction until the chariot of a very
exalted official necessarily drives all before it or compels them
to cast themselves for safety into the ditch?"

"It is indeed true," admitted one of those who a moment
before had supported Tang-hi; "and this person was once most
objectionably mutilated between the wall and the chariot of a
mandarin of the second degree in a narrow street of Ping Chow."

"Yet mandarins of the higher ranks are not inevitably more
weighty than those below them," continued Kai Lung, "nor
are the longer instruments destined to be used throughout their
length, but are carried solely to denote the skill and consequence of their owners."

"Your words are invariably well-considered, O estimable
story-teller," observed a person who stood on the outside fringe
of the hearers; "and it would ill behove one of my obscured
mind and unsuccessful career to enter into the matter contro-
versially with yourself. Therefore the detail is put before you
after the manner of one seeking enlightenment: that upon an
occasion at the house of one of his wife's wealthy kinsmen this
person was shown a printed book containing the picture of
one pierced in the manner described by the honourable Tang-
hi, with a shaft protruding both before and behind."

"The argument is advanced in a fitting spirit of moderation and due self-abasement," replied Kai Lung approvingly: "and this one will not seek to involve so discreet and respectful an enquirer in ridicule or contempt. There exists such a book, indeed, and the illustration is displayed in the manner spoken of, but had you been able to read the meaning of the characters standing at the side you would at once have understood that the person there depicted is not an afflicted one being restored by the operation indicated but an ordinary dweller of one of the outside countries lying much nearer to the moon. These barbarian ghosts – as many of the most scholarly and intelligent standing about can testify – have the advantage of being born with a hole through their chests, so that in their country there is no necessity for sedan chairs as when one is desirous of making a journey a suitable pole is put through him and he is borne away on the shoulders of stalwart carriers."

"It is uncontroversial," agreed the greater number of those who formed the gathering. "The country indicated is well known to us all, and though we have not actually ourselves beheld one of the persons in question yet we have conversed with many who have known those who have."

"O amiable Kai Lung," observed a silkworm-keeper who had contributed to the collecting bowl without taking any part in the subsequent discussion, "the arrival of the illustrious Hong Ngou appears to have evicted us somewhat from the purpose for which we drew together at the sound of your uplifted voice. Will you not, therefore, putting aside all such comparisons and impolite references to shrubs and trees, turn our minds to more lofty images by relating the history of the incomparable Wan-taing to whom you have so flatteringly alluded?"

"The reproof is a just one," replied Kai Lung, "and although the story is not one lightly to be presented upon an ordinary occasion, yet the circumstances out of which it arises and the becoming attitude of the request cannot be honourably ignored."

1

IN AN IMPORTANT TOWNSHIP in the eastern part of Shan-Si there once lived a worker in lacquer named Sha-kien. Being the representative of his line – of a House, moreover, which had formerly occupied a position of dignified eminence – Sha-kien possessed an unusually large number of ancestral tablets and to worship fittingly before these, and, if possible, to restore to the family some of its extinguished brilliance, he caused his only son Cheng to receive a more varied and profound education that was really consistent with his poor condition. To this end Cheng persevered and meanwhile, by his dignified yet becoming attitude on all occasions, he disarmed adverse criticism. He had, it is true, an intimate knowledge of the twenty four Dynastic Histories and was able to repeat the Five Classics from beginning to end, yet with amiable broad-mindedness he did not hesitate to kow-tow respectfully to rich but illiterate merchants who approached his father's door.

When Cheng reached the age of early manhood he could not fail to become aware that the encouraging and well-satisfied cast of his father's expression towards him was changing into the settled lines of apprehensive doubt and it cannot be denied that although the youth sacrificed before the ancestral tablets with a refined elegance hitherto unknown in Lin-fi, the accomplishment failed to contribute anything to the family maintenance, and the result of his almost too-assiduous devotion was such that the time could not be far distant when there would be nothing more in the house to sacrifice.

Before this period had actually been reached an entirely new condition of affairs had come to exist. Chancing one day to hear his father enquiring, in a tone of voice from which every sympathetic modulation was absent, whether any person could account for the disappearance of a dish of silver carp which had been destined for his noon-day repast, Cheng, whose thoughts instinctively leapt back toward the ceremony and details of the morning sacrifice, deemed it expedient to pass unobserved from the house in a state of exalted mental abstraction and to spend the next few hours in a contemplative melancholy among the mountains. Here he encountered a devout woman whose particular gift enabled her to foretell the future, and also, to a somewhat less evident extent, to see through walls and rocks and into the substance of the earth. For this purpose she was widely employed to determine favourable spots for tombs, to detect the presence of hidden dragons and to read omens and cast horoscopes as the occasions arose. When Cheng first observed this opportune being his mind was heavy with the thought that the members of his own family certainly did not present any appearance of definite encouragement towards his pursuits, and filled with a reasonable curiosity to know what amount of sympathy he might rely upon elsewhere he approached the woman and courteously requested her to search into the future for the name of the maiden who was destined to occupy the crimson-covered chair of his wedding procession.

"Certainly," replied the accommodating witch, spreading before her a number of emblematic parchments and arranging them into a diversity of combinations as she proceeded; "the desire is a natural one. Before you this person sees outlined a varied and adventurous course. Across your path will fall the malignant shadow of one wearing a black pig-tail; beware such a person. There are also the indications of a journey to a distant land, dangers both ordinary and supernatural, and a final triumph.

"As regards the maiden," continued the wise woman, "the lines of destiny are so displayed that there is no possibility of doubt. She is Tsing-ai, only daughter of the wealthy Chin Paik, and although she has not yet gathered the experience of ten summers of life she is well named 'Loving Heart' from the grace and tenderness which already mark her nature. Furthermore it is assured that from this union will spring a prolific generation

which will resemble Tsing-ai in their external features and
inwardly perpetuate the valour and benevolent virtues of the
enlightened Cheng."

"So definite a pronouncement is a satisfying testimony of
your powers, O expert sorceress," said Cheng gratefully, for
the rank and position of the maiden were much higher than
anything to which he could reasonably have aspired. "Add an
even more convincing proof by predicting an early date for the
appointed ceremony."

"That is the one detail of the craft of prophecy which it is
the least prudent to engage upon," replied the wise woman.
"Be well satisfied that it will take place within its destined hour,
or this person will cheerfully return to you the gold with which,
out of your overflowing munificence, it is your intention to
reward her exertions."

"Is there not any special warning touching those whose faces
may be adversely set towards this one's destiny?" enquired
Cheng.

"I see one, indeed," admitted the woman. "One whom you
have hitherto trusted as of your household. Yet, by infallible
portents, he is treacherously inclined beneath all and has
formed a design to possess himself of a competence which in
honourable justice should be yours."

"How unfailing is your knowledge," exclaimed Cheng admiringly. "He has already succeeded in his abandoned scheme
and that piece of gold which you accurately divined it was my
intention to bestow has been engulfed together with the rest.
Nevertheless, when the more affluent future which you have
obligingly predicted unrolls itself the obligation will not be forgotten, and bear away an assurance, both in Tsing-ai's name
and my own, that the sound of your approaching footsteps will
ever be welcome at the hour of the evening meal."

It chanced that as this venerable person was returning to
Lin-fi she met Chin Paik and being desirous that her prolonged
exertion in research should not be without material benefit

more tangible than the anticipation of Cheng's honey-spread millet cakes, she bargained with him and for a sum of money much less than a person of his consequence would have been obliged to pay by the ordinary rates of divination she assured him that Cheng, son of Sha-kien of the Waste Expanses, was destined to become his son-in-law.

When Chin Paik thoroughly understood the nature of this revelation and further learned that Cheng was fully acquainted with the matter also his words and actions became so offensively unpresentable that they have wisely been allowed to pass into oblivion, but it is significantly recorded that two of those persons into whose hands the care and well-being of the district had been entrusted hastily thrust him into a passing chair, and muffling his voice within their ample flowing robes caused him to be carried at a rapid pace to the security and isolation of his own dwelling.

"Alas," exclaimed Chin Paik, when his emotions had subsided to the extent of enabling him to relate the happening coherently to his wife, "at such a moment the truth of the observation 'Even the falling dew is fatal to the beautiful maiden, but she of the down-trodden features will not drown in mid-ocean,' comes home to one with the force and precision of an expertly-wielded battle-axe. To what purpose have we held the umbrella of personal affection over Tsing-ai for a period of ten years and assiduously surrounded her with a heavily-spiked barrier of strategy and guile if she is destined to become the property of the low-born and poverty-stricken house of Sha? Apart from the indignity of such an alliance the pecuniary loss will by no means be slight."

"'Though it is certain to rain tomorrow, do not barter your sandals for an outer garment until today's journey is accomplished,'" said the wife of Chin Paik consolingly. "The arranged and premeditated lot of a person is not to be regarded as definitely as if the bridal chair was already at the door. Who, in the first place, is Cheng of the Waste Expanses?"

"A person of immature years and even slighter attainments," replied Chin Paik with undisguised contempt, "and with finger nails of no particular length. So abject are his instincts that the only view of his lineaments which he has presented to this one has been a repeated survey of the back of his head as he prostrated himself in the dust with a zeal that savoured more of an innate love of grovelling than of polite obeisance. Such elaborate servility in one who plainly regards himself as worthy to meet us on terms of equality must either spring from a sordid imagination or from a reprehensible passion for vain display, and in either case the jewel-like Tsing-ai would be sacrificed and the cost of her food and raiment for these ten years a loss beyond recall."

Then replied the wife of Chin Paik, "The insatiable curiosity which led the evil-minded Cheng to enquire of so delicate a matter as the name and position of his future wife will assuredly lure him into an endeavour to gaze upon her unveiled face before marriage – probably within a period to be counted by days. To that point this slow-witted person's preparations will tend and in the meantime let her lord pass the damp cloth of obliteration across the perturbed tablets of his mind in the full assurance of an early extrication."

In order to account more reasonably for Chin Paik's discreditable behaviour upon this occasion and for his wife's deep-seated if less grossly-expressed resentment, it is now to be explained that Tsing-ai was the most perfect and heaven-adorned maiden who has ever existed. So baffling were her charms and so diffuse the confessed enchantment of her manner that every historian of the time has turned aside from the task of describing her with a self-contemptuous feeling of total inefficiency and as a consequence no single detail of her fascinating personality has been handed down. Some, indeed, at this point have left an unwritten space in their parchments, with the obvious purpose either of returning to it when they had become more expert in the art of describing maidenly perfection, or of searching ancient records for adequate terms which they might fittingly employ; others have taken the more honourable course of asserting generally that each one of Tsing-ai's features would have conferred a lasting reputation for beauty upon a person otherwise deformed.

The advantages which might reasonably be expected from the possession of so charming a being did not long escape Chin Paik's sordid imagination and with the ill-advised obstinacy that marked many of his actions he determined to discourage every suitor of less rank than a mandarin of the ruby button, nor did his innermost thoughts hesitate to dwell upon the sublime Emperor himself. For this reason Tsing-ai was educated in the most expensive manner possible and walled in with a solicitude which, at that time, rendered her appearance unknown to any but a few.

Such perfection could hardly escape the malice of one or other of the many vindictive spirits which are ever on the alert to display their enmity towards all that is good and prepossessing. Fortunately the enlightened astrologer who had been consulted at an early period was able to learn that the danger would be at its zenith when Tsing-ai attained the age of five years and her parents were thereby enabled to take added precautions. To this end, before the indicated period arrived, Tsing-ai was one night secretly conveyed to an obscure part of the house and a carefully-selected pig, somewhat resembling her in size and superficial outline, was with equal despatch established in her place. This highly-favoured animal was on all occasions ostentatiously referred to as "Tsing-ai," it wore her delicately perfumed garments, occupied her ivory couch by night, and received frequent marks of ceremonious affection at the hands of Chin Paik and of his wife. The crafty stratagem proved entirely successful; the revengeful demons failed to notice that matters were not proceeding exactly as before, and on the very night to which the trustworthy wizard had pointed a specific warning the occupant of Tsing-ai's couch was seized by a mysterious languor and quickly passed beyond although no mark or external indication whatever could be found upon its body. After a sufficient period of mourning had been observed Tsing-ai was cautiously and gradually restored, but in order to safeguard her existence against the curiosity of any ill-disposed spirit who might be passing she was occasionally addressed as 'thou intellectual sow,' 'highly trained animal,' and other appropriate disguises, and it was commanded that she should be openly spoken of as 'the little pig' by the slaves and attendants.

It was with the memory of this providential deliverance still floating in her mind that the wife of Chin Paik resolved upon a similar course of evasion; but as a young man expecting to see a maiden of reasonable attractiveness is by no means so easily imposed upon as an implacable demon who has no personal interest in the matter would be, a more speciously-contrived project became necessary. Procuring the head of yet another pig, suitable in dimension and of not too ferocious an expression, the wife of Chin Paik removed the forefront portion and submitting it to the purifying action of spice and embalming herbs she fashioned it into a natural mask which was at once life-like and in no way objectionable. She then instructed Tsing-ai in her allotted part and laid upon the attendants commands of more than ordinary precision.

Upon the evening of the same day there came to the outer gate of Chin Paik's courtyard one having the robes and external manner of an aged woman, yet so hastily had the disguise been assumed and so deviously inexact were his footsteps as he endeavoured to move forward upon the extreme points of his feet that no one he encountered had any doubt whatever in recognising him as Cheng, the son of Sha-kien of the Waste Expanses. Nevertheless the keeper of the gate saluted him fittingly as he entered and passed to him the greeting of a jest only suitable for the perception of an aged woman, so that Cheng turned his face towards the meaner part of the house with every assurance of success.

"Behold," he exclaimed to the slave maidens who stood about the open door, "convey to your mistress, the magnanimous image of the inner chamber, the information that a cringing mendicant with her sleeves full of new and miraculous face and body essences and certain alluring breath spices from the Garden of the Twilight Nymphs is awaiting her refined permission to enter and display her wares. Also introduce a graceful compliment to the effect that the perfumes in question are admittedly unnecessary but add that they are produced by magic and are very cheap. Do this expertly and to a successful end and a phial of oil for narrowing the eye-brows will not be deemed too great a reward."

Then said one of the slave maidens, "Truly. Perchance she of the inner chamber may deem that she herself stands in no need of such arts but there is one whose deformities may lead greatly to your advantageous traffic. Have you, by any hap, philtres or charms which transform uncouth bristles into lustrous silken hair, endow a harsh brindled skin with a peach-like bloom, change protruding tusks into pearly teeth, and convert an exterior admittedly animal into the semblance of a human face?"

"The requirement is a somewhat unusual one," replied Cheng with no great certainty of tone; "though doubtless much could be accomplished by unceasing perseverance and the proper distribution of written spells. But for whom is so drastic a course of adornment required?"

"Who indeed but for the little pig of the inner chamber," replied the slave maiden. "Does it appear, thou aged and purblind beldam, that the one before you stands in need of such enchantment?" and she concentrated upon Cheng (who had hitherto not mixed freely in the society of slave maidens) a glance which impelled him to make a brilliant and complimentary reply and at the same time deprived him of all power of speech.

"There is a whisper about the walls that matters of some import will shortly take place concerning the little pig," remarked another, as the first slave departed to obey Cheng's behest. "It is credibly asserted that many years ago a more than usually prescient sorcerer discerned that before the tenth anniversary of her birth a simple-minded and ingenuous youth would approach Tsing-ai, and drawn on partly by an inexorable destiny and partly by the undoubted fascination of the grotesque and misshapen to which the ill-balanced are particularly exposed, would carry her away and honourably fulfil the obligations of marriage towards her."

At this moment an attendant carrying in her outstretched hands a wooden bowl of broken meat approached the house and would have entered, when the second slave maiden detained her, saying pleasantly,

"What is that mixture which you bear, O Hya? Surely the creatures have by this time been fed and driven back to the pastures?"

"Assuredly," replied the attendant. "This is destined for the little pig-faced one within. A brief span ago, between her fitful slumbers, she suddenly professed an insatiable craving for a repast of the kind she most loves, and this I have been bidden to prepare."

"Tarry then a moment," said the other, as the first slave maiden returned acquiescently, "for this skilled and opportune person is bidden to display her enticing profusion within, and it is not seemly that an unknown one should see our little pig in the act of feeding as her nature prompts." Thereupon Hya retired and Cheng was conducted through an intricacy of passages and into a sumptuous inner chamber. Even as he entered the unmistakable sound of a long-drawn-out and unnaturally sonorous breathing which rose and fell behind the silk-hung drapery of an inlaid couch, did not tend to reassure his mind.

"O aged woman," said the wife of Chin Paik, after courteously requesting Cheng to sit upon the floor and remove his shoes and outer garments, "it is reported that you possess very subtle preparations for adding lustre and dignity to the features of even the most commonplace. As far as this unambitious person is concerned she is now reconciled to the prospect of passing into the Upper Air with the same face as that which she has always worn, but there is one on whose account she is justly perturbed, and if your art can effect any beneficial and lasting change your mouth cannot be opened too wide in naming your reward."

"The exact requirement has not yet been definitely expressed," said Cheng, who in spite of his hopeful words began to have a very oppressive feeling on every side. "Certain allegories and ornamental flowers of conversation were, indeed, discreetly made use of, but to this person's ears they partook of the nature of amiable and affectionate raillery, as one may say to a mirthful companion 'thou genial hound,' or address a not unflattering comparison to a light-spirited maiden under the form of 'O vivacious kitten.'"

"Alas," replied the wife of Chin Paik, concealing for a moment her gracefully-proportioned head among the lace-embroidered cushions in order to screen her uncontrollable emotion, "the infliction is one of all too conspicuous actuality. It is indeed a heavy penalty to have to pay for a guiltless if unreasonably-indulged passion for sparsely-broiled pork, to have an only and tenderly-regarded child thus made the means of perpetuating her mother's indiscretion, perhaps through countless generations and to the ultimate end of peopling the Middle Flowery Land with a pig-headed and self-conceited race who will become a mock and a by-word among nations now admittedly barbaric. So far Tsing-ai's refined and complaisant disposition has shown few indications of relapsing mentally into an uncouth state of nature, yet—"

"What is this added terror?" exclaimed Cheng, as the wife of Chin Paik paused; "what new infirmity is to be heaped upon the already tottering endurance of those whose destiny it may be to become connected with the maiden? Speak, O obscure-mouthed wife of Chin Paik!"

"Who can tell the nature of the verse from the appearance of the brush, the ink, and the unwritten parchment?" replied the other. "The internal signs are yet but trivial: perchance thou, O venerable and mature-witted woman, can divine somewhat of the intention of the deities." With these words the wife of Chin Paik approached the couch from which still proceeded the ill-omened sounds and pulling aside the silken curtain indicated by a gesture that he should draw near.

The imagination of Cheng had been in a measure prepared for the sight which meet his eyes but the full circumstance was beyond his innermost dread, for the mask had been so skilfully prepared and attached that it was impossible to read in it any suggestion of not being a fixed and inherent member. As he gazed, unable to withdraw his eyes, Tsing-ai awoke and raising herself in anticipation of the bowl of food which was being prepared, moved her head forward towards Cheng, at the same time dextrously aping the continuous sounds of somewhat glut-tonous approval with which the creatures whose similitude she feigned greet an approaching meal. For yet a moment Cheng tarried, but when the disconcertingly clammy snout was thrust confidingly into his hand all thought of disguise or of ceremo-nious leave-taking passed from his mind and abandoning his cramping shoes and the greater part of his garments he pro-pelled himself rapidly through wall after wall until he reached the outer air where he was presently seen surmounting every obstacle and recklessly spreading his limbs across the country in an undeviating line towards the Waste Expanses.

In the solitude of his own chamber Cheng passed in review before his mind the many-hued incidents of the day. He now understood that the approving countenances of the maiden's parents towards one in his inferior circumstances would be by no means so remarkable and disinterested an attitude as it had first appeared to be. Next there arose a disturbing emotion regarding his own father's face towards the matter, conferring, as such an alliance would, honours and definite remuneration by no means to be lightly rejected in their necessitous condition. The pointing of insidiously-worded reproaches that one who was so zealous in offering up even the mid-day meal of another should hesitate to sacrifice himself for the common good, would, Cheng felt confident, occupy the greater part of the conversation within his home, and whatever possibility there might be of escaping one's destiny in an ordinary course, there could be little doubt that destiny assisted by two deeply-interested and self-willed families would in the end be unevadable.

From the meshes of this doubly-strung net flight seemed to offer the only unguarded channel. This decision to one who had ever been of a tame and affectionate nature was not alluring, but as he weighed the various surroundings an added incentive fell heavily into the balance for amid the pangs of separation he found himself dwelling on the thought of leaving Tsing-ai with a palpable regret. Now that the full effect of her disconcerting appearance was no longer before his eyes he had begun to question within himself whether the matter was really so pronounced as it had at the time appeared to be, and whether he had not been guilty of an undignified haste in coming to a definite decision and acting upon it. If (to express the reasoning as it now presented itself to him) Tsing-ai's features did chance to be rather more concave than those of maidens in general, there were not wanting philosophers of the highest excellence who had declared that beauty designed by a rigid adherence to fixed principles was most intolerably monotonous and devoid of charm. This inconsistency on Cheng's part was undoubtedly owing to two causes: for the wife of Chin Paik had, at the last moment, found herself reluctant to make the adorable Tsing-ai seem more unnatural than was necessary and had, in consequence, selected the most prepossessing and daintily-proportioned pig that she could find, while Tsing-ai's admitted fascination was so great that it had the power to shine through and embellish as it were even the inflexible mask which she wore; so that, to this day, the saying 'Like Tsing-ai's mask, – without Tsing-ai behind it' has remained as a compliment of doubtful application. To Cheng's mind, however, his indecision had another source, for when he had reached the point of assuring himself that the maiden's nose was really not ungracefully poised, her eye-brows little more than delicately arched and her complexion merely that of a rich and interesting pallor, the words spoken by the second slave suddenly recurred to him. No longer doubting that he was a person of ill-balanced mental outlook and that he was even then passing under the spell of Tsing-ai's deformity he at once gathered together his possessions, took up a staff, and leaving the house secretly – for the night had fallen – turned his face towards the north.

In the meantime Chin Paik had not been passing the time pleasantly in his own company. He was, it has been remarked by those who were the best acquainted with his usual manner, a person who would have succeeded in whatever he undertook had he been sufficiently discriminating to leave the matter entirely to his wife and to bar himself within his inner chamber until it had been accomplished. On this occasion, instead of following her solicitous advice and retiring for a few days to a summer pagoda which he had built on the extreme point of a pleasantly-situated mountain until she sent him tidings that Cheng had definitely fled from the neighbourhood, he set out to return to Lin-fi on the plea that he had already pledged himself to meet one with whom he was desirous of trafficking for the purchase of a goat. Entreating his wife not to await him but to retire to her couch at the usual hour as the self-willed animal might embarrass and retard his returning footsteps, Chin Paik set forth and would doubtless have returned either with the object of his quest or with an honourable account of the circumstances by which the deficiency arose had he not chanced to encounter the wise woman who earlier in the day had obliged Cheng in the prediction of his future.

As a final resort Chin Paik's wife had imposed upon him a bond of secrecy respecting all that had taken place. It cannot be doubted that he would have rigidly upheld this obligation as far as it concerned persons who were in no way involved, but, as Chin Paik repeatedly protested to his wife on after occasions, it did not seem reasonable to be continuously upon one's guard with a person of supernatural attainments. As the one in question was able to penetrate into an obscure and far-removed future with little inconvenience to herself, so recent an event in the past must of necessity be practically before her eyes in precise and vividly-outlined details. Not regarding the meeting in the light which it subsequently appeared would have been the prudent one to adopt, and being at the time in a magnanimous and austerity-bending mood, when every circumstance and surrounding object seemed to be very brilliantly illuminated and festively-inclined, Chin Paik approached the sorceress and proceeded to explain the stratagem of events connected with Cheng's discouragement, ingeniously devising the narration into the semblance of a fable which from time to time contained subtle jests at her expense in the matter of predictions and diverting allusions to the consternation of those in the Upper Air when they found how dextrously Cheng had been led aside. When he had finished instead of replying in a similar amiable strain, as he had expected, the aged woman suddenly turned upon him with an expression of most tiger-like resentment.

"O mean-spirited and injudicious Chin Paik," she exclaimed, and at the tone of her voice and the sight of the mystic characters which she began to trace upon the ground with her staff most of the excessive radiance faded from Chin Paik's surroundings and the involved problems of life appeared to be quite as numerous and insoluble as before, "thou weasel-headed one with the heart of a grasshopper, the voice of a corncrake, and the lower limbs of a paralytic elephant, how hast thou presumed to thrust in thy objectionable body between the Upper

Ones and their fixed purpose, rendering their pronouncements outwardly illusory and destroying this hard-striving person's prophetic reputation in Lin-fi by openly displaying her as an eater of her own words and one whose omens are ineffective and whose visions cannot be relied upon?"

"Behold!" exclaimed Chin Paik in some confusion, "—"

"It is well said," continued the aged person, regarding Chin Paik as though he were one who had no actual existence on the spot, "that the snail may travel a thousand li by sitting on the camel's tail, but the ill-witted outcast who attempts to press in between the deities and one of their authentically-inspired soothsayers will find himself in the unenviable position of the person who remained beneath the avalanche in order to protect his chrysanthemums. Having thus expressed her own private opinion and being desirous of passing on to matters of greater import this one, Aing Nu, possessor of a fragment of the Tooth and reader of the illuminated sky-signs, having completed the necessary charms and invocations now makes a definite request that she and the space about shall be surrounded by demons—"

"Alas!" protested Chin Paik, "—"

"that the ground beneath shall be thickly peopled with dragons of the earth, that shadows and apparitions shall fill the air above and that spirits of all kinds shall be in readiness to carry out her words whatever they may be."

"Tarry yet a—"

"Being well convinced that these precautions have been efficiently carried out she now proceeds to throw herself into a responsive condition and to speak the words that are placed within her understanding: Although it is sometimes permitted, Chin Paik, that creatures of the lower world should hold their faces inflexibly against high decrees and should appear to proceed towards their own ends yet the arms of the Upper Ones are as long as the chain of the Pe-ling Mountains, their grasp as wide as the range from The Wall to the Bitter Waters of the

South and their nails as smoothly curved as the flight of an eagle's wing, as sharp as the lightning's edge. That which you have moved to avoid shall come to pass, O Chin Paik, and as a reward for your obstinacy it shall be attended by poverty, loss of friends, severe pains in your limbs, and by other disagreeable indications of celestial displeasure. Cheng and Tsing-ai shall long continue to live happily together in Lin-fi and by their affable and charitable conduct they will reflect upon themselves the honourable distinction that has been totally deficient in your life. As regards your real punishments, which will commence when you reach the Upper Air, they will consist—"

At this point Chin Paik, who suddenly came to the narrow-minded conclusion that his own comfort would be in no way increased by remaining, encircled his arms as completely as he could about his head and thus protected cast himself upon the invisible barrier of spirits and succeeded in forcing his way through. Without pausing he continued in flight until he reached his own house. Incredible as it may appear, with the intolerance of the dull-witted, Chin was still determined to oppose the intentions of the deities, but in order to guard himself as much as possible in his impiety he resolved to move to a considerable distance from Lin-fi. To this end he commanded his wife to follow him with all his possessions at a more convenient leisure, and taking Tsing-ai by the hand he set out to escape to the south without making any further preparation whatever.

It so chanced that at the Bridge of the Eight Directions he encountered Cheng, fleeing to the north. Tsing-ai, who was compelled by the impatient haste of her father's footsteps to leap continuously forward by his side, still wore her little mask; for in the turmoil of departure it had been forgotten and she was of too amiable and respectful a nature to protest against the inconvenience which she suffered. At that moment the great sky-lantern passed out from behind a cloud and displayed the features and unnatural pallor of the head in an even more disconcerting prominence than before, so that Cheng cast himself to the ground unreservedly scarcely doubting but that the two persons had learned of his intention and were urging their footsteps to the Waste Expanses to bargain with his father before he left. Chin Paik, for his part, plainly recognised Cheng lying prostrate in his usual attitude before him, and at once springing to the conclusion that the one in question had detected the imposition and was hastening to demand Tsing-ai in marriage, he pressed forward with redoubled speed.

As they passed each gave the other the dignified greeting of courteous formality, "Slowly, slowly; walk slowly," but so rapid were their movements that before their words were well uttered, both had melted from the possibility of the keenest vision. Cheng did not pause until he had effectually eluded pursuit by losing himself within one of the most obscure and involved quarters of Pekin; while at the same moment Chin Paik, with every satisfaction at having placed such barriers of distance and obstruction behind him, crossed the furthest limits of Shan-Si and entered the province of Ho-Nan.

2

"Alas! To what purpose are the allurements of a maiden who resides in the barbarous district of western Ho-Nan where there are none but earth-tillers and hereditary mendicants to hear the report! Can it justly be a matter of reproach to one thus positioned that she has reached the humiliating span of fifteen rice harvests without being made the object of a fitting offer? Let it not be regarded as an indelicate utterance but if the one who is now openly expressing her mind were again transported to her native province, the future would soon be arranged very differently from what there is every likelihood of its remaining in this abandoned clime."

The one who revealed her innermost feelings in this lucid and dignified manner was a maiden of exceptional but well-matured beauty who stood alone on the southern bank of the Hoang Ho, and waved her hands in ornamental gestures of despair towards the inopportune waters which separated her from the well-remembered province of her earlier years. Having thus disclosed her words and sentiments it cannot reasonably be withheld that the one in question was the maiden called Tsing-ai, and in order to make the matter less complicated this may be freely admitted.

As she stood, involved in a meditative depression, there approached by a path on the riverside a young man of high and commanding appearance, very sumptuously apparelled, and followed at a respectful distance by an imposing company of bearers and attendants. Seeing so fair a creature he tactfully commanded his followers to conceal themselves lest the unexpected sight of so many persons of the opposite sex should disconcert her unduly. Having by this delicate precaution safeguarded her emotions he went forward alone and standing in a courteous attitude before her he enquired whether out of the magnanimity of her nature she could describe to him the residence of one Quang-te Nung of that place, spoken of as a Watcher of the Waters.

"O solitary passer-by," said Tsing-ai, "if your remark were one of ordinary triviality, this maiden must certainly have ignored your not inelegant personality altogether, but your question reveals some connection with a matter which concerns herself. Are you not, indeed, Wan-taing, by repute the most skilful and relentless pain-extractor of the Capital?"

"Touching the name and the manner of occupation the facts are undeniable," replied Wan-taing modestly.

"Of the other details this one will doubtless be able to form an unbiased judgement on her own account," replied Tsing-ai, with an expression of her eyes plainly intimating that she entertained no concern as to the nature of the judgement alluded to; "for she is the only daughter of the Quang-te Nung in question. His residence is that marked by two tall crimson poles of ornamental design and even on the blackest night it can generally be recognised by the unrestrained cries proceeding from it – of agony if this person's father is suffering from a more than usually close embrace of his malady, or of rage and derision if he is engaged in the ordinary formalities of social intercourse."

"Alas," exclaimed Wan-taing, "is he then a person of so disputatious a nature and one whom it is difficult to approach with honourable proposals?"

"Not to an absolutely insuperable degree," replied Tsing-ai, tempering her reply equally between the fact as it existed and a desire not utterly to discourage the one before her. "Formerly he was of light and genial nature but since this person's mother passed beyond and her restraining influence vanished it is undeniable that he has developed a more assertive and pugnacious disposition. Yet it cannot be doubted that this is principally due to the intolerable weight of his affliction. Will you not, then, journey thither with all speed to the end that this may be removed without delay?"

"Assuredly," replied Wan-taing; "yet a certain time must elapse in ascertaining whether the conditions around are favourable towards the enterprise, as well as preparing the necessary spikes and implements, and already the sun has passed behind the mountains. At an early gong stroke of the morrow, however—"

"It is reasonably said, 'The person who speaks of "Tomorrow" to a supplicating maiden will reply "The year after next" to his wife's petition,'" recited Tsing-ai reproachfully. "Lightly do you condemn this one's father to another period of acute suffering and herself to an enforced contemplation of the unseemly cries and remarks thereby wrested from him."

"There is yet another cause," replied Wan-taing, advancing a step nearer to Tsing-ai and holding towards her his right hand which shook somewhat. "Behold the hand that has never trembled in its exacting duties, not even when it was necessary to push a long spiked instrument completely through the sacred shoulder of the sublime Emperor himself. When the deviation of a single tremor from its appointed line might be fatal how can so irresponsible a member be relied upon; and whence, O maiden, springs its unwonted frailty?"

"It is said that the night air arising from the marshes of the river may produce such an effect," replied Tsing-ai, yet addressing herself rather to an illuminated figure upon the heavily-gilt fan which she carried than to the one before her. "Perchance—"

"Perchance," exclaimed Wan-taing, advancing another step nearer to her and holding out both his hands, "perchance it is because there stands before him one whose glances are sharper and more destructively-inclined than the most highly-burnished instrument in all his store, whose smile is more gratifying than the most successfully-carried-out perforation; one, moreover, who seems to be agitating subtly within his mind the end of an elusive thread of which he cannot grasp the beginning. The mists arising from the Hoang Ho may indeed be ague-laden, but the danger of gazing upon one who—"

But at this point Tsing-ai formed an opinion that that matter was being expressed too closely as regarded her own attributes for her to remain, whereupon she fled in high-minded agitation. Wan-taing then ordered certain of his attendants to erect his tent in that place, and throughout the length of the night he remained with his head unceasingly pressed to the ground on the spot which Tsing-ai's delicately proportioned feet had last occupied.

At this point some details of Chin Paik's existence since his flight from Lin-fi may be suitably brought to light. As he had abandoned the lucrative appointment which constituted his sole means of support it became necessary that he should obtain some other official position without delay; for, not possessing a sufficient intelligence to grasp the requirements of any commerce or profession, no other manner of livelihood was open to him. In this he was aided by a friend of high position in the Department of Shelves and Protests who pointed out to

those in authority that unless Chin Paik was given this opportunity of supporting himself he must inevitably be maintained
at considerable expense out of public funds. Readily percciv-
ing the economy which they thereby effected these persons
conferred on Chin Paik the office of Watcher of the Waters
and Repairer of the Hoang Ho Banks for the district in which
he resided. The appointment is one at no time very enviously
regarded from the nature of its disadvantages; for the annual
amount allotted to the repairing of the banks is considerably
less than that actually necessary to carry out the work with
a systematic and diligent exactitude, and as it is an essential
detail that the Watcher of the Waters shall live upon the banks
under his charge, a total disregard of the obligations, although
it may for the time prove very remunerative, is destined to
overwhelm him fatally sooner or later. Nevertheless Chin Paik
accepted the offer without demur, cheerfully remarking that
doubtless favourable occasions for securing an adequate recompense would present themselves, and adding that one could
not expect to be created a Receiver of Customs or appointed
to negotiate international treaties until one had shown a capacity for making the best use of smaller opportunities.

Assuming the official title of Quang-te Nung and approaching his duties in the tolerant and broad-minded spirit already
indicated, Chin Paik (as he may still be fittingly referred to, when
addressing those who are in possession of the full circumstances)
zealously began to carry out the first part of his service and for
a period he watched the waters with untiring diligence. For the
space of three moons he found the government allowance equal
to his requirement, but about that time there arose disquieting
rumours of the approaching Season of Much Rain and the conversation of those with whom he talked was invariably of the
exposed position of his house and of the relentless havoc that the
escaping waters had wrought in every former year. Perceiving
that his own house was, indeed, the nearest to the river, which
even in ordinary times stood some paces above the level of the

surrounding country from which it was restrained by earthen banks, Chin Paik experienced an emotion of disgust that his predecessor had not carried out his duties more thoroughly, for it was plain to see that the barriers, and especially those on his side, would prove contemptibly inefficient.

In this emergency Chin Paik addressed himself to the inhabitants of the village of Ko, distant only a few li from his residence, pointing out to them the danger under which they existed and urging them to strengthen the river walls without delay. This appeal proved completely futile, for the village in question chanced to be peopled by a race directly descended from the Incomparable Philosopher, and as a mark of Imperial recognition it had been decreed that persons of this tribe should be exempt from the necessity of engaging in manual labour. So highly esteemed was this privilege that for many generations past those of Ko had done no work whatever, nor did the threat of an impending calamity disturb them. "Doubtless," remarked the most venerable, "the illustrious Waterman little anticipated that simple villagers would possess so refined a sense of dignity, but though poverty-stricken in the extreme we of the line of the Imperishable Sage cannot be bought." The others, also, to whom Chin Paik spoke replied in a like strain, holding it to be a very honourable end, that of being drowned in defending their principles.

On the north bank of the river stood the village of Yun, whose inhabitants were of a frugal and industrious disposition. These persons agreed that those who prophesied floods and devastation spoke with their eyes and not their imagination; but asserting out of the remembrance of former experiences that it was less painful to be drowned than to be starved to death, they resolutely declined to leave the harvesting of their rice until Chin Paik would recompense them in advance; nor could the most specific promises of written and signet-bearing undertakings entice them from this decision. Deeply regretting this ill-bred display of short-sighted mistrust, Chin Paik withdrew for a time in dignified unapproachableness, but finding that it was not the intention of the villagers to seek him out with reduced demands – while each day the waters of the Hoang Ho rose by a perceptible finger breadth – it soon became necessary for him to return to Yun bearing with him the amount of money demanded.

The result was that which every prudent observer must have anticipated. The degraded outcasts of Yun repaired their own bank with untiring energy and skill, but being assured within themselves that nothing would prove effective against the ever-increasing waters, and not unreasonably desiring that the expected deluge should take place on the side furthest removed from their own interests, they naturally weakened the endurance of the southern bank, undermining its defences and secretly conveying the material to add to the stability of their own barriers. From this cause the day very soon arrived when Chin Paik for the first time understood the meaning of the tall ornamental poles standing in his courtyard.

It need scarcely be a matter of wonder or reproach to Chin Paik that from that time forward he steadfastly declined to sacrifice any part of his income either on the north or the south bank of the Hoang Ho, or to take any interest whatever in the river's movements beyond duly reporting at stated periods that matters were going on as satisfactorily as before and that the defences were visibly growing as the season advanced. Yet in spite of this economy Chin Paik was not really comfortable. The necessity of spending the greater part of his time with the lower half of his body submerged beneath the flood which was now an ever-present actuality at his door began, with advancing years, to press heavily upon his mind so that the genial effusiveness that had formerly been a part of his nature melted away as it were and none but strangers unacquainted with his too-often irrelevant words and gestures greeted him with the polite "Slowly, slowly; walk slowly," or the well-intentioned "How is your inside?" when they encountered him wading with

uncertain movements in the neighbourhood of Ko or of Yun.
To add to his discomfort the wife who was so necessary to his
welfare languished unaccountably and finally passed into the
Upper Air; nor, when the facts of the situation were thoroughly
understood, could Chin Paik persuade anyone of suitable descent and attainment to fill her place. Tsing-ai, indeed, still
remained by his side and by her adorable perfection she would
have transformed a seat beneath a leafless poplar in the middle
of a burning desert into a cool and thirst-assuaging oasis but
even in this Chin Paik's deformed perception found no relief
for it had been the aim and beginning of his evasion and the
cause of all his subsequent misfortune that none of less rank
than a mandarin of the first degree should approach Tsing-ai,
and he now found, so unenviable was the repute in which the
district was held, that he could by no pretext induce even a
minor official to make the required journey. In an access of
despair he was contemplating going to the Capital himself and
imploring certain high nobles to return with him (for the expedient of taking Tsing-ai did not occur to his already failing intellect) when the imprecation revealed by the wise woman Aing
Nu gradually closed in about him and severe pains declared
their presence in his lower limbs. When the floods again appeared Chin Paik found himself incapable of taking his daily
wade and by the time they receded he was unable to leave his
couch save by the painful and undignified action of rolling off
onto the floor. A Yun extractor of pain (who also taught logic
and trafficked in abandoned garments) was summoned and
after measuring Chin Paik's dimensions and testing his faculties by means of coloured powders, he asserted that the most
reasonable expedient would be to hew away the limbs utterly
as they were manifestly of no real service where they were, but
on the contrary inflicted suffering upon the entire body and
necessitated an expenditure for apparel. In this extremity Chin
Paik chanced to hear of Wan-taing, of whom it was credibly
reported that he had never yet been compelled to sever any

portion of the body and had even replaced and healed an arm which had been removed by an inferior and less adventurous one, and by offering an unusual reward for his inimitable services he induced him to come to his assistance.

Wan-taing was at that moment the most expert and highly-rewarded extractor of pain within the Capital. In spite of his riches – for jewels and priceless fragments of porcelain were almost daily dropped into his sleeve by grateful ones – and of the company of praise-chanters which ever surrounded his chair, he did not present the external appearance of being completely happy and it was chiefly to escape if possible from the funereal vapour of an indefinite yearning that he allowed Chin Paik's really insignificant offer to have any influence over his movements.

In order to grasp more intelligently Wan-taing's unique position and his manner of extracting pain it must be understood at once that he was not one of those – like the obscure and incompetent person of Yun – who without any definite and settled method apply to every case submitted to their operation the remedy which seems to be the best fitted for the occasion – administering decoctions of rare bones and relics, removing a seemingly unpropitious influence, or binding up the afflicted parts with inscribed charms, more or less at a confessed venture. To Wan-taing's acuter perception this inconsistence involved a great and avoidable risk, as it would be conceivable for an excessively ill-destined person never to chance upon the correct remedy in the case of a single person, whereas by applying the same specific in every emergency it must inevitably be of use occasionally. Nor can it be ignored that those who adopt a special and well-defined method of removing pain, adhering to it on all occasions, receive higher rewards than do the variable and are permitted to reside in a healthy and very honourably-esteemed quarter of the city.

Of the nine distinct branches of the art of pain dispelling to which custom and the classical records give approval none appeared, on deep reflection, to be so reasonable to Wan-taing as that which consists in thrusting needles and other spiked objects into the seat of the disorder, for by no other means is the contending element (which not infrequently takes the form of a revengeful demon) afforded a free and uninterrupted way of escape. Only the method of scarification seemed in any way comparable with the obvious advantages of acupuncture and to Wan-taing's thorough and resolute mind scarification did not go deep enough into the matter; yet it is an admitted fact that up to that time needle-thrusting had suffered one deficiency and this became evident when the cause of the malady resolutely declined to avail itself of the opportunity for escape. Some who practised the art were driven in such cases to the use of specially prepared implements with barbed extremities, by which they hoped to drag out the most stubborn disorder; but added to the objection of never knowing at what point they had achieved success was the continual loss they sustained through the barbs becoming too firmly embedded to be withdrawn. It remained for Wan-taing to make his brand of treatment effective beyond question, by the inspired device of gradually heating the protruding shaft of the implement until an internal condition was created which not even the most obstinate demon could resist.

At an early hour of the day following that on which Tsing-ai had bewailed herself upon the banks of the Hoang-Ho, the beating of many hollow stones, wooden bowls and other musical instruments in the neighbourhood of Chin Paik's house announced the approach of some person of consequence. Preceded by attendants who displayed aloft needles and spiked instruments of gigantic proportions, to the concern and admiration of all the inhabitants of Ko and Yun, and surrounded by a full retinue appropriate to the position of a high official, Wan-taing presented himself before the leaf-shaped door and commanded that tablets, bearing his name, degrees and attainments, together with some graceful verses containing a special reference to the fact that he had completely punctured the jade shoulder of the benign and many-sided Emperor, should be carried to the chief one within.

It was one of the indications of Chin Paik's malady that although he was never really conciliatory at some times he was much more offensively-disposed than at others, but never, in the estimation of those whose lot it was to stand in his presence, was he so far removed from presenting an agreeable surface as upon this occasion. With no thought of engendering a feeling of resentment in his mind Tsing-ai had told him of the arrival of the expert young pain dispeller and had related some portion of her unsuccessful appeal, but to Chin Paik's mist-obscured mind this necessary postponement took the form of a deliberate and contemptuous insult. He had passed the night in alternately trying to lose himself in the Middle Air when his sufferings grew too acute and in blindly groping to return to the condition of a wakeful existence when dragon-dreams became unbearably oppressive, and incapably persuading himself that Wan-taing was directly responsible for these inflictions in that he had not come at once to prevent them, he was prepared to greet him as unbecomingly as the circumstances would permit without becoming legally malicious.

"Ha, daintiest of needle-men," he exclaimed, not offering the really essential hospitality of ceremonious tea or even attempting to descend from his couch, "perchance your habits are so leisurely-inclined you will make whole the deficiencies of this person's robe while you are engaged with your implements," and Chin Paik, searching, feigned to discover a rent in the sleeve of his robe.

"A torn garment can be restored, an afflicted body healed perchance, but the mind that is wilfully tangled and the heart that is obstinately bad cannot be reached from without," replied Wan-taing in a tone of impassive dignity. With these words he offered to Chin Paik a spike of formidable dimensions, adding, "Search yourself internally, thou caster of pointless jibes."

At this moment the person of Yun, who had thrust himself into the chamber on the pretext of being engaged in the operation, approached Wan-taing, and being totally deficient of the one-to-another etiquette he explained unbidden, "Honourable greeting, O brother of the pale pink powder and the scraping irons! Can it be, as it is confidently reported, that you intend to subject the amiable Quang-te Nung to the doubtful process of perforation? Would it not be more discreet to cleave away the lower portion of the body at once, by reason of the following logical—"

By this time Wan-taing, who was accustomed to be deferentially supported in all his pronouncements by the highest and most venerable pain dispellers of Pekin, recovered sufficiently from his unassumed surprise to move his eyebrows slightly in a preconcerted sign, whereupon two of his attendants seized the intolerable person of Yun by the extremities and placed him carelessly among the ornamental rocks which lay at a distance beneath the window. At a further gesture four others surrounded Chin Paik's couch and threw back the loose portions of their dress in readiness to obey their master's next commands no matter what they might involve.

"O really accomplished spike-user," cried Chin Paik, "surely this adroit display of the highly-trained vigour and harmonious precision of your engaging slaves is lost upon this commonplace being." In spite of his presumptuous words and general manner of standing upon those with whom he conversed Chin Paik was in reality quite deficient of courageousness and at the sight of Wan-taing's firm but unassuming preparation his heart began to slip elusively from his internal grasp.

"Men speak upon all sides of you with a smooth tongue, Wan-taing," he continued; "yet it cannot be denied that your manner of commencing the enterprise savours more of the captain of a band of Chu-san pirates than of a peaceable-minded remover of pain. Call off your somewhat bloodthirsty-looking attendants, therefore, and then this person's mind will become flattened out into a more confident feeling of assured tranquillity."

"'Fallen water is hard to pick up,'" quoted Wan-taing, plainly referring to the irrevocable contempt of Chin Paik's greeting. "'Yet when the wolf disappears within his lair the watch-dogs may be prudently recalled.'" With these words of reconciliation the lenient Wan-taing commanded the attendants so that they stepped back a pace from surrounding the couch but did not completely disperse from about Chin Paik, then drawing near he spoke for that one's ear alone, saying, "Listen well, O contumacious Quang-te Nung, and decide. Already I have pierced the subtlety of your malady and speaking with unvarnished lips it is no boastful word that I alone can restrain it."

"Your manner inspires confidence," replied Chin Paik. "Do not hesitate to begin."

"There is yet a detail," continued Wan-taing. "The flavour of your reception has already obliterated any agreement between us, and were there no added incentive this person's face would already be turned away from the inhospitable region of western Ho-Nan, leaving you in full possession of your afflicted extremities. But, unconsciously, a benignant spirit has intervened on your behalf and the remembrance of your enchanting daughter's perfections is strong enough to hold back my footsteps and to make me willing to regard your general offensiveness in the light of the ordinary courtesy of the neighbourhood. Remove your trivial little offering of gold, therefore, and let the more glittering being alluded to stand in its place as the reward of success and this one will persevere to an inspired victory even though it should involve the use and destruction of every spike and needle in his possession."

"Alas," replied Chin Paik, "the outlook is not alluring. The absence of the melodious Tsing-ai and the presence of the intolerable demon in this person's extremities are two considerations which evenly balance one another. Is there no other alternative?"

"To a definite end has it been spoken," said Wan-taing, already displaying on a table near at hand a profusion of implements and beginning to test their qualities.

"Yet," continued Chin Paik, "it had ever been the intention of those concerned that Tsing-ai should marry one not less in degree than a mandarin of the highest rank."

"Doubtless a mandarin of the first degree is acceptable among the wilds of western Ho-Nan," replied Wan-taing, concealing his refined disdain not unmingled with amusement at being compared with a person of such ordinary distinction, "but in Pekin one who has been endowed with the Three-Eyed Peacock Feather and granted the privilege of riding with purple reins, as a reward for the intrepid dexterity with which he pierced the left shoulder of the all-knowing Emperor, employs mandarins of the first degree to open the door of his chariot or to fan him to sleep."

"Yet if the perforation were unsuccessful and this person still remained a prey to his malignant disorder?" demanded Chin Paik, in no wise impressed by the recital of Wan-taing's exceptional honours, chiefly because he was so closely occupied with his own remarks that he paid practically no attention to those addressed to him.

"In such a contingency," replied Wan-taing, who always looked at failure with closed eyes, "the advantage would necessarily lie either with you or with the demon concerned, for this one would be compelled to return to his own land carrying with him neither maiden nor money."

On this avowal Chin Paik declared himself ready to submit to the trial whereupon the other selected a weapon of suitable proportions and manipulating it so skilfully that it bent to his touch in whatsoever direction he willed, as gracefully as a swallow in its flight among the tangled branches of a forest, he drove it among the bones of Chin Paik's knee until it reached the innermost point of the disorder. By subtle indications as he withdrew it he at once knew that the object had been achieved, so that with an enlightened triumph in his voice he bade Chin Paik rise from his couch and test his regained powers.

"Alas!" exclaimed Chin Paik, affecting to make the attempt unsuccessfully, "alas, the matter stands for all essential details as it did before."

"Other and more effective means must then be tried," said Wan-taing, not by the faintest deviation of his voice admitting that he had pierced the guile of Chin Paik's unworthy strata-gem. "Ho, slaves, prepare the charcoal brazier!"

At these words, and the understanding of what they her-alded, Chin Paik suddenly attempted to leap from off his couch but the four attendants, to whom such a manifestation was by no means unknown, flung themselves upon him and withheld him, each seizing a limb and heaping the lavishly-ornamented cushions upon his head.

"Truly the demon is not yet driven forth," remarked Wan-taing, again inserting an instrument and applying the pan of fire to the protruding shaft; "and it is a most usual proceeding among creatures of this class to throw those whom they are afflicting into a frenzy when they learn that their period of mastery is at an end. Do not fear the ultimate end, O intrepid Quang-te Nung, but endeavour to lose yourself for the time in the inward contemplation of some simple and mind-compos-ing occupation, such as the imagined numbering of a flock of goats passing through a narrow opening."

After the first outburst Chin Paik had restrained himself but at the mention of the ill-savoured word 'goat' those who held his limbs were observed to sway to and fro, in spite of being attendants specially selected on account of their massive and enduring frames, like bamboos in a wind-storm. Wan-taing still continued to apply the fire, remarking, "The conflict has every promise of becoming a desperate one, O heroic sufferer, and this one's head aches for you, but do not despair. Those around will not slacken their embrace nor abandon you to the subjec-tion of so intolerable a spirit; and with the illuminated image of the ultimate reward before him, this infatuated pain extractor will cheerfully reduce every implement in his possession to a shapeless mass of molten iron rather than admit defeat and leave empty-handed." Thereupon the four attendants took a more tenacious grasp upon Chin Paik's limbs although by this time their faces were concealed behind the mists of their exertion and the cracking of their teeth as they were driven one into another in unquenchable determination resembled the continual firing of matchlocks.

"The shaft already glows redly," observed Wan-taing, so that Chin Paik might know that his conscientious efforts were not relaxed. "Presently it will sink into a dazzling whiteness which in ordinary cases is of almost irresistible potency. Should this not be effective, and the too pertinacious demon still continue to defy the high-principled Quang-te Nung, it will be necessary to employ really—" but at this point the voice of Chin Paik was heard faintly protesting that he already felt better, and asserting that he had no doubt whatever that the cause of his affliction had at last been subdued and driven out.

"The admission is a generous and an unqualified one," remarked Wan-taing, "and the beneficent consummation is in a large measure due to your own characteristic persistence. Abandon your couch now, O deep-headed Quang-te Nung, and give a display of your restored agility so that those around may be convinced of its reality. Otherwise there might arise a whisper that you do but speak out of the overflowing channels of your unfathomable good nature, and in order to safeguard his reputation this person may be driven into the use of more formidable persuasion."

In the face of this suggestion Chin Paik descended from his couch and although the violence of the exertion was so highly-sustained that even his pig-tail projected in a rigid and self-reliant attitude he succeeded in walking unassisted round the room and returned to his couch to receive the well-merited congratulations of all.

"The removal of any trivial appearance of inflexibility will be in the nature of a gradual fading away, brought about by the mitigating and unaided passage of time," continued Wan-taing. "Also, in future profit by the example of the sagacious crane and when journeying to and fro in the season of inundation raise yourself above the waters by means of capable but insensible substitutes. Now, my venerated father-in-law, whose name shall henceforth be regarded in my devotions as second in importance to that of my own sire alone, let the minstrels be summoned, and bid they of the inner chamber prepare the red silk veil."

"Truly, it is written, 'Expedition in an official and tardiness on the part of a suitor cease to be virtues,'" admitted Chin Paik, "but there are many details of more or less elaborate necessity and lengthy preparation which it is scarcely seemly to ignore. The amiable exchange of mutual gifts—"

"'"Today" is a secure footing for an army; "tomorrow" will scarcely support one man clutching with his hands and feet,'" quoted Wan-taing. "For a gift accept this auspicious needle which will ever serve to remind you of your own distinguished endurance. Upon it is inscribed the appropriate remark, 'Like Tohung Ling's sword when opposed to treachery – only one blow but that always decisive.'"

"How oppressive would be Tsing-ai's emotions to go forth without a proper concealment of pearls," continued Chin Paik, with no immediate appearance of acting as the other had suggested. "What but misfortune could follow a neglect of the emblematic fire—"

"Pearls would lose their lustre in despair and crumble into dust if opposed to such fairness," replied Wan-taing. "For the ceremonious fire nothing could be more fitting than that Wan-taing should receive his bride over this censer by which he has won her,"

"Nevertheless," persisted the refractory Chin Paik, moving towards the door and disclosing an expression of obstinacy in no way friendly towards Wan-taing's ambition, "there are yet many things to be adjusted before the arrangement can be definitely complete."

At this avowal of perfidy Wan-taing plainly recognised that a moment of action would be more effective than a day spent in the closest deliberation. "*Ho, slaves—*" he cried aloud, but there was no necessity to express the matter more fully, for so benumbing was the impression created on Chin Paik's mind by Wan-taing's former manner of acting that at this well-remembered and awe-inspiring summons he threw up his hands and commanded that Tsing-ai should be prepared for the ceremony without delay.

A very brief span of time later Tsing-ai was led forward into the room and by the most meagre essentials of words and formalities she was thenceforward separated from all ties of kinship other than those of the house of Wan-taing, and ceremoniously received into the possession of that one to have every authority over her which did not involve cruelly breaking any important bonds. Wan-taing, on his part, specifically bound himself to maintain her fittingly both in years of plenty and of famine; not to disown her for less cause than the seven just motives of childlessness, habitual jealousy, leprosy, talkativeness, a propensity to theft, wantonness, or persisting in a disrespectful attitude towards his parents; and to provide for her a sufficiency of flowers for the hair, ear-rings and bracelets of jade and metal, and suitable raiment.

Wan-taing next gave certain instructions to his carriers who presently laid at his feet a number of sacks containing silver and gold pieces in unlimited profusion. These the munificent pain-dispeller proceeded to distribute with large hands among the assembled crowds from Ko and Yun, and so unstinted was his benevolence that even Chin Paik could not restrain himself from drawing near and under the pretext of brushing away such coins as were descending near him securing no inconsiderable portion within his capacious sleeves. Bales of merchandise were then thrown open and from these Wan-taing, acting in the mild and conciliatory spirit that had inspired him throughout the enterprise, invested his father-in-law in many changes of rich apparel and made fitting gifts to all of his household. Nor were his own attendants forgotten; such as hitherto had been slaves obtained their freedom from that day, together with an added sum of money, while the free-born received great stores of coarser traffic, each one being at liberty to bear away as much as he could carry of corn, of dried fruit and of cotton cloth. Yet this unsparing liberality had but touched the outside edge of his store, so that when he led forth Tsing-ai, still wearing her veil, by the hand and laid all that remained at her feet a cry of wonder and admiration was raised on every side and all freely admitted that no more worthy person that Wan-taing could have been discovered.

The sun had already gone down on the heat of the day. Courteously declining to be carried high upon the shoulders of a chosen band through Ko and Yun, so that the mentally afflicted who had been left behind might be agreeably amused and perhaps even improved by the sight of his engaging countenance, Wan-taing commanded his bearers to bring forward the two chairs which had been specially prepared in the meantime. "Doubtless in the future opportunities for renewing the pleasurable social intercourse of the past few hours will arise," he added to Chin Paik, "but at the present moment this person's feet are aching to carry him to his native town of Lin-fi, and there hastening to the Waste Expanses, to prostrate him dutifully before the revered sire from whom a great peril – now happily surmounted – has withheld him for five interminable years."

"Lin-fi! and the Waste Expanses!" exclaimed Chin Paik, drawing nearer and searching Wan-taing's features with an expression of ever changeful feeling. "Who, and living by what manner of existence, is the one in question, O thou disturber of dust-strewn memories? And is thy name indeed Wan-taing?"

"The one referred to is Sha-kien of the cave by the ancient plantain grove, now and in the past a frugal and painstaking worker in lacquer, and shortly, to mark his unworthy son's

Imperial success, to be adorned with the Open-work Umbrella, the Plastic-sided Sandals or the title 'Ferocious,'" replied Wan-taing. "Concerning the one who is now addressing you, it is an undeniable fact that his milk-name was Cheng, but it would be an act of disrespectful treason for one who has pierced the shoulder of the supreme Emperor to call himself by the same name as that which described him when he was merely an ordinary person, so that for all general and official purposes Sha Ah-cheng is now Wan-taing."

"'The Hoang Ho may again change its course but the fixed purpose of the deities is immovable,'" exclaimed Chin Paik with tardy but deep-seated conviction. "Now this person for the first time grasps that which seemed familiar in the pre-possessing outline of your lowered head. Had you but once prostrated yourself his mind would unhesitatingly have leapt to an immediate recognition."

"One who wears the Three-Eyed Peacock Feather, who possesses full authority to ride even up to the gate of the Forbidden City with purple reins, and who can, moreover, make two needles meet within any part of a person's body, has very little use for such an accomplishment," replied Wan-taing with a well-assured belief that Chin Paik would never adequately realise the distinguished nature of his son-in-law's attainments. "But of yourself, O darkly-speaking Quang-te Nung – who are you who hint of these forgotten things?"

"In the past," replied Chin Paik, hesitating in doubt as to how much he might prudently reveal and how much he could not safely conceal, "there was one, Chin Paik—"

"Chin Paik!" exclaimed Wan-taing, no less astonished. "Is the peerless and incomparable Tsing-ai the same – she who was formerly designated the little pig of the inner chamber?"

"Undoubtedly such a name may have had some application once," admitted Chin Paik, deciding not for the time to disclose the artifice more fully, "but however ill-balanced her features may have been in the unformed years of childhood, it is a sincere word that owing to the self-sacrificing effacement of one in authority over her – who has thrust aside official preferment and more than poetically-speaking submerged himself alive so that Tsing-ai should experience the invigorating climate of western Ho-Nan and disport in the peony-laden breezes of the Hoang Ho – the one in question will now be described to posterity as beautiful above all who have gone before, and only comparable to the rainbow, the phoenix, and the full moon."

"It is well spoken: yet the greater part is not told," replied Wan-taing, for the first time prostrating himself – but not in the direction of Chin Paik. "With reason is it written, 'Destiny has three and thirty feet, each eleven li long, and is a thousand eyed. Do you think, O person of weak mind, to outstrip him?'"

"The remark is an inspired one; for there are those who, although they are unable to lay their hands upon an ordinary four-legged goat, think to leave behind them in flight the Many-Footed One and to discredit the unalterable fate that was written in unchanging letters of iron before their birth," exclaimed a voice rising from the ground behind, and all turning in amazement beheld an ancient person who to Chin Paik and Wan-taing appeared in the guise of the wise woman Aing Nu. "Chin Paik," continued this opportune vision, "in consideration of your confessed submission to the decree of the Upper Ones your period of suffering is now at an end. Return without delay to Lin-fi, for there friends will be restored to you and a more remunerative office than any which you have yet held awaits your acceptance. By a consistently benevolent life henceforward you may even diminish the threatened torments in the Upper World. Prosperity, O Wan-taing and Tsing-ai; a hundred sons and a thousand grandsons, all reflecting honour and renown upon their line!" With this auspicious remark the aged woman was lost to their vision, her disappearance being concealed by the discharge of countless crackers and the burning of many coloured fires; while at that moment the blowing of conch shells announced the arrival of chairs before the door.

Colophon

Seven of the stories in this volume have been published before. One was written in 1923, and the other six were probably written in 1940 and 1941. This list gives the place and date of the first publications.

Ming Tseuen and the Emergency
> *The Specimen Case,* September 1924

Lam-hoo and the Reward of Merit
> *Punch Almanak for 1941,* 4 November 1940

Chung Pun and the Miraculous Peacocks
> *Punch,* 20 November 1940

Yuen Yang and the Empty Lo-Chee Crate
> *Punch,* 11 December 1940

Sing Tsung and the Exponent of Dark Magic
> *Punch Summer Number,* 26 May 1941

Kwey Chao and the Grateful Song Bird
> *Punch,* 11 June 1941

Li Pao, Lucky Star and the Intruding Stranger
> *Punch Almanak for 1942,* 17 November 1941

The other four stories have never been published before, but were written between 1900 and 1905.

COLOPHON

The story 'Yuen Yang and the Empty Lo-Chee Crate' was published in *Punch* as 'Yuen Yang and the Empty Soo-Shong Chest', but here appears as in the original manuscript. The differences between the versions are minor except for the large introductory section, up to the paragraph starting "As Yuen Yang bent his footsteps", which was removed completely from the version in *Punch*.

The cover illustration is taken from 杨柳鸣禽图 (Willow Warbler Picture) by 金礼赢 (Jin Liying) (1772–1807).

Set in Monotype Baskerville, 11/13

Lightning Source UK Ltd.
Milton Keynes UK
UKHW012345280622
405094UK00002B/9